THE
GOLDEN BOY
OF PYE
CORNER

CRUDD'S
HOUSE

SAINT

THE OLD NICHOL

ST. PAUL

RE...

WILKI...
Crudd...

DEC 07 2019

THE CLEANSWEE...

MADRONA

THE MATCHSTICK

EAST END

TOWER
OF LONDON

ELEPHANT
AND CASTLE

SOUTHWARK

LONDON
BY NAN
AND CHARLIE

NEW
CROSS

A STORY BY
JONATHAN AUXIER

AMULET BOOKS

NEW YORK

SWEEP

THE STORY OF A GIRL
AND HER MONSTER

LIBRARY OF CONGRESS CATALOGING-IN-PUBLICATION DATA

Names: Auxier, Jonathan, author.

Title: Sweep: the story of a girl and her monster / by Jonathan Auxier.

Description: New York: Amulet Books, 2018. | Summary: In nineteenth-century England, after her father's disappearance Nan Sparrow, ten, works as a "climbing boy," aiding chimney sweeps, but when her most treasured possessions end up in a fireplace, she unwittingly creates a golem.

Identifiers: LCCN 2018014305 | ISBN 978-1-4197-3140-2 (hardback)

Subjects: | CYAC: Golem—Fiction. | Chimney sweeps—Fiction. | Homeless persons—Fiction. | Orphans—Fiction. | Great Britain—History—19th century—Fiction. | BISAC: JUVENILE FICTION / Family / Orphans & Foster Homes. | JUVENILE FICTION / Social Issues / Homelessness & Poverty. | JUVENILE FICTION / Fantasy & Magic.

Classification: LCC PZ7.A9314 Swe 2018 | DDC [Fic]—dc23

TEXT COPYRIGHT © 2018 JONATHAN AUXIER
ILLUSTRATIONS COPYRIGHT © 2018 DADU SHIN
MAP ILLUSTRATION COPYRIGHT © 2018 JONATHAN AUXIER
BOOK DESIGN BY CHAD W. BECKERMAN

Printed and bound in U.S.A.

10 9 8 7 6 5 4 3 2 1

ABRAMS The Art of Books
195 Broadway, New York, NY 10007
abramsbooks.com

For those who have saved me

⊰ Mary, Penelope, Matilda, and Hazel ⊱

Golden lads and girls all must,
As chimney-sweepers, come to dust.
~ *William Shakespeare,* Cymbeline

⋄ ⋄ ⋄

The imagination is the true fire,
stolen from heaven, to animate
this cold creature of clay.
~ *Mary Wollstonecraft*

⋇ PART ONE ⋇

INNOCENCE

⊰ THE GIRL AND HER SWEEP ⊱

*T*here are all sorts of wonderful things a person might see very early
in the morning. You might see your parents sleeping. You might see
an ambitious bird catching a worm. You might see an unclaimed penny on
the sidewalk or the first rays of dawn. And if you are very, very lucky, you
might even catch a glimpse of the girl and her Sweep.

Look! Here they are now, approaching through the early fog: a thin
man with a long broom over one shoulder, the end bobbing up and down
with every step. And trailing behind him, pail in hand, a little girl, who
loves that man more than anything in the world.

The girl sticks to the man like a shadow. If he hops over a puddle, she
hops, too. If he skips along a rail, she does the same. It is clear just by looking at them that the little girl belongs to the man, just as the man belongs
to the little girl. And as they pass between sleeping houses, they sing at the
top of their lungs:

> With brush and pail and soot and song!
> A sweep brings luck all season long!

The song is not particularly special. Their voices are not particularly sweet. But when they sing, the most unusual thing happens. Instead of people snapping their windows shut to block out the sound, they rise from their beds, one by one, throw back the curtains, and decide to love the world just a little bit more. Parents suddenly feel the urge to hug their children. Children suddenly feel the urge to let them.

And every person, young and old, spends the rest of the day softly humming the song of the girl and her Sweep.

For as long as the girl could remember, the Sweep had been at her side. First he carried her in a sling over his back and fed her bottles of milk. When she got a bit older, he would let her ride upon his shoulders and pick apples from the trees they passed. And when she got older yet, they walked together like true equals.

The Sweep shared everything with the girl. If he had a scarf, he would let her wear it during the cold days and take it for himself on the hot ones. If they found a loaf of bread, the girl would eat half and pass the rest to the Sweep; he would eat half of what remained and then give it back to the girl; then she would eat half again; and so on. They would trade the loaf back and forth like this until the bread was gone and their bellies were full.

The Sweep let the girl share in his work, too. First he just had her scoop ashes from the hearth, but when the girl became a bit stronger, he let her climb chimneys with him. From the start, the girl was a natural climber.

She had long limbs, just like the Sweep, and her thin frame could wriggle through even the tiniest flues.

Being inside a chimney is a frightening thing; it's so dark and cramped that one can scarcely tell which way is up. And so when the girl and her Sweep climbed inside a chimney, they would sing to each other. The Sweep, who always went up first, would brush out soot and nests and cobwebs, singing all the while. And the girl knew that all she had to do was follow his voice and she would be safe.

Eventually the two of them would emerge from the top of the flue, filthy and triumphant. The view from a chimney stack is a truly majestic thing. For miles in every direction all you can see are rooftops and more rooftops, like tiny dunes stretching to the horizon. Many times the Sweep remarked that kings and lords couldn't wish for a better view—and he should know, because he had swept a few palaces in his day.

Of course, life was not always easy for the girl and her Sweep. Many nights were cold and wet. Many days were humid and hungry. More than once they entered a new town and quickly found themselves surrounded by a band of disgruntled local sweeps. Whenever this happened, the Sweep would ask the girl to watch the tools while he and the other sweeps talked things through in the alley. He would emerge a few minutes later, limping slightly, his clothes a little torn, but smiling as broadly as ever. He would report to the girl that the other sweeps had told him of a neighborhood just a few miles off with some particularly good houses. In thanks for this valuable information, he had decided to give them all the money in his pockets.

When the Sweep did secure work, he would get paid a coin or sometimes even two coins. On his way out the door, he would always warn the homeowner to burn the chimney hot all night long—just in case any sparrows tried to make a nest up there. (This was a special joke between the girl and the Sweep, and it was all the girl could do not to spoil things by laughing.)

Later that night, once the sun had set and the town was asleep, they would return to the same house, and the girl would clamber up the rain gutter to the edge of the roof and let down a rope for the Sweep to follow after her. Then, walking very carefully, so as not to make any noise, they would lay blankets against the smoking chimney stack, which was warm to the touch, and make their beds.

Most children despise bedtime and will do anything to avoid it. This is because they are forced to sleep under scratchy covers inside stifling houses. If they could sleep like the girl and her Sweep—on warm rooftops beneath a canopy of stars—they would understand just how magical bedtime could be.

As they stared into the infinite dark, sometimes the Sweep would tell the girl stories about their day. Other times they would just lie in silence. But every night ended the same way: with her falling asleep against his chest as he stroked her hair and sang her their special lullaby:

With brush and pail and soot and song!
A sweep brings luck all season long!

As the Sweep sang these words, the girl would drift off—dreaming of stars and seas and adventures far, far away.

This was life as the girl knew it. And every night she slept soundly, knowing that she and the Sweep would have each other forever.

⊰ VOICES IN THE DARK ⊱

Nan, tell us about the Sweep."

It was dark in the coal bin, but Nan could tell it was Newt who was asking. Newt was newest to Crudd's crew. He was barely six years old; he didn't know all the rules. The first rule was you never asked another climber about his life Before.

There were five climbing boys in the coal bin: Newt, Whittles, Shilling-Tom, Roger, and Nan. Nan wasn't a boy, but you'd never know that to look at her. She was as grimy as the rest of them. "Who told you about the Sweep?" Nan said. "Was it Roger?"

"Keep me out of it, Cinderella," Roger muttered. He called Nan "Cinderella" because he thought it annoyed her. He was right.

"No one told me," Newt said. "I *dreamed* about him. Last night I slept in your corner. I dreamed him and the girl were both singing to all the people. Only I woke up before I could hear the words."

This was a thing that happened: the dreaming. Every so often one of the boys would say that he had dreamed about the Sweep. Nan couldn't explain it. It seemed to happen whenever one of them fell asleep close to her. All she knew was that she didn't like it. The Sweep was *hers*.

"It was about you, wasn't it?" Newt whispered. "You're the girl from my dream."

"No," Nan said. "I'm the girl who wants to go to sleep." She'd spent fourteen hours climbing chimneys and knew there were more waiting for her tomorrow.

"You're splashing in the wrong puddle, Newt," said a raspy voice by the slat window. It was Whittles. He was only eight, but his voice sounded like an old man's on account of breathing too much chimney soot. "Me and Shilling-Tom been dreaming about the girl and her Sweep for years. Not once have we gotten Nan to fess up that it's her."

"Aye," said Shilling-Tom. He was Whittles's best mate. "You might as well try to get a second helping from Trundle's pot." Trundle was the woman who cared for them. If you could call it that.

"I won't fess up because it's nonsense," Nan said. And it *was* nonsense. How could two people have the same dream?

"Is the Sweep a real person?" Newt asked. "He sounds lovely. Much nicer than Master Crudd." He whispered this last bit. Just in case Crudd could hear him upstairs.

"Sweeps aren't supposed to be lovely," Nan said. "They're

grimy and tough as stone. Just like chimneys." Maybe *lovely* was a fine thing to call a person in Newt's old life, but he was a climber now. He wouldn't last long if he kept using words like that.

She heard the boy move closer. "Please, Nan?" Her eyes had adjusted to the dim light, and she could see the outline of his head. With his curls shaved off, he really did look like a newt. They had named him well. "Just tell me if he's real. I promise I won't tell the others."

"Don't beg. A climber never begs." That was another rule.

"Maybe I can sleep here next to you?" He clasped her arm. "Then I'll dream about him all on my own?"

Nan knew what the boy was saying. He thought that somehow the dreams were coming from *her*, which was impossible. She pulled away. "Find your own corner."

"Aw, go easy on the kid." It was Whittles. "It's only been a week since he . . . you know . . ." He didn't say the rest. None of them knew what had happened to Newt's family to have him end up here, but it had to have been bad. It was always bad.

"I'm not begging," Newt said. "But it's a true fact: I can't sleep without a bedtime story. My mummy always says . . ." He corrected himself. ". . . always *said* . . ." His voice faltered. "It's just I thought hearing a story about the Sweep might help me fall asleep."

Nan remembered when she had felt the same way. That was a long time ago. That was Before.

"*I* can tell you about the Sweep." Roger had crawled out from his spot under the stairs. "He was Cinderella's old master before Crudd snatched her up." Roger was the oldest climber on the team and knew about her life Before. She hated him for that. "Only to hear Nan tell it, that Sweep was like a prince stepped right out of some fairy story. But he's no prince, believe me. Why, she was hardly your age when that Sweep of hers up and—"

"That's enough," Nan said.

"I'll say what's enough," Roger shot back. "Do you know the really sad part? Five years on, and she still thinks he's coming back. How's that for—?"

"YOU SHUT YOUR MOUTH." There was violence in her voice. She could feel everyone in the room watching her.

Whittles broke the silence. "A fight between Nan and Roger? Now, *that* I'd pay to see."

Shilling–Tom laughed. "I got a shilling here that says Nan lays him out flat."

Nan heard him flip his prized coin and catch it. In all her years of working with Shilling–Tom, she had never actually seen the coin, which he kept hidden safely so that other boys wouldn't take it.

"Save your money." Nan didn't need them goading Roger into a fight. He was twice her size and fought dirty. She glanced up at the window. Dawn would be coming in a few hours, and they would all be back on the streets, brooms in hand. She suddenly felt very tired.

"Go to sleep," she whispered to Newt. "You've got your first climb tomorrow, and we wouldn't want you to nod off in the flue." This was meant to be a joke, but it was not a funny one, because that had happened once to a boy named Hi-Ho. He had broken both legs and ended up a beggar.

Nan listened as Newt made a sort of whimper and retreated to the far wall of the coal bin. He would cry himself to sleep, as he'd done the nights previous. But eventually he would get over it.

Nan brushed the loose clumps of coal from the floor and rolled over on her side, knees to her chest. It was the way she had always slept—like an infant waiting to be cradled.

The stone floor was cold. Her only pillow was a burlap sack, turned black from years of hauling loose soot. Nan reached a hand into her coat pocket. Inside she found a charred clump of soot—a treasure she kept with her always. She called it her "char." It was small and crumbly and unnaturally warm, like a little ember in her pocket. She couldn't explain how, but the thing seemed to burn with its own inner heat, which radiated year in and year out, no matter the weather. It was the only thing she had left from Before.

Nan took a deep breath and closed her eyes and willed herself to sleep.

But she did not sleep.

Instead, she remembered the Sweep.

⋅≼ THE SWEEP'S GIFT ≽⋅

*T*he girl was just six years old when it happened.

She and her Sweep had both gone to bed as they always had, nestled against a chimney stack beneath the starry sky. But when the girl woke the next morning, her Sweep was gone.

She did not worry straightaway. Chimney folk are natural rovers, as rootless as the four winds. She assumed her Sweep had nipped off to forage for breakfast—they called these little trips "belly quests." He would come back any moment now, with ripe figs stolen from a low bough or quail's eggs swiped from a nest or even (if they had money) day-old rolls from the baker.

But the Sweep did not come back with figs or eggs or rolls.

When morning turned to afternoon, the girl began to let herself worry. They had only just recently come to this new town—the great kingdom of London. The Sweep had told her all sorts of stories about dragons in the *river and banshees in the fog, and she wasn't sure which of them were true and which were play.*

The Sweep liked to pass the time by telling stories. And so the girl now told herself stories. She made up fanciful tales about magic bookshops, talking fruit trees, and blind thieves who could open any lock. The stories were all brilliant. But no matter where she started, every story always led her back to that rooftop—alone, hungry, waiting for her Sweep.

The girl scolded herself for becoming afraid. For all she knew, this was some sort of new game. The Sweep was probably hiding behind one of the chimney stacks, waiting to jump out and surprise her. "Ha-ha!" he would say, and scoop her up in his arms. "My little sparrow has flown at last from her nest!"

The girl got up and started to check the rooftop. She checked the stacks and peered over the eaves. She could just make out the words on a sign hanging by the entrance of the house directly beneath her—

~ WILKIE CRUDD, Esq. ~
"The Clean Sweep"

The girl remembered how funny she found this at the time: the idea of a sweep being clean.

She widened her search. She checked the rooftops across the entire block, taking care to look behind every stack, even poking her head into the chimney pots.

At last she returned to the spot where she had started, more frightened than before. She took up the Sweep's coat, which lay folded beside her sootbag.

And that was when she saw the hat.

There is nothing more sacred to a chimney sweep than his hat. It remains with him at all times—even in the privy and the bath. "To lose your hat, even for a moment," the Sweep often told her, "is to summon a thousand tragedies." He was always telling the girl stories about foolish chimney sweeps who mislaid their hats, only to have a church steeple or a wild elephant come down on their heads. He had also promised that someday, when he became too frail to climb, the hat would be hers.

And so when she saw the Sweep's hat, which he had concealed beneath his coat, she knew something had gone horribly wrong.

Her first thought was that the Sweep had tumbled from the roof in his sleep. He usually tied a rope around his waist to prevent this, but perhaps he had forgotten. But somehow she knew that the hat was no accident.

He had left it for her.

The girl knelt and took the hat in her small hands. The brim was warm to the touch. She smelled the sweet aroma of kindling. When she leaned close, she saw that there was something inside the crown.

She reached inside and removed a small clump made of ash or coal or soot—she could not tell which. It was about the size of her fist. The outside was crumbly, but it would not break when she squeezed it. And it was very warm.

Imagine discovering that the only person you have ever known and loved was now gone without a word. Not a note. Not a message. Only a strange lump of flickering char.

The girl's first emotion was anger. She very nearly threw the char over the edge of the roof. But something within her checked this impulse, and she clasped the clump to her breast. She held it so tight that it could have turned into a diamond.

Without the Sweep, the girl had nothing to do and nowhere to go. And so she waited on the roof, hoping the Sweep would return. She clung to the piece of char, her only inheritance. Even in the bitterest cold, it kept her warm.

Indeed, it was the thing that kept her alive.

⊰ THE CLEAN SWEEP ⊱

N an woke from a dead sleep to the bells of St. Florian's Church. She'd heard once that St. Florian was the patron saint of chimney sweeps. She thought if that were true, then he shouldn't make his bells ring so early. Nan rubbed soot from her eyes. She had been dreaming of Before. It was a thing she tried not to remember—but the dreams wouldn't let her forget.

"Get a move on, you lot!" a voice yelled from upstairs.

The boys were on their feet in a flash. No time for yawning or stretching. They stampeded up the wooden steps, pushing against one another to get to the kitchen before the bell finished its five o'clock toll.

Nan sprang up and started to run with them.

But then she stopped, feeling her coat. "My char!"

It must have fallen from her pocket when she got up. This

happened a lot. No matter how tightly she held on to it in the night, by morning it would find a way to slip from her grip—almost as if it had a mind of its own. Nan dug through the scattered coals along the east wall. It was like finding a needle in a needlestack. Finally she uncovered it—warm and familiar. It was where she usually located it, right beneath the window that looked out toward St. Florian's churchyard.

Nan paused for a moment, looking more closely at the char in the early light. She noticed two small divots in the face, equal in size. They looked for all the world like a pair of *eyes*.

"Step lively, Cinderella!" Roger called from the top of the stairs. "You know what happens when that bell strikes midnight." He shut the door. Nan heard the lock click behind him.

Nan cursed Roger under her breath and stuffed the char in her pocket. The bells continued ringing as she clambered into the coal bin's chimney, which connected to the kitchen hearth above it.

By the time Nan reached the main floor, the boys were already seated along the table, slurping up bowls of hot gruel. Porridge was thick and filling and needed to be eaten with a spoon, but gruel was different. It was mostly water. You could drink it straight from the bowl. This was the only food they could expect today.

Nan squeezed between Whittles and Newt and reached for her waiting bowl—

Whap!

A wooden spoon came down on her hand. She shrieked, clutching her fingers.

"You're late, missy," Mrs. Trundle said, looming over her. Trundle was a widow, and Nan always thought her late husband was probably glad to be rid of her. The woman was mean as a weasel in winter. Her apron was splattered gray and smelled awful. She kept a giant iron pot perched on her hip like an infant. The inside of the pot was caked with brown muck that had once been food. "That last bell was well rung by the time you sat down." She jabbed the end of her gruel-covered spoon at Nan. "You know the rule: Stragglers starve."

Nan clutched her throbbing hand. "Sorry, ma'am." She sucked the bits of gruel from her knuckle and forced herself not to cry. In five years she had not once let herself cry in this home. She knew Crudd would enjoy it too much.

Trundle snatched Nan's bowl and poured the uneaten gruel back into the pot. "Never you fear. It'll be waitin' for you tomorrow."

For as long as Nan had lived in the house, she had never once seen that gruel pot cleaned. Every morning a few more ingredients were added. It was impossible to tell where one batch ended and another began.

A door creaked behind her. "Brooms up!" She and the other climbers all leaped to attention as Wilkie Crudd stepped into the room.

"Mister Crudd," Mrs. Trundle said in an almost girlish voice. "Good morning to you." She bent her knees in something like a curtsy.

"It's not good yet," Crudd replied. "That will depend entirely on whether these imps do their jobs." He talked the way Nan imagined a ship's captain might talk.

"I got your boots, sir," Roger said. "Shined 'em up real good."

"Used his tongue and everything," Whittles muttered.

Shilling-Tom started to laugh, but a look from Crudd cut him short.

Crudd took his seat at the head of the table. Roger rushed to meet him with his boots. They really were shiny.

Wilkie Crudd had built a reputation as "the Clean Sweep." Instead of the blacks of a proper sweep, he wore a green velvet jacket with gold piping. His shirt and breeches were spotless white. Even his brush was clean. This was not vanity but calculation: He knew that wealthy customers preferred to work with someone who looked like them—so they could forget just how filthy the job really was.

Nan couldn't see it, but she knew from the way housemaids talked that Crudd was quite handsome. The widow Trundle was the latest in a long line of romantic conquests. Every few months, Crudd brought in a new woman to cook and keep house. Nan was fairly certain these women worked for nothing—perhaps in the hope that Crudd might see their value and make an offer of marriage. He never did.

Mrs. Trundle set a covered plate in front of him. "I've fixed up a special breakfast for you, sir." With a flourish, she removed the cover. Delicious, hot smells assaulted Nan's nose. "Roast pheasant with bread sauce. Your favorite."

Crudd pushed the steaming plate away without even looking at it. "None for me, Missus Trundle. I'll be eating my fill on the job—three weddings."

Weddings were a tidy business for chimney sweeps. Everyone knew that paying a sweep to attend your wedding guaranteed years of happiness. And no sweep was in such high demand as the Clean Sweep. "Days are getting shorter since autumn's begun. I shouldn't plan to be home before dark."

"Too busy kissing the brides for luck, eh, sir?" Roger said, helping Crudd don his overcoat.

Nan saw Mrs. Trundle wince slightly, as if she'd just pricked her finger.

Crudd glanced at the table, specifically at the empty space in front of Nan. "We seem to be a bowl short." He gave Trundle an inquiring look.

"The girl was late for breakfast," the woman said. "And she knows my rule."

"*Your* rule, not mine," he said. "I've a business to run. I can't have my best climber start the day on an empty stomach." This was not so much a compliment as a slap aimed at Roger.

"Of course," Trundle said. "Only there's none left in the pot." A dirty lie.

"Let her have my breakfast, then." Crudd nodded toward the pheasant.

"But, Wilkie!" the woman protested. "The bird alone cost half a shilling."

"Psssh," Shilling-Tom muttered. "That ain't so fancy. I could buy two."

"Don't worry yourself about the cost." Crudd walked to the front door and took up his broom. "Only the best for my best."

Nan could feel both Trundle and Roger glaring at her. She kept her eyes on Crudd, who was watching her with an expectant smile. "Well?"

She breathed in the smell of the food. It nearly made her knees buckle. She lowered her head. "I'm not hungry."

·¾ FIRST CLIMB ¾·

N an walked briskly through Tower Hamlets. Shabby houses lined the narrow street. The granite setts were cold against her bare feet, and she could just make out her breath as she turned down Whitechapel toward the heart of London. She kept one hand on her brush and the other buried deep in her pocket, clutching her char to ward off the early-autumn chill. She thought again about the "eyes" she had seen in its face. Surely it was just a trick of the light?

The smell of warm rolls filled her nostrils as she passed Hob's Bakery on the corner. She felt a violent stab in her gut. She wondered if it had been a mistake to turn down Crudd's offer of the pheasant, but then she told herself that a bit of hunger was preferable to taking part in Crudd's little game.

She and Roger were the oldest climbers on the team. For years Crudd had been promising to make one of them apprentice when they came of age. And that day was fast approaching. Being an apprentice meant less work and actual pay. Being passed over meant the streets.

Crudd wielded this promise as both carrot and stick. He would alternately praise one of them and ignore the other. Lately he had been unusually kind to Nan. And for good reason. Roger didn't care a whit for hard work. If a corner could be cut, he'd cut it twice . . . and leave someone else with the blame. On a given day, Nan cleared twice as many chimneys with half as many complaints. Her sootbag was always full to bursting. Shilling-Tom and Whittles both said she was a sure thing. Still, when it came to Wilkie Crudd, there was no such thing as a sure thing.

Nan hated climbing for Wilkie Crudd, but what other choice did she have? She had learned quickly that no person would hire a six-year-old girl without a proper master, and so she had been forced to indenture herself. For all she knew, the Sweep had left her at Crudd's house for that very reason.

Nan found the others at the Matchstick on Pudding Lane. The Matchstick was a giant stone torch built to commemorate the Great Fire of London, when a baker's chimney caught fire near that spot and burned the whole city down. For a farthing you could take the stairs up and look out from the viewing platform. Folks said you could see clear to America from up there. Nan wouldn't know—she'd never had a farthing to spare. Sweeps and climbers used the Matchstick as an informal place of business, probably to remind folks of what would happen if they didn't clean their chimneys.

Whittles was sitting on a low wall, carving a stick into what looked to be a smaller stick. Shilling-Tom was window-shopping outside a haberdashery. Newt was trailing behind Roger, peppering him with questions about climbing. Up to this point, Newt had only had to fill ash pails and haul ropes. Today was his first climb.

"But what if I get stuck?" he was asking as Nan approached.

"No 'what if' about it. You *will* get stuck." Roger was chewing something that looked suspiciously like a pheasant leg. He must have swiped it when Trundle wasn't looking. "And once you're stuck, there's only three ways out. Up, down, or in the arms of angels."

"That means dead," Newt said sagely.

"If I had to guess, I'd say you'll be buried by May Day. If you're lucky, you'll just fall and break your neck. But there are worse ways to go. Much worse."

"Like what?" Newt sounded nervous.

Roger sucked the last bits of meat from the knuckle. The smell made Nan's stomach tremble. "There's soot wart," he said. "That's a disease that eats your guts from the inside till there's nothing left. But even soot wart don't hold a candle to getting stuck. You're climbing along, easy as pie, and then suddenly, before you know it, your knees are up to your chin and you're wedged in there like a cork."

"But if you're stuck, can't they get you out again?"

"They can try. Easiest way is to open the chimney cap and toss a few bricks down. That might knock you loose enough, and you'll fall the rest of the way."

Newt's eyes widened. "Doesn't that hurt?"

"Not as much as the next way. If bricks don't work, Crudd'll send up another climber with a silver hat pin to jab you in the heels hard as he can." He poked the end of his pheasant bone into Newt's face. "Once you feel that, you can bet you'll work yourself free." He tossed the bone into the street, where two dogs promptly began to fight over it. "But sometimes that don't work, neither. And then it's time for . . . *the Devil's Nudge*."

Nan rolled her eyes. Of course Roger would tell him about the nudge. "Just ignore him," she said to Newt.

Newt kept his eyes on the older boy. "Wh-wh-what's the Devil's Nudge?"

"Can't tell you." Roger licked his fingers. "It's too horrible. Let's just say that if Crudd uses the Devil's Nudge, you'd better hurry and say your last prayers, 'cause soon you'll be screaming all the way to potter's field."

"Leave him alone, Roger," Nan said. "You're scaring him."

"I'm telling him the way things are," Roger said. He folded his arms. "Name one thing I said that ain't true."

Nan grit her teeth. She remembered her first climb. Even all these years later, she still felt a whisper of that old terror every time she stepped into a hearth. "You're small," she said to Newt. "You'll be fine."

"But what if I get stuck?" He wiped his nose to reveal a smear of pink skin beneath the grime. "What if they have to . . . nudge me?"

Nan set down her broom and knelt. She looked Newt dead in the eye. "I'm not going to tell you it's easy or that you shouldn't be scared. But being scared's not the whole story of it. There's another reason we climb—one that makes all that danger worth it. It's the *view*. There's nothing in the world like it." She took off her hat and put it over Newt's eyes. The way the Sweep had done with her before her very first climb.

"Imagine it," she whispered. "You go up that long, dark flue, coal sack over your eyes and mouth, legs and arms scraped and aching. But then you reach the top, feel that cool air on your skin. You take the bag off and what do you see . . . ?"

She pulled the hat away. The boy blinked. "What do I see?"

Nan smiled. "Everything."

Newt's eyes shone as if he could really see everything. He turned toward her. "Will you go up with me?"

Nan pulled back from him. "Me?"

"Aw," Roger said in a mocking voice. "Looks like Nan's got herself a pet."

She wiped her hands on her coat, as if they were dirty. Which they were. "I'm afraid training is Roger's job." She fit her hat—the Sweep's hat—back on her head.

"Just for my first climb!" Newt grabbed at her arm. "After that I'll be brave—I promise I will!"

"Brave's got nothing to do with it," called Whittles. "Nan Sparrow climbs alone. Always has. Always will."

This was true. Nan didn't need dead weight slowing her down. "You're a climber now." She gave Newt a not unkind shrug. "You can't depend on folks to protect you from the world. Because someday there won't be anyone but you to do it. Not Roger, not Crudd, not me—"

"What's that mean, *not you*?" Newt said. "Are you leaving?"

"Not if I can help it," Nan said. "I got soot in my veins." But that was the problem: She couldn't help it. Things were changing. *She* was changing. Nan was nearly twelve now. She had seen girls her age who had graduated from the workhouses, seen the way they had grown plump and awkward. "Blossomed," people called it. She tried to imagine one of those girls wriggling up a chimney flue. It was impossible.

Church bells across London struck the hour. "Speaking of . . ." She stood with her brush. "It's time we all got to work."

The little boy stared up at her. His tiny chin quivered. "What's the point of seeing *everything* if there's no one to see it with?"

Nan didn't have an answer for this, so she just took up her soot-bag and walked away.

⊰ NAN'S SONG ⊱

Nan tried not to think about Newt climbing into his first flue. The others had learned not to work chimneys with Roger. And now Newt would learn.

She knew her best chance at getting something to eat would be to find a job near a wealthy home in the West End. The servants in nice homes could be counted on to give you a bit of food once you'd finished the job. She supposed she was a reminder of where most of them had come from. Seeing her made them grateful not to be her.

The sun was just coming up now. The first fallen leaves of autumn were scattered across the dewy streets. All along the city, she could hear the chorus of climbers shouting their trade.

> *Sweep!*
> > *Sweep O!*
> > > *Sweep for your soot!*

Of course, Nan had her own way of getting work. It was the way the Sweep had taught her.

She saw a cluster of children on the steps of St. Paul's. They were all crowded around a filthy boy who had an enormous bag at his bare feet. Perched on his shoulder was a little white rat with horrible red eyes. "No pushing, gentlemen!" said the boy in a loud voice. "There's treasure enough for all. Whatever your need, Toby Squall's Emporium has *just the thing.*"

"Does it have a kick in the backside?" Nan muttered.

The boy somehow heard her. He waved his cap, revealing a head of wild orange curls. "Hullo, Smudge!" He was always calling her that. She hated it even more than Cinderella. "Care to browse the emporium?"

The "emporium" was what Toby called his junk bag. It was rumored that Toby's bag was magical and bottomless. On any given day, he could be seen hawking buttons, candle ends, playing cards, string, pocketknives, snails, cutlery, eye patches, wishbones, and even once a set of false teeth. He proudly described himself as an *entrepreneur.* Nan called him a pest.

Toby Squall was a mudlark. He spent his days wading along the banks of the Thames searching for rubbish and things he could repair and sell. Most mudlarks found only junk. But Toby had an eye for treasure—if there was a good bootlace or hairpin in the river, you could bet he would find it.

"I'm busy," Nan said.

"Just a peek!" Toby clasped a hand to his heart. "Everything's half price for my best girl."

Toby was also always calling Nan his "best girl." He claimed to have loads of other girls, but Nan was his best.

"Go dunk your head," she said, walking more quickly. Her cheeks were burning, and she was grateful they could not be seen beneath the grime.

Nan and Toby had been having exchanges like this for the better part of five years. No matter what route Nan took each morning, Toby Squall somehow managed to be on the way.

She cut up Bride Street to Farringdon Market. Girls and old women sold watercress and oranges and fresh oysters for a penny. Maids and butlers and servants rushed about on errands while their masters and mistresses slept late into the morning. The Sweep had never understood how a person could sleep through the sunrise. "It's like Heaven itself is offering you a gift you're too lazy to open," he used to say. Then he'd wink and add, "Ah, well. More for us."

Nan stopped in the middle of the market. People flowed around her like water around a stone. She closed her eyes, and sang.

With brush and pail and soot and song!
A sweep brings luck all season long!

When Nan sang like this, she could almost hear the Sweep singing with her—his voice high and bright. She kept her hand in her pocket, clasped tight around the Sweep's char. It almost felt as if she were holding his hand. Sometimes she thought that if she could just sing loud enough, the Sweep would hear her . . . and would be drawn back to her by the song.

As she sang, everything around her seemed to go quiet. Merchants and servants slowed their pace. Even beggars raised themselves from the gutters. She knew every one of them was thinking the same thing: How could such a voice come from a person so filthy?

Nan opened her eyes to find her first customer. It was a woman in a black shift with a pinched expression.

"Morning, mum," Nan said, and tipped her top hat. It was much too large for her, and she kept the inside stuffed with newspaper so it wouldn't cover her eyes.

The song was over, which meant the spell was broken. The woman now eyed Nan as though she might bite her. "Who's your master, boy?"

Nan didn't bother correcting the woman about her being a girl. "I work for Wilkie Crudd." When Crudd's name drew no response, she added, "The Clean Sweep."

"The Clean Sweep?" The woman's cheeks flushed red. "I may have heard . . . *something* about him." Nan was pretty sure that "something" had to do with his being handsome. The woman touched the back of her hair as if it were made of glass. "Will, er, your *master* be attending the task personally?"

Nan pretended not to understand what she was asking. "I'll be doing the flues, mum. But the master always comes round to settle the bill and give a *final inspection*." She let this last bit hang in the air like a promise.

"Of course," the woman said. "Follow me."

The woman led her up Holborn and Oxford Street. Nan glimpsed an abandoned mansion in Bloomsbury with more chimneys than she could count. The house was famous among climbers. They called it "the House of One Hundred Chimneys." Everyone knew it was haunted. It was bad luck to even look at the place.

The woman's heels clacked sharply against the wet sidewalk. Nan wondered what kind of house let the maid wear high boots. It didn't seem practical, but then rich folks never were. Nan's own feet were bare—her soles hard as leather from years of climbing rough brick. She didn't mind. Besides, in the wrong part of town, a pair of boots could get you killed. No one could steal what you didn't have.

At last they reached an imposing house in Marylebone. "Here we are," the woman said, removing her gloves. Nan looked up at the tall building—stone, not brick—with a flat front and many windows. No gables, no proper stoop. And far too few chimney stacks.

Nan heard a pianoforte playing from one of the rooms on the second floor. A chorus of small voices sang along with it:

> *How doth the little busy Bee*
> *Improve each shining Hour,*
> *And gather Honey all the day*
> *From every opening Flower!*

A few of the voices were pretty. All of them were eager. Nan listened to the singing and felt a nervous clench in her empty stomach. "What kind of home do you keep?"

The woman feigned insult. "I do not 'keep' a home. This is Miss Mayhew's Seminary for Young Ladies." When Nan did not respond, she added, "A *seminary* is a formal word for a—"

"I know what it means," Nan said. She adjusted her bag on her shoulder. "Let's get on with it."

·⊰ WHAT IT'S LIKE ⊱·

Nan hated schools. They did not pay well, and the chimneys were always filthy on account of children burning all sorts of rubbish they weren't supposed to.

There were other reasons, too.

The woman, who turned out to be something called a "house-mistress," took Nan around back to the servants' entrance. Nan followed her into the kitchen on the ground floor, which was where the main chimney began. The air was warm and steamy from what smelled like pease pudding.

The cook eyed Nan with open disgust. "Get that trash out o' my kitchen before she blacks my biscuits."

Nan silently gave up any hope of getting scraps. She made a point of letting the end of her brush rake across the wall as she passed—leaving a long streak of soot on the plaster.

The housemistress led Nan to an enormous hearth on the back wall. It reeked of drippings and offal. "It's this one here, the rest are upstairs," she said.

The cook pushed past Nan and collected some kippers that had been smoking above the fire. "Keep them hands in your pockets. I've counted every morsel of food in the larder—and if I find even one bite missing, I'll reach into your mouth and pull it from your belly myself."

Nan was eager to get to work—and away from the smell of food. It was clear that the fire had been doused only moments before her arrival. The bricks radiated heat. She squeezed the char in her pocket for good luck. She removed her coat and top hat and closed her eyes.

If you have never climbed inside a chimney, perhaps you are wondering what it's like. Imagine holding an open book. Maybe you are holding one right now? Imagine a black tunnel exactly that size—an endless, winding tunnel with no light at the end.

Imagine that the walls of the tunnel are sharp enough to cut your skin bloody. Imagine some of the walls will crush you if you touch them wrong. Imagine some of the walls are on fire.

Now imagine placing a cloth over your head.

Take a deep breath, if you still can.

And crawl inside.

·⊁ A PUZZLING QUESTION ⊁·

Nan reached the roof before the parish bells struck nine. She was shaky from hunger. From this height, she could see clear to Tower Hamlets, where she lived.

She wondered where Newt was right now. She wondered if he had made it safely through his first climb.

What's the point of seeing everything if there's
no one to see it with?

His question rang in her mind. Louder than bells. She told herself that it was better this way—leaving Newt with Roger. The boy needed to learn that he couldn't depend on anyone but himself. That was part of growing up.

She reset the chimney cap and climbed down the drainpipe

to collect the loose soot for her bag. By the end of the day, it would be as big as her. Soot was valuable to master sweeps—almost more than the fee they collected for cleaning chimneys. They sold it to farmers as fertilizer to make things grow. Nan always liked the idea that the soot she scraped might end up helping feed an apple she might one day buy in the market.

She thought about eating apples.

Then she tried not to think about eating apples.

With the main stack clear, Nan reported back to the house-mistress, who led her up to the first floor. "The next fireplace is just this way," she said, leading down a hallway lined with doors. "Mind you don't track on the rugs."

Nan heard the sharp *tap-scritch-tap* of chalk against a slate board. A woman's voice spoke from behind a closed door. "You will transcribe this poem in your finest hand, along with the answer. Any girl who provides a correct answer will receive—"

Nan never learned what the girls might receive because that was when the housemistress opened the door. The room went instantly quiet. There must have been almost twenty girls in the classroom.

All in pretty bows.

All seated at pretty wooden desks.

All staring at her.

This was the real reason Nan hated schools: the students. Most ordinary folks try to be polite and not stare. But schoolchildren do the opposite. They stare and stare and stare until you feel like there's nothing left inside you.

"What . . . is . . . *that*?" a girl in the front row whispered. Plenty loud enough for everyone to hear. There were some nervous titters from the others.

Nan didn't say anything. She knew what she looked like. Every inch of her was caked in soot. Only her eye whites and teeth stood out from the mass of grime. She could have washed for a week, and you still wouldn't know the color of her hair.

The teacher was staring just like the rest. "It seems we have a guest," she said, not looking away from Nan.

"Forgive the interruption, Miss Bloom." The housemistress extracted a speck of lint from her sleeve. "But this little fellow here'll need to get through to the chimney. Miss Mayhew ordered it be done before first frost. We'll need you and the girls out of here so as they don't get soot on their pinafores. Seems your little poetry lesson will have to wait." Nan got the sense that this woman was taking some pleasure in disrupting the class.

The teacher—Miss Bloom—said nothing. She still had the chalk in her hand, suspended between thumb and forefinger. She had been writing a sort of riddle on the board.

Feathers and bone without and within,
I am that and this and that once again.
Borne aloft among the winds,
I encircle new life within my limbs,
I bear the seed that bears the seed—
And by spring's end, small mouths I'll feed!
What am I?

Nan read and reread the words—anything to avoid the staring eyes. The letters were long and elegant and perfectly formed. "I shouldn't be long, your grace." She was unsure of how to address a teacher.

"Goodness . . ." The woman stepped closer, peering at Nan as if she were some sort of curio. "You're . . . a little *girl*."

Nan heard a sort of horrified gasp from some of the students. But the teacher did not look horrified. She looked concerned.

Nan shifted her weight. She wanted to say something to the woman—to show she was more than a filthy climber. Her eyes returned to the riddle on the board. "You have a very pretty hand," she said. "My letters are rubbish." This was true. Nan knew how to read, but writing was more difficult.

Miss Bloom looked from Nan to the blackboard and back again.

"You can . . . read that?" If the woman seemed surprised before, she now looked positively astonished. "What sort of sweep are you?"

"A filthy one," someone muttered.

Nan kept her eyes on the teacher. "What am I?" She tipped her hat. "I am . . . an *egg*." Without another word, she marched past the woman and set to work in the hearth.

Some of the girls laughed at this strange response. Miss Bloom said nothing. Nan could not see the classroom, but if she could, she might have noticed the look on the teacher's face—a dazed expression and an open mouth, slowly forming into a smile.

⊰ CHARITY AND FOLLY ⊱

Nan wasn't sure why she had answered the riddle on the board. She supposed she had wanted to impress Miss Bloom. Most climbers were illiterate, but she was different. She knew how to read. The Sweep had taught her. "The man who can read is a king among paupers," he used to tell her. "Better than a king, I'll warrant. For there's plenty o' royal folk who don't know their A— from their E—!" The Sweep would always chuckle at this last part, and Nan had never quite known why.

The Sweep hadn't been able to afford proper books. But words were everywhere. On bits of trash. On hanging signs. In shop windows. Nan's favorite lessons were when they visited cemeteries. The Sweep would lead her to the headstones, and she would read the names. She would run her fingers along the deep grooves in the stone, and the stone would speak to her. A sweep lives by his fingertips—reading the grooves and faults within dark flues. It was fitting that she learned to read by touch.

Nan was proud of being able to read. She knew it made the other climbers a little afraid of her. And it meant Crudd sometimes trusted her with written instructions—something Roger hated. She'd once caught Roger trying to read one of Crudd's instruction sheets that he had salvaged from the trash. He had been holding it upside down. She and the boys had had a good laugh over that.

Just as Nan expected, the upper chimneys of the school were horrible—nine inches square with half a dozen switchbacks. Climbers called such flues "dread shuttles" for the way they weaved back and forth, picking up other flues on their way to the top. In theory, she could reach any other room in the school from this one snaking flue.

The chimney was a tight fit, and she was making slow progress. The rule for safe climbing was "elbows and knees," but there wasn't even enough room for that. Nan thought with wry dismay how useful it would have been to have someone small like Newt helping her on this job.

She squeezed herself through a tight corner where two flues intersected. She heard voices echoing from somewhere close by.

". . . would never have believed it if I hadn't heard it with my own ears," said one voice. "*I am an egg.*"

"Tosh," said another voice. "She was probably just thinking of breakfast. I'd taken her down to the kitchen before that—"

"I'm telling you, Lottie," said the first voice. "She *read* the riddle. And she solved it faster than any one of our girls."

Eavesdropping was one of the few perks of the job. From a single flue, a climber might hear a dozen different scenes playing out. Nan was fairly sure that it was Miss Bloom talking to the housemistress. And it sounded as if they were talking about *her*.

The voices were coming from a dirty flue just above Nan's head. It was dangerous to climb into a flue that hadn't first been brushed—the walls could come down around you. But Nan *had* to hear what the women were saying. She braced her elbows and forced herself into the narrow passage. A sharp bit of brick cut a fresh wound into her side, but she ignored the pain.

"I'll kindly ask you not to take that familiar tone, Miss Bloom," the housemistress said. "And may I ask why you are bothering me with all this when you've a class to teach?"

"A class *you* interrupted. And I'm telling you because a girl like that deserves better than sweeping filth. The seminary has charitable patrons. I know they—"

Here she was interrupted by a laugh. "There's charity, and then there's folly. If you think a girl like that would ever be let into a place like this, you are even more mistaken than I thought." Nan heard footsteps as the woman moved across the room. "We might as well take in lepers and ragmen while we're at it."

"Perhaps Headmistress Mayhew will see it differently." Miss Bloom followed after her. "If we can just . . ."

Nan listened as the voices receded. She wanted to kick the housemistress. But more than that, she wanted to know what the teacher was saying.

If she could find the chimney path to the next room, perhaps she could hear them. She released her elbows from the wall to drop back to the main stack.

And that's when she discovered that she was stuck.

·⊰ STUCK ⊱·

So much of Nan's life involved forgetting things. She lived with the grime by forgetting what it was to be clean. She scaled heights by forgetting to look down. She squeezed through a flue by forgetting she was in a flue.

Once Nan realized she might be stuck, however, that was all she could think of. *I'm stuck*, she thought. *I'm stuck!* And when she tried to forget this fact, her mind shouted even louder—

I'M STUCK!

She tried to push her body down and then up but only managed to wedge herself in more tightly.

"Nan, you fool," she muttered. How many thousands of chimneys had she gotten through without a hitch? And yet here she was, packed tight as a musket ball. The worst part was that she knew it was her own fault. If she hadn't been so desperate to hear what Miss Bloom was saying, she wouldn't be in this predicament.

And why did it matter what that woman said? She was just another grown-up.

Nan still had a burlap cloth over her head. It was meant to protect her eyes and nose from loose soot. Usually she could make out light through the fibers, but not now. The chimney cap high above her was too far away to let in even a speck of light.

"Hello!" she called.

Not even an echo came back.

She could feel her heartbeat pounding in her ears. The burlap on her head suddenly felt suffocating. Her brush hand was tight against her cheek, and so she let go of the handle and pulled the cloth from her face. Soot sprinkled down in her eyes, but she didn't care. She could breathe.

"HELLOOOOOO!" She called again.

This time someone heard her.

"Who is that?" said a small voice.

It was coming from a room beneath her. Nan felt a wave of relief. She had heard stories of climbers who got stuck and weren't found for days. She pitched her head toward the voice. "It's the sweep," she called down. "I'm stuck in a flue!"

"The sweep?" the voice said, confused. "We haven't any sweeps here. Are you sure you're not . . . an *egg*?"

Nan heard the sounds of suppressed laughter. It was the girls from Miss Bloom's class. Apparently they still hadn't cracked the riddle. Not that that mattered right now.

Nan took a calming breath. "I need someone to fetch my master," she said. "His name is Wilkie Crudd."

"I didn't know eggs could talk," the girl said. "I must be imagining things."

Nan *imagined* ripping the girl's pigtails clean from her scalp. "Please?" she called. "I am trapped in here, and I need help."

She heard a murmur of voices below as someone else entered the room. "Girls? Get back from there." It was the teacher, Miss Bloom. "Hello?" Her voice rang up through the flue. "Who is that?"

"It's the climbing girl," Nan called. "The one who reads!" She didn't know why she said that part. What other climbing girl could it be? "I'm stuck in a flue, and I need someone to fetch my master."

There was a flurry of activity and voices. Nan waited in the darkness while maids were sent out in search of Crudd. "Help will be here soon," the teacher called up to her. "Please forgive my students for not responding with the grace and concern befitting a Mayhew girl." Nan could tell from the teacher's tone that every one of them would be in trouble. That was something, at least.

Nan's panic slowly subsided and was replaced by hunger and embarrassment. If the Sweep could see her now, what would he say? She could feel the char in her pocket—uncomfortably warm against her leg. She had always thought of the Sweep's gift as a lucky talisman. Not lucky enough, it seemed.

She closed her eyes and shuddered to think what Crudd would make of such a mistake. This was not the sort of thing an apprentice did.

Finally, after what felt like hours, Miss Bloom's voice returned. "We've found someone to help you," she called up. "He's coming now."

Nan heard footsteps on the roof. There was a scraping sound directly overhead, and bits of soot sprinkled down as the chimney cap was pulled away. She blinked at the ray of blinding light above her. "Master Crudd?" she called.

A silhouette blocked out the light as someone peered down at her.

It did not look like Crudd.

"Well, well, well," said a thin voice. "If it isn't Cinderella."

⊰ ROGER ⊱

For as long as Nan had known Roger, they had been rivals.
The two had first met shortly after Nan had lost the Sweep.
In fact, it had been Roger who had discovered her on Crudd's roof
and taken her to his master. Nan had the vague impression that
Roger had hoped to make a friend of her. But Crudd had made that
impossible. "I am not running a charity," he had said once Nan had
scribbled her initials on a seven-year contract. "I cannot afford
to feed another climber. Each day, whichever of you sweeps more
chimneys gets supper. The other one gets slops."

So every day they swept.

And Nan got supper.

And Roger got slops.

Nan knew all this. But she could not know—not truly—how
this rivalry had shaped the boy. In the years that followed, she had
become a sort of mortal enemy to Roger. The source of his every
misery. The eternal obstacle standing in his path.

And now she was at his mercy.

"Are you going to help me or not?" she called up from the darkness. She knew it was important not to sound scared—that would only make Roger realize how much she needed him.

The boy peered down at her, his head dark against the sky. She could not see his features, but she knew he was smiling. "Oh, dear," he said. "It seems the great Nan Sparrow has got herself stuck in a flue."

"I bet you're loving this." Nan adjusted herself. "Where's Crudd?"

"The master's off on weddings," Roger said. "So I guess it's up to me to pull you out." He rapped some hardened soot with the end of his brush. Chunks tumbled down the length of the chimney and pelted Nan in the face. "Afraid it's a bit narrow for me to climb. I'm getting too big for these square nines. So are you, it seems."

"Send Whittles, then!" Nan called. "Or Shilling-Tom!"

"Sadly, I gave the boys the afternoon off. Seems you're stuck with me." There was something about the way he said this that made her uncomfortable.

"I'm here, too, Nan!" a smaller voice called. Newt's face appeared in the top of the chimney. "I can get you out!"

"No," Nan said firmly. Newt was too inexperienced for a chimney like this. She didn't need another stuck climber to worry about. "Let Roger handle it."

"And handle it I will!" Roger rubbed his chin. "Only it's a bit tricky. You're wedged pretty far down. And from what I can see there's no hope of getting rope or rig around you." He was right about this. "Only way I see out of this is if you get *yourself* free. And for that, we'll need special *motivation*."

Nan felt a prickle of nausea as she realized what he was saying. "You can't mean . . ."

"I can, and I do!" Roger leaned back from the opening. "Newt, this morning you asked about a thing called 'the Devil's Nudge.' I say it's time we showed you."

⊰ THE DEVIL'S NUDGE ⊱

Nan felt a cold sweat forming on her brow. "The Devil's Nudge?" For a moment, she thought Roger might be joking. But this was *Roger*. Roger, who cheated by adding sawdust to his soot. Roger, who stole coins from beggars' cups. Roger, who kicked dogs just to hear them yelp. Roger, who would do anything to prevent Nan from making apprentice.

"Roger!" she shouted, straining against the walls of the flue. The char in her pocket was snagged against the rough brick, preventing her from moving up or down. "Please, listen to me!"

But he was already gone. She could hear footsteps running down the edge of the roof. She thrashed her head, trying to pull herself free. She had to get out of the chimney. Had to get free before—

"Miss me?" called a cheery voice beneath her. "Just sit tight, and you'll be out in no time. Most of you, anyway."

Nan took a deep breath. She knew Roger wasn't trying to kill her. He wanted to hurt her, certainly. But he didn't understand just how stuck she was. "Roger, listen to me!" She tried to keep her voice calm. "I know you think this will work, but—"

"That's the first rule with the Devil's Nudge." Roger was talking to Newt. "Don't let them talk you out of it. They may have to break a few of their own bones to get out, but they'll get out just the same."

"But what *is* it?" Newt's voice echoed up. "What's the Devil's Nudge?" He sounded even more scared than Nan.

"It's just what it sounds like. A nudge."

Nan closed her eyes. She could almost hear Roger reaching into his coat pocket and removing a single match.

Newt cried out, "You'll burn her up!"

"You sit still or I'll shove you up there with her!"

There were sounds of a struggle, and then she heard Newt yelp.

"Leave Newt alone!" Nan screamed.

She heard more commotion as the door swung open. "I heard shouting." It was the teacher. "Is the girl all right?" And then, "What are you doing with that match?"

"Official sweep business, ma'am. Stand back." There was the sharp *scratch* of phosphorus against stone. Nan caught the sharp smell of sulfur. "Everyone thinks you're the better climber,

Cinderella," Roger's voice hissed up from below. "Let's see if they still think that when you're too cooked to hold a broom."

"Roger!" Nan shouted. "Roger, no—" Her cries were cut off by a hollow *whoof* as the match hit the coals. Air sucked down through the chimney, like a beast drawing a deep breath.

First came the smoke, a thick black tendril that slid up the flue and snaked around her neck. She coughed and felt her eyes water.

Next came the heat. It started as a prickling sensation on her back and heels, then spread up her legs. Within seconds, the warmth had turned to a blistering heat. "Roger, you win!" she shrieked, releasing her last lungful of air. "I'll quit Crudd! I'll quit climbing! Just PUT OUT THE FIRE!"

She could hear Roger holler something below, but his words were swallowed by the roaring of the flames.

Her entire body felt as if it were burning from the inside out. The char in her pocket had gotten so hot that she thought it would burn a hole clean through her. Both of her eyes were stinging, and tears were streaming down her face.

Animal instinct took over, and she clawed and wriggled, desperate to climb free of the smoke. She heard a sickening *pop*, and a terrible pain ripped through her right shoulder.

She ignored the pain and kept climbing higher. The heat was no longer just coming from below. The char in her pocket had somehow caught fire and was searing her thigh like a brand. The flue seemed to tighten around her like a fist. Smoke slithered down her throat and into her lungs.

"Help . . . ," she gasped with her final ounce of life. "Help . . ."

And then Nan Sparrow burned.

⋇ STORY SOUP ⊱

Sometimes, on nights when there was no food to eat, the girl and her Sweep used to make story soup. The girl would fill her pockets with trash that she found on the streets—scraps of paper or trampled strings or bits of colored glass. At the end of the day, she would present these things to the Sweep. "Make story soup!" she would tell him.

"Oh-ho!" the Sweep would always exclaim, rubbing his belly with both hands. "You've brought us ingredients for a right feast!"

He would look at the ingredients, holding each one between his blackened fingers like a crown jewel. "Mmm," he would say slowly. "Very interesting, this one. Lots of potential."

"Into the pot!" the girl would shout. She used to go mad with impatience. The Sweep always took too long with this part.

The Sweep would remove his hat in a special way—rolling it between his fingers like a magician. He would nestle the crown in his lap and put the ingredients inside. He would mix them around with the end of his broom. Sometimes he would hum. He used to close his eyes and pretend to smell the story cooking inside. He would add imaginary pinches of salt and pepper. And then he would open his eyes and serve up a piping hot story.

He might reach into the hat and produce half of an oyster shell. "There once was a haberdasher who made caps for fairies. But one day he entered his workshop to find that his caps had been stolen. . . . His only clue: one strand of hair left on the ground." And so saying, he might produce a tattered bit of string. The Sweep would take out each object as he talked, weaving it into the story. Before long, he would have worked in the glass and paper scraps and whatever other ingredients she had brought for story soup.

And even though they had eaten nothing, the girl still ended her day with a belly full of story—which sticks to the ribs even better than mutton.

There was one pot of story soup that the girl would never forget. The Sweep had been collecting ingredients for a long time—gathering them and keeping them but never using them. She would watch him review the objects before bed, placing each one in the crown of his hat. "A doll's eye for wonder . . . ," he would mutter. "A feather for kindness . . . a thimble for mending . . . a wooden chessman for courage . . . a swaddle for warmth."

The girl knew these ingredients. She could not remember where the Sweep had gathered them, but she had the sense that he had been collecting them for many years. She knew they were important.

"Can we make story soup tonight?" the girl said one night. "If you are too tired, I can make it." The Sweep had not eaten any food for many days. The girl thought story soup might make him feel better.

The Sweep looked at her, and his expression carried something she could not understand. "Not yet." He folded a scrap of soft blue cloth and gently laid it in his hat. "There is one final ingredient."

"What is it?" The girl leaped to her feet. She thought it might be a new sort of game. "I'll bet you've hidden it for me to find!"

"No." The Sweep closed his eyes. The spaces beneath his lids were hollow and dark. "It is not hidden."

"Tell me, and I can fetch it," she said.

The Sweep shook his head and secreted the ingredients back into his pockets. His hands were shaking. "Soon enough you will know the story." The way he said this, it made the story sound like something he did not want to tell.

Of course, this made her want to hear it all the more.

But the girl never heard that last story.

She never learned what that final ingredient was.

·⊰ ALIVE ⊱·

Nan Sparrow was not dead.

She had been dreaming of the Sweep. They had been together, making story soup—something she had all but forgotten about. Little Nan had crawled inside his hat to find the ingredients, and the crown of the hat had turned into a burning chimney. She remembered crying out for the Sweep, trying to escape. And then . . .

She was alone.

Nan released a whimper. She could feel a cold wooden floor beneath her. She must have lost consciousness during the nudge. But if so, how did she escape?

She tried to swallow. Her throat was cracked and dry. A carapace of soot encased her lips and nose and eyelids. She scraped the soot from her eyes, which stung and watered. She blinked, trying to see where she was.

She saw rafters directly above her.

She saw her own breath.

She saw cobwebs and shadows and a thin shaft of moonlight.

She was curled up in a ball on a bare floor. When she moved, motes of dead ash rose from her body, swirling in the light.

How long had she been there?

Nan saw hunks of charred rubble scattered around her. She put her hands on the floor and forced herself to sit up. Her shoulder winced in protest, but she persisted. Nan's eyes had adjusted to the moonlight. She could see a chimney stack that had collapsed in on itself—a black abscess of bricks and mortar devoured by fire. It was the seminary chimney.

Nan was in a low crawl space above the attic—barely large enough for her to stand in. A porthole window at one end let in shafts of pale light. She ran her fingers over the seam of a dusty trapdoor. It looked like it hadn't been opened in years. Nan turned back to the destroyed chimney. She rubbed her throbbing head. The last thing she remembered was crying for help. She must have pushed a hole through the wall of the burning chimney the moment before she passed out. How else could she have escaped?

She looked down at her clothes, which were charred and tattered. She noticed the place where her pocket had burst into flame. The skin was pink and new—tender, like the flesh beneath a scab.

She checked her arms and legs and even the soles of her feet. Somehow she had not gotten one single burn.

She should have been crushed by the rubble, burned by the fire. But somehow she had survived. Had she been passed out long enough to heal from her injuries? Surely not.

The ache in her head had subsided to a dull throbbing, and she now realized that she was very cold. She looked around for something with which to cover herself, to fend off the chill. She noticed something on the floor beside her. It was small and round and dark gray.

It was her char.

That little clod of soot had warmed her on many a cold night. It must have tumbled from her pocket when she broke through the chimney wall. Nan pulled herself to her knees and crawled toward it. She reached out a trembling hand. But as she did, something unusual happened—

The char *moved*.

It did not move far. It rolled only far enough to escape her grasp. Nan had seen the char roll before. It would sometimes tumble from her open palm in the mornings. But never with such intention.

She shook her head clear and reached for it again—

The char moved again.

Now Nan was certain it had happened. There was a gray smear on the floorboards where it had rolled. She crouched on her heels and readied both hands. "If you think you can get away from me, you've got another think coming." She lunged forward—aiming not where the char was but where it would be when it tried to dart away.

"Got you!" she cried as she crashed to the floor. She had the thing cupped in her hands. She could feel it twitching against her fingers—flustered, panicked—expanding and shrinking like a racing heartbeat.

Nan's heart was racing, too.

She sat up and slowly, slowly opened her hands, staring at the thing inside.

She knew the Sweep's gift as well as she knew her own self. It was the same lump of charred soot she had carried with her for five years—every pock and divot was where it had always been. Only something had changed. It was trembling. It was *alive*.

Whatever happened inside that chimney must have changed the char—brought it to life. All thoughts of thirst and cold and pain left Nan. All she could think about was this little *thing*. It seemed so frightened. And it was so small.

"Don't be afraid," she whispered. "I won't hurt you." She ran her thumb gently along the side. She didn't know why.

The thing became still. It settled into her palm. Again she noticed the two divots etched into its face—dark as a shadow's shadow. They looked so much like *eyes*.

Nan stared at the thing. The thing stared back. Its warmth radiated up her arms and through her whole body. She did not question whether the Sweep had meant for this to happen: She knew at once that this little creature was not a mistake.

Her vision blurred with tears, and she blinked. "Hello, little thing," she whispered. "I've waited so long to meet you."

The thing blinked back.

·⊁ A NAME ⊀·

The Sweep had raised Nan to believe in impossible things. He had told her countless stories of genies and dragons and witches and fairies. He had made her believe that a thousand wonders were waiting around every corner. But she had learned through hard experience that those stories were not the real world.

The real world offered no miracles.

No "once upon a time."

No "happily ever after."

And yet, here in this dusty crawl space, she held a miracle in her hands. A miracle with eyes and a heartbeat and a crumbly gray body.

How many times had she almost thrown the Sweep's gift away? "I don't understand," she said. "Why now? After five years, *why today*?"

The thing was no longer looking at Nan. It craned its body

to take in the space beyond. Its gaze moved from one thing to another—rafter, window, cobweb, the collapsed chimney.

"Did you do that?" Nan said, pointing to the crumbled bricks.

The thing looked up at her. And then it nodded.

"You . . . can understand me?" she said.

The thing nodded again. It screwed its body into her palm. Its eyes tightened in concentration. Nan saw a thin crack appear along the bottom of its face—long and uneven, like a scar.

"You have a mouth," Nan said, her own mouth breaking into a smile.

The thing opened its mouth. It made a rasping sound like two bricks being dragged against each other. It was a hollow, mewling cry that seemed to move through Nan's ears straight into her bones. It was not a beautiful sound.

The thing had not spoken any real words, but Nan felt very much that it had just told her something about the fire. "Is that so?" she said. "You must have been very frightened."

The thing nodded gravely.

It rolled itself off her hand and spoke as it moved around the crawl space. Again, she felt she somehow understood. The thing was telling her about what had happened inside the chimney.

"You must be very tired," Nan said when it had finished its story. "It's not every day someone is born."

The thing nodded.

Nan sat back on her heels. What did soot creatures eat? Did they wear clothes? How was she meant to care for it? "I suppose we should start by giving you a proper name," she said. "I can't very well keep calling you my char."

The thing made a noise that sounded very much like agreement.

"All right, then." Nan tapped her chin. "The best sort of name tells folks who you really are." The Sweep had believed that. That's why he and Nan both had the name Sparrow—because they nested under the eaves, like little birds. "So first let's figure out who you are."

The thing nodded.

"Let me think," Nan said. She lay down on her stomach and stared at the creature in front of her. It smelled like crackling embers on a cold day. Its surface was soft as a bed of ashes. It was as dark as fresh coal. "Maybe your name can be about how you're made of burned-up things," she said. "We could call you Sootly."

The thing wrinkled its face.

"Ashkin?"

The thing made a retching sound.

"Emberton?"

The thing glared at her. It screwed up its face, and a gust of flames burst from its body.

"Ow!" Nan cried, pulling back. "You nearly took off my nose." The thing gave a sort of *harumph* and rolled away from her, burning a trail of char in the floorboards. "I'm trying the best I can," Nan called. "You don't have to be rude." But the thing would have no more of it.

Nan scratched the back of her neck. It was clear that the thing didn't want a silly name. She supposed this made sense. She thought of how it made her feel when Roger called her Cinderella. She thought about what she had called the thing before it had come to life. "What about a real person name, but with the word 'char' in it?" she said. "Maybe . . . Charlemagne? Or Charles . . . or just Charlie?"

The thing turned toward her.

"Charlie?" Nan said again. "Do you like that name?"

The thing opened its mouth and made a sort of croaking sound. "*Kkrraaa–rreeeee . . .*" It sounded nothing like "Charlie."

Nan smiled. "I like it, too."

⊰ FRUITCAKE ⊱

Nan and Charlie stayed up through the night. They were both too excited to sleep. After a little exploring, Nan found an ancient tin of fruitcake beneath a loose floorboard—no doubt stashed there by some long-ago student who hadn't wanted to share with her classmates. The cake was stale and far too sweet . . . and the best thing Nan had ever eaten. Charlie nibbled at the edge of some burned bricks.

Nan found they were able to converse about basic things with little trouble. Charlie could not speak, exactly, but the sounds he uttered made a sort of sense to her. She told him all about what he was: How she had first found him on the rooftop all those years before. How she carried him in her pocket. How he warmed her on the coldest nights in Crudd's coal bin. And, finally, how she woke in the crawl space to find him *alive* and watching over her.

Charlie listened to every word with unblinking eyes. When she had finished, he made her tell it again.

Nan decided it was the fire that had made Charlie come to life. As though all these years he had been a piece of kindling, waiting for his spark. "Thank you," she said. "I don't know what would have happened if you hadn't gotten me out of there." But she did know. She had seen it before. Masons would come and pull apart the bricks and drag out a tiny charred body, and no one would ever speak of her again.

She wondered if the Sweep had really known what Charlie was. He must have. Perhaps he had thought that Nan would burn it straightaway for warmth? But she hadn't. Instead, she had kept it.

A pink light crept over the crest of the porthole window. Charlie jumped back and hid behind Nan's leg. "It's fine," Nan said. "It's only daybreak."

Charlie made a sound like a question.

"You'll want to see this." The window was decorative, and had no latch. She wiped grime from the glass with her sleeve and set Charlie on the sill. Outside, the sun woke over the whole East End. She could actually see it erasing the shadows, street by street, until it broke from the horizon and flooded the space with golden light.

Nan watched Charlie watching his first sunrise. His eyes were impossibly wide.

"It's like Heaven itself is offering us a gift," she whispered.

The first sounds of morning had begun: bells and carts and the cries of eager sweeps. Far in the distance, she could make out Crudd's house, hidden in the shadow of St. Florian's Church. "See that tower there?" she said, pointing. "That's home."

"*Hhooommm?*" Charlie said, trying his best to repeat her word.

Nan tried to think of a fitting explanation. "Home is a safe place to put your things so burglars can't touch them."

Charlie nodded, and then hopped off the sill and rolled into Nan's pocket. The place she had kept him for five years. "*Hhooommm,*" he said.

Nan took him back out again. "I'll take my pocket with me, don't worry." She looked back toward the East End. Toward Crudd's house. Worry fluttered into her gut. She could only imagine what Roger had told Crudd about the fire—that Nan had started it herself, maybe even on purpose. Even without Roger, it was bad. A chimney fire was expensive and embarrassing. Crudd would not be happy.

Nan heard voices echoing up from the house below as the cook and the servants began their day. There were shouts from the street, and then—

"Brooms up!"

The voice was so close it made Nan jump back. Footsteps echoed directly above them. "Someone's on the roof," she said.

Charlie turned toward her. "*Rrroooo—?*"

"Shh!" Nan crawled back from the window.

There were more footsteps. "Nothing down this one," a voice echoed down through the flue. It was Shilling-Tom.

"I'm tellin' you, she's dead!" called a raspy voice. That was Whittles. "The fire burned the whole stack to rubble. Me and Tom were up and down twice yesterday. It was all we could do to keep it from catching the house."

An icy voice echoed up from somewhere below. "If she's dead, then there will be a body. Look again."

Nan felt a clench of panic. "It's Crudd." In that moment, hearing his voice, she knew she could never go back to him.

A door slammed downstairs, and Nan heard tense voices. It sounded as if Crudd was arguing with some other men—inspectors from the Board of Works. "And why not fine *the school* for keeping filthy chimneys?" Crudd snapped. "The whole thing is a ruse to allow the girl to escape her legal obligation to me. You will not get one farthing from me unless I see the body!"

There were shouts of alarm. She heard sounds of footsteps climbing a staircase to the attic. "Nan Sparrow!" his voice roared directly beneath her. "I know you're hiding!"

Nan dropped to her knees and started to push bricks atop the trapdoor in the floor. "He's coming," she whispered. "We have to get out of here!"

The bricks jumped as Crudd pounded against the other side of the door. "Nan!" his voice boomed. "Show yourself!"

Nan could feel Charlie shaking in her palm. She looked around, panic-stricken. There were no other doors. The chimney was being watched. She scrambled to the window at the end of the crawl space. She wrapped her fist in the tatters of her sleeve and broke the glass.

More shouts as the trapdoor shuddered again. "Unhand me!" Crudd shouted, apparently pulling himself free from the inspectors.

Nan dragged herself through the round window and spilled out onto the roof. Sharp glass cut her shin, but she bit her tongue to stop from crying aloud.

She heard a crash as the trapdoor broke open and Crudd climbed into the crawl space. "Nan!" he bellowed.

Nan pressed herself against the roof, hiding from Crudd's view. Had he seen her? She could hear him inside, rifling through the rubble.

"Nan?" a small voice said beside her.

It was Newt, standing at an uncapped chimney, clutching a rope in his tiny hand. His face was pale, even beneath the grime. "They . . . they said you were dead . . ."

Nan stared at him, eyes wide, imploring. "I am."

She took a step back and dropped from the gable.

THE HOUSE OF
·⊀ ONE HUNDRED ⊁·
CHIMNEYS

N an stumbled between two wagons on her way past Euston Station. Her body was weak and trembling. Blood was running from her shin and she thought she might have turned her ankle when she dropped down from the rainspout. Growlers and omnibuses crossed in every direction—the whole city was a confusing swirl of hooves and wheels and shouts. The September fog meant she could scarcely see twenty paces in front of her. She didn't know where she was going. She only knew she needed to get off the street before Crudd found her.

She hoped, desperately, that Newt wouldn't tell what he'd seen.

A hulking train rumbled out of the station, shaking the ground. Nan glanced behind her shoulder before slipping into a mews that cut into Bloomsbury. She remembered Charlie in her pocket. He was probably terrified. She lifted him out. "That was a narrow escape," she said. "I hope I didn't scrape you when I squeezed through that window."

Charlie stared at the narrow alleyway. Empty stables ran along one side; on the other, doors to servants' apartments. "*Hhooommm?*"

Nan shook her head. "Not here. But we do need a safe place to hide." She thought she might be able to find lodging at a doss-house in the Old Nichol. Or maybe get work in a factory along the river. But Crudd would surely search in all of those places. Besides, she wasn't sure she could make it that far in her current state. The longer she was in the streets, the more certain she would be spotted. "We need to go somewhere close by," she said, scanning the rooftops. "Somewhere no sweep or climber will ever think to look."

And that was how she found herself standing before the House of One Hundred Chimneys.

The door was barred, and all of the windows were shuttered and locked. Nan thought her best way in would be one of the chimneys. The stacks were tall and decrepit. Most climbers wouldn't have risked scaling them without rope, for fear of breaking their necks. But Charlie needed a home, and so Nan climbed.

The inside of the stack was choked with spiderwebs and rats' nests and goodness knows what else. But these were old chimneys, built for the burning of wood, not coal, which meant that the walls were at least free of hard soot. Nan could feel Charlie shivering. And so she sang to him, the way the Sweep had sung to her.

She slowly made her way down until she reached a hearth. "Here we are," she said, and drew Charlie from her pocket. She thought they were in a servant's bedroom—though it was hard to tell for sure. The windows were boarded up, and there were gray tarpaulins covering the furniture.

Nan set Charlie on the floor. She felt her way across the room until she found a wooden chair. She turned it upside down and broke off one of the legs. She tore a strip from a tarpaulin and tied it around one end. "We have a torch. We just need a match."

Charlie made an excited sound and then scrunched up his face in intense concentration. After a moment, a thin trail of smoke began to waft up from his body. A tiny flame appeared just above his right eye.

"Perfect!" Nan lit her torch, which filled the room with flickering orange light. Everything was coated in a thick layer of dust. "It's like snow," she whispered. She didn't know why she whispered.

Charlie sneezed and rolled backward. "*Sssnnnoo?*" he said, righting himself.

Nan wasn't sure she could explain snow. "I wouldn't want to spoil the surprise," she said. "You'll just have to see it for yourself."

They walked down the narrow stairs, guided by their torch. Each step issued an angry creak. "That's just the house saying hello," Nan said.

Charlie tried to say "hello" back.

The house was enormous. Each room led to another room and another and another. Nan made a practice of watching her own footprints in the dust to make sure she wouldn't become too lost. By her count, there were fourteen bedrooms, three parlors, a drawing room, a smallish ballroom, one giant study filled with books and another filled with maps—not to mention a labyrinth of hallways and staircases and closet passages.

Nan told Charlie, "They say this old house belonged to a famous captain and explorer who died at sea. It's been haunted ever since."

Charlie made a questioning sound.

And so Nan explained ghosts to him. But no matter how she tried, she couldn't make him understand the concept of death. Finally she gave up. He would learn about death in time. Everyone did.

At last came time for sleep. Nan told Charlie he could sleep in any room he wanted. He picked Nan's pocket. After all that ghost talk, she supposed she couldn't blame him.

Nan chose the grandest bedroom for herself. She thought it must have been where the captain slept. It had a fireplace large enough for her to stand in. The closet was bigger than Wilkie Crudd's entire coal bin. A chandelier fashioned from an old ship's wheel hung from above. But none of that compared to the bed. The bed had four tall wooden posts that nearly touched the ceiling.

In all her life, Nan had never touched a bed. Not with the Sweep, not with Crudd. Her only beds had been rooftops and stoops and open fields and coal bins.

She approached the captain's bed and pressed a hand on the embroidered duvet, leaving a dark print. The duvet was stiff and covered in dust. She coughed and pulled it onto the floor. The sheets beneath glowed white in the darkness. Nan wasn't sure how to get into the bed, which was nearly as high as her chin. She decided that that was what the posts on the corners were for. She climbed the post and then set an uncertain foot on the mattress. She fell over at once.

Nan had fallen many times in her life. To her, falling meant hurting herself. But when she fell on the bed, she did not get hurt. Instead, she felt herself engulfed by softness. Was this what sleep felt like for rich people? "It's like lying on a cloud," she said.

Charlie did not ask her about clouds. He had rolled out of her pocket and was jumping up and down on the mattress. It looked like fun, so Nan tried jumping, too.

They jumped for probably an hour.

Finally, exhausted and elated, Nan flopped back down. "We should sleep now," she said.

She drew a cover over her body and put her head on a pillow. Charlie rolled beside her and tucked himself in close.

Within moments, she was asleep.

·⊀ A ROOM FOR EVERYTHING ⊱·

Nan spent the first few weeks in constant fear of discovery by Crudd or the police. But she soon discovered that the rest of London had little interest in the House of One Hundred Chimneys. Still, she was careful to keep the shutters closed and never to approach from the street, entering instead from a turret window on the top floor.

As days wore on, the House of One Hundred Chimneys became a true home for Nan and Charlie. Their first task had been to dust and scrub every inch. Nan discovered she didn't mind the work so long as Charlie was there to keep her company. Together they inventoried all the interesting artifacts that the captain had brought home from his travels—spears and shrunken heads and treasure maps and arrowheads and sextants and clay pipes and pressed flowers and insect husks and even a real cannon. (Nan tried to shoot Charlie from the cannon, but it didn't work.)

It is a quiet marvel to watch another person grow up before your eyes. With each passing hour, Charlie seemed to be changing more into himself.

After an unfortunate incident in which Nan's pillowcase caught fire in the middle of the night, Charlie had been made to sleep in a pile of loose soot in the fireplace. Every morning the pile of soot would be a bit smaller and Charlie would be a bit bigger.

Charlie seemed to acquire language with remarkable ease. Individual words soon gave way to little broken sentences of two or three words strung together. Nan was exceedingly grateful for this. She had always disliked babies for their inability to plainly say what they needed. "Babies just cry and cry and make you guess what's the matter," she said. "But you can just come out and tell me."

Nan figured the more words Charlie heard, the faster he would learn. So she made a habit of narrating everything that she did. "I am trying on this suit of armor," she might say. Or "I have a bit of watercress stuck between my teeth, and so I'm using this rusty cutlass to pick it out." Or "I am making a pincushion in the shape of Toby Squall."

Nan remembered how the Sweep had done the same thing for her when she was small. Even when there was little to say, he would say that, and then some. The Sweep's words were the music of her childhood. It was probably the reason that, even though she could barely remember his face, she could still remember his voice.

The dreams helped with that, too. Ever since Charlie had been "born," her dreams of the Sweep had become more vivid and varied. And they didn't feel like dreams anymore. They felt almost like memories—chapters of her life she had long since forgotten rising to the surface. Nan felt fairly certain that the dreams were somehow connected to Charlie. But any time she asked him about it, he seemed unable or unwilling to respond.

Even with shelter, food remained a concern. And so once Nan felt strong enough, she decided to take Charlie climbing. She bought a new brush and scraper by pawning a vase from the captain's den. Charlie was too big for her pocket, and so she made a sling for him that hung from her shoulder. "You're nearly a month old," she told him. "It's time you saw something of the world."

Nan had at first been nervous to step back into a chimney—she was still recovering from the horrors of the nudge. But Charlie changed things somehow. She knew that if she acted afraid, then Charlie would notice and become afraid himself. "It's easy as apples for folks like us," she told him the first time she forced herself up into a flue. "We got soot in our veins." And in saying this, it began to feel true.

She kept to the West End—miles from where Crudd or any of the boys might spot her. She and Charlie swept houses up and down Paddington and Westminster and Kensington, singing for jobs as she had always done. The homes were large and beautiful, the streets lined with orange-leaved oaks. She kept Charlie in her sling while she climbed, and the two of them would talk the whole day through.

With the cold days of November fast approaching, there was no shortage of work. Whenever customers asked the name of Nan's master, she would tell them she worked for "the Captain." This was a little joke between her and Charlie. Having no master meant she was regularly stiffed. But Nan didn't mind, because she was able to sell the soot she collected to a dustman named Horace Nobbs, who paid a fair price and asked few questions. "How a little slip of a girl manages to bring in two bushels a day is beyond me," he would often say.

By the end of the month, the captain's house was properly turned out, and they set to reorganizing. "We need to make this place our very own," she explained. The house was so big that they could make a room for everything. They had a Tantrum Room (filled with cushions and pillows), a Dress-Up Room (full of capes, hats, and regalia), a Banging-Pots-and-Pans Room (self-explanatory), an Inventing Room, a Gauntlet (which was where Nan made mazes for Charlie to roll through), and a Rubbish Room (which they had to stop using because the smell of the food scraps became so bad).

Nan named all the rooms except for one. Charlie had requested that he do one room all by himself.

"Do not peek on it," he said to her. "I want the room to be a surprise." Nan had said he could use the attic, which was enormous and crammed full of unused furniture that she was too lazy to sort. Charlie spent several days working on his room. Nan would hear occasional crashing sounds as pieces of furniture tumbled down the staircase. She had no idea how a creature without arms and legs could move furniture. Perhaps Charlie was stronger than she realized.

At last he came to her with an announcement. "I have finished with my room," he said.

Nan followed him up to the attic. The climb was difficult on account of the stairway being full of broken furniture. She opened the door and stepped inside and looked around.

"What do you think?" Charlie asked.

"I . . ." Nan did not know what to say. "It's . . . enormous."

"I will call it 'the Nothing Room,' " he said. "Because it is full of nothing." This was true. Every piece of furniture and every trunk and every crate and cobweb was gone. All that remained was a grove of chimney stacks—stretching from floor to ceiling like brick tree trunks.

Nan nodded. "That is a good name." She hesitated. "What is it for?"

Charlie took a deep breath. "For being quiet, and things like that."

Nan sat down next to him. "A Nothing Room is just what this house needed."

Charlie got so warm his head smoldered. He was that proud.

Nan and Charlie stayed in the room all through the afternoon and into the night.

Just being quiet, and things like that.

⊰ BONFIRE NIGHT ⊱

The late-autumn sky was a cauldron of swirling gray. There was a smell of ash and mischief in the air. Dead leaves danced across the streets like brittle phantoms. And everywhere Nan went, she heard the whispering words—

Remember, remember, the fifth of November.
Gunpowder, treason, and plot!

"What did you say?" Charlie asked, rolling closer.

Nan must have been muttering the song under her breath. "It's an old rhyme to remember Bonfire Night," she said. "That's the name of a holiday."

"A holly-day?" Charlie said.

"Holidays are special times when folks dance and sing and play games and eat big meals."

"Oh, yes," Charlie said. "We do a lot of holly-days."

Nan pulled on her coat and grabbed the torn bed curtain she had been using as a muffler. "A long time ago there was a guy named Fox, and he tried to blow up the king with gunpowder, but they caught him. And now folks celebrate every year by setting off fireworks."

Charlie's eyes widened. "I do like fire."

"I know you do." Nan tied the curtain around her neck. "And fire*works* are even better."

Nan wanted to take Charlie out for Bonfire Night, but she needed a way to transport him. In recent weeks, he had grown too large to go climbing with her. He was nearly the size of a winter squash now, and heavy. Nan led him down the hallway. "I thought you could ride in this." She brought out the old perambulator that she had found in a closet—it was frilly and powder blue and felt out of place in the home of a seafaring bachelor. It hinted at some mystery in the captain's life that Nan could not quite piece together.

"This is a pram," Nan said. "Nannies use them to take babies out of doors."

Charlie looked up at the perambulator. "For babies?" He pushed his head against the back wheel. It squeaked. "I do not think I want to be in that."

"I can't have you just tumbling down the street by yourself." She patted the handle. "You'll love it in here."

Charlie scooted back. "I am *not* a baby."

Nan rolled her eyes. "You're certainly acting like one. Get in."

✦ ✦ ✦

It turned out that pushing the pram over granite setts was much harder than Nan had anticipated. The nannies made it look so easy. It probably didn't help that Nan's pram had three bent wheels. And that Charlie was a lot heavier than a baby.

"Is . . . ! walking . . . ! always . . . ! this . . . ! bumpy?" Charlie said.

"Keep your voice down." Nan grunted, forcing one of the back wheels out of a rut. "We don't want anyone noticing you."

Not that folks were noticing much of anything. The city was alive with Bonfire Night preparations. There were apple sellers and turnip lanterns and soul cakes everywhere.

A pack of children ran past Nan and Charlie. They had a sort of scarecrow on their shoulders made from rags and straw. It had a long mustache and large nose and a barrister's wig.

The scarecrow was a Bonfire Night tradition. Children collected donations from adults to pay for the evening's celebration. "Who is that man they're carrying?" Charlie asked. "I hope he does not fall."

"That's the Guy—Guy Fox. It's a doll. They made it to look like the man who tried to blow up the king. Tonight they'll set him on fire."

"Oh, yes," Charlie said. "Like Roger set you on fire."

"Penny for the Guy, mum?" one of the boys said, holding out a cup. He must have thought Nan was older, on account of the pram. That or the fact that Nan had started taking regular baths.

Nan gave the boy a penny. Ordinarily she would never have wasted money like that, but she was feeling magnanimous. However little she had, these children had less.

Nan continued down Marylebone Street toward Portman Market. She glimpsed the top of Miss Mayhew's Seminary—white smoke serenely rising from the stacks. Nan wondered about the teacher, Miss Bloom. She wondered if she would be out celebrating Bonfire Night, too.

The market was teeming with every sort of person selling every sort of thing you could imagine—hay and onions and squashes and cut poppies and tin kettles and coffee and rags and fireworks and masks. "That's what we've come for," Nan said. "Masks."

She pulled the shade over the pram, keeping Charlie hidden from view, and perused the stalls.

She found a burly man selling paper masks with long mustaches. "Guy masks! Guy masks! Two for a penny!" Nan paid the man and took two masks—one for her and one for Charlie.

She pushed the pram over to an old woman selling fireworks out of an open crate. "Bangers! Roman candles! Catherine wheels! Red sizzlers!" she crowed. "What's Bonfire Night without a little pop and shimmer! Shipped direct to you from the Far East!"

Nan pointed to the side of a crate. "It says Dover."

"Well, that's east, innit?" The woman showed a toothless smile. "Don't worry where they come from, lovey. Think how a little set o' sparklers will bring joy to your wee baby's shining eyes."

Nan dug into her pocket. She had enough money to buy one firecracker. She let go of the pram and inspected the wares—dozens of poppers and rockets and fountains neatly resting in a bed of straw. She breathed in the flinty smell of gunpowder. Behind her, the shouts of the market filled the air to create a sort of song.

"Oranges! Sweet oranges!"

"Oi! You touch it, you buy it!"

"Rabbits! Hampshire rabbits!"

"... Tuppence, and not a farthing more."

"Coo, what a sweet little baby ..."

The last voice Nan recognized. It was the fireworks seller. And she was talking to Charlie. "Wait!" Nan spun around to see the woman reaching into the pram. "Don't touch—!"

"AHHHH!" The woman cut her off with a piercing shriek. She was pointing at the pram—hand shaking, eyes wide. *"M-m-monster!"*

By now others in the market had taken notice and were crowding around the pram. Someone prodded one of the wheels with a broom handle, and the pram fell over with a crash. Charlie rolled out onto the street and everyone screamed.

"Hello," he said, righting himself. "I am Charlie."

There were new cries as more people leaped back in fear. One man fainted right on the spot. A few others held brooms and ladles out like weapons.

"It's hideous!"

"Don't touch it!"

"Someone fetch the police!"

"Charlie!" Nan shouted, trying to push through the crowd. And then "Leave him alone!"

A burly fishmonger grabbed her by the arm. "Careful, girl! There's a monster on the loose!" He thought he was protecting her. Nan fought against his grip. She caught a glimpse of Charlie in the middle of the street. He was staring at the angry faces, shifting one way and then another, his eyes wide with terror. Nervous trails of smoke were wafting from his body.

"It's burning like brimstone!"

"It's a demon!"

"Someone fetch the priest!"

A farmer took a swipe at him with a baling fork. Charlie rolled back, crying out in fear. "N-N-Nan?" he called, white smoke billowing from his head. Bits of loose straw crackled and burned beneath him. "Nan, why are these people trying to hurt me?" He bumped against one of the crates marked "Dover," and Nan caught the sweet aroma of burning wood.

"You're scaring him!" she shouted, finally breaking free from the fishmonger's grip. She sprinted toward Charlie. "Get back, before he—"

POP!

POP!

POP!

The entire crate of fireworks went off—red, yellow, silver, and blue sparks sprayed across the market, landing on stalls and carts. Horses reared and stampeded. Men and women staggered blindly through the sulfurous smoke, screaming for help. Nan dove behind a barrel of herrings and covered her ears from the explosions as more and more fireworks went off.

At last the explosions stopped. People were yelling and sobbing along the street. Police whistles sounded in the distance.

Nan knew she needed to get Charlie out of there before he was caught. She stifled a cough and pulled her muffler back over her mouth. The air was so thick she could scarcely see her own feet. "Charlie?" Her throat burned from smoke. "I'm coming!"

Nan crawled toward what remained of the fireworks stall. By now the smoke had dissipated, revealing a husk of charred splinters. Scorch marks ran along the granite setts. *"Charlie?"* she shouted, throwing aside chunks of smoldering wreckage.

But Charlie was gone.

⋈ THE BELLS OF ST. FLORIAN ⋈

Nan searched the area around the market for any sign of Charlie. Then she checked all of Marylebone and Westminster. She realized that Charlie would probably have rolled downhill, and so she traveled east—into the streets of her old life.

The sun had long since set, and Bonfire Night was in full swing. The streets were now filled with masked revelers. This was one of only two days each year that the rich and the poor celebrated together. At nearly every corner she saw crowds burning Guys. Seeing the flaming effigies, she recalled her own experience in the seminary chimney. Suddenly Bonfire Night didn't feel like a holiday at all.

Nan passed a crowd gathered outside Mansion House, which was where the Lord Mayor lived. Men and women were shouting and waving torches—factory workers from the look of them. Labor riots like this seemed to be happening more and more in the city. Not that they changed anything. There was a crashing sound as someone threw a brick through one of the mansion windows. A whistle sounded and the policemen broke into the crowd with batons. Nan kept her head down and rushed along Lombard Street. She didn't want to get caught up in the trouble.

As Nan entered the East End, she put her Guy Fawkes mask over her head. Doubtless there were climbers about—someone who might recognize her. She checked the alleys. She checked the stoops. She checked every place she could think of, but there was no Charlie.

"*Chaaarrliieeee!*" she called for the hundredth time. Her voice was raspy from shouting. She cursed herself. If she had been paying more attention, if she hadn't strayed from the pram, Charlie would still be safe.

She tried not to think about whether Charlie was hurt. She didn't even know if he *could* be hurt. She had seen him fall from some pretty great heights without complaining, and fire didn't burn him. She eyed the river. Bonfires along the south shore of the Thames reflected off its shifting surface. Could Charlie float?

Bells across London struck ten o'clock. She took a deep breath and tried to think like Charlie. If she were lost, where would she go? She thought of him in the morning. He was always up with the bells, staring out the window that faced east.

Nan had assumed he was looking toward the sunrise.

But maybe he was looking at something else?

She remembered Charlie before he was Charlie, back when he was just a lump of soot. She thought of how some mornings he managed to escape her pocket and roll to the window in Crudd's coal bin—as though something were drawing him in that direction.

Nan turned up her collar and walked down Whitechapel Road, toward her old home. She knew it was foolish. Even with a mask, any number of people might recognize her—including Crudd. The November wind had turned brittle and cold. She balled her fists in her pocket and wished she still had the Sweep's hat. She wondered what had happened to it after she escaped from the nudge. Perhaps it had burned in the fire.

As she walked, she saw landmarks she had always known: the Matchstick, the Tower of London, London Hospital. They all looked smaller than she remembered.

Finally Nan caught sight of St. Florian's, rising up from the hill in the east. The church steeple cast a shadow over Tower Hamlets. She moved slowly, keeping in shadow. Fireworks echoed off distant streets, lighting the sky overhead.

Nan searched along the outer gates of the church. She took off her mask and called, "Charlie?"

She saw something moving in the darkness. "N–N–Nan?" a voice said.

Nan ran toward the voice. "I'm here!" She found Charlie nestled beside one of the stone steps.

"Is it really you?" His voice was so small.

Nan collapsed to her knees and scooped him up in her arms. "I looked everywhere for you. You scared me half to death." She felt tears in her eyes. "You're shivering."

"I was very frightened," he said. "But then I heard him."

Nan wiped her eyes. "Heard who?"

"He was singing," Charlie said. "He sang and sang, and I followed his singing, and it led me here. And then you came."

Nan looked up at St. Florian's Church—huge and square like a castle. Skeleton trees stretched up from the grounds beyond like grasping hands. Nan had never been this close to the church before. She was afraid of what she might find. "You mean, you heard the bells," she said.

"No." Charlie shook his self back and forth. "It was . . . *He* was singing." He looked up at her. "It was the Sweep. Not out loud, but I could hear him."

Nan looked at Charlie, unsure how to answer. She took her muffler and wrapped it around him. She could feel his heartbeat racing against her own. "Come on," she said. "I'm taking you home."

Nan did not say much until they were sitting safely on the captain's rooftop. Her mind was filled with questions she didn't know how to ask. Questions she wasn't sure she wanted to hear the answers to.

"Charlie, what did you mean when you said you could hear the Sweep?" Charlie was nestled in her lap. She could feel his flickering warmth. It warded off the autumn chill.

"Sometimes, I think I can hear him calling me." He shifted. "It feels like maybe he is trying to tell me something. Tonight, I was very close, but . . . I couldn't find him." He sounded disappointed in himself.

Nan stared out at the endless rooftops. "That doesn't make sense. Why would you be able to hear . . . ?" She didn't even know how to finish the question.

Charlie seemed to understand what she was asking. "I think . . ." He paused for a long moment. "I think . . . there's something he wants me to tell you."

Nan caught her breath. For five years, she had forced herself to believe that the Sweep hadn't abandoned her, that he was coming back. And now Charlie was telling her he had a message. "What is it?" Her voice was shaking. "What does he want you to tell me?"

Charlie turned himself to look at her. "I . . . I don't know." He lowered his eyes. "I am sorry."

Nan sighed. "That's all right." She squeezed him. "I'm sorry for losing you."

Charlie flinched as a firework popped somewhere close by.

"It's fine," Nan said. "We're safe up here."

A green rocket shrieked above the rooftops, illuminating the low clouds. It arced and fizzled and then scattered into flickering ash, drifting back into the dark streets below.

"The sounds are painting the air," Charlie said. "I like fireworks much more from up here."

Nan watched Charlie watching the display. "Me, too."

A silver light streaked up from afar and burst into a thousand glittering stars that crackled and drifted down.

"Nan?" Charlie's voice was small. "What is a monster?"

He was recalling the word from the market. Even now, Nan could hear the screams of the crowd. " 'Monster' is a word for something that frightens folks. Like a creature of some kind."

"Oh," he said. And then, "Am I a monster?"

Nan hesitated a long moment before answering. She thought about Crudd and Trundle and the cruel indifference of every person in the city who didn't care if she lived or died. "I've met monsters before," she said, resting her head atop his. "And you are not one of them."

⊰ KINDNESS ⊱

*T*he girl and her Sweep had been walking between towns along the shore. The air had turned cold—colder than it had any right to be at that time of year. There was a wind from the east—bitter and wet—pushing against their faces as they walked. The Sweep carried the girl in his arms, just as he had when she was much smaller. That way she could keep her face turned from the wind.

The howling was so loud that the Sweep could not sing or speak to pass the time. The girl pressed her face against his neck, listening to his labored breaths as he trudged over the muddy path. She thought it sounded like the breathing of an old man.

At last they came upon shelter. "Behold! A miracle," the Sweep cried, and he dropped the girl, nearly falling with her. It was an abandoned smithy's shed, open on all sides. The tools were rusted and useless. The foundation crumbled. But in the middle—a furnace with a tall stone chimney. Even in this wind, a fire could be lit inside this furnace. The girl and *her Sweep got to their knees and cleared away the cobwebs. The girl noticed that the Sweep's hands were shaking. They scraped the floor of the furnace until they had found enough bits of coal to burn.*

"Tonight we shall roast like a pair of plucked pheasants!" the Sweep said, rubbing his hands together. "We might as well put ourselves on spits and—" He fell into a rattling cough that lasted too long. When he took his handkerchief from his mouth, it was stained black. The girl watched and wondered if he had swallowed a shadow.

The girl removed a match from her pocket and—shielding it from the wind—struck it on the side of the furnace. The flame glowed warm against her skin. She lowered the match to the coals.

"Wait," the Sweep said.

He grabbed her wrist. His hand was so cold.

The Sweep reached into the corner of the furnace and removed something small from the shadows. He held it up to the dying light of the match.

It was a feather, small and downy.

The girl looked at the feather, gripped tight between his thin fingers, fluttering in the wind. The match went out. "What does it mean?" the girl asked.

The Sweep crawled into the mouth of the furnace. He picked the girl up and put her on his shoulders—pushing her up into the stone flue. The girl saw something high in darkness, half lit by the moon. It was a nest. And nestled within it were three baby birds. They opened and shut their mouths, making the most pitiful cries.

cheep!

        cheep!

                cheep!

The girl was horrified. She had not heard the cries over the howling of the wind. She had almost burned the birds alive. She had dislodged her share of empty nests before and knew what to do. But when she reached up to clear the nest, the Sweep told her to stop. He told her if they touched the nest, then the parent birds would abandon it, and the babies would starve.

He let the girl down from his shoulders. "It seems tonight we will have no fire." And then he lowered his head and said something she had never heard him say before. "I'm sorry."

He scuttled the coals with his boot and picked up the girl and their brushes. She could feel his arms shivering as wind howled around them.

They continued walking into the night.

·A PERFECT K·

W hat am I?"

Nan was taking a bath when Charlie appeared in the
doorway. "I know I am not a monster," he said. "But I am also not a
human bean. What am I?"

"You're a thing made of soot," she said, wiping soap from her
eyes. "Also, you aren't supposed to come in without knocking."

"Oh, yes," Charlie said. "You are doing *privacy*."

Nan had only recently told Charlie about privacy. Privacy was
what she "did" when she went to the toilet or had a bath. But sometimes Charlie forgot.

"I will go to the Books Room," Charlie said, rolling back into
the hall. "And I will read about what I am." Charlie couldn't read,
so Nan wasn't sure what he would find.

Nan finished her bath and dressed herself. She found Charlie
in the captain's study. Books and loose soot were scattered across

the floor. She watched as Charlie rolled himself across the room at full speed and slammed himself into the bookcase—*Whump!* The case shuddered, and a few books fell to the floor.

"That looks painful," Nan said.

"I am having . . . trouble reaching . . . the books." He was out of breath from the whumping.

"I'm not sure these are the sorts of books that will help." Nan knelt and picked up a book on cloud formations. She looked at Charlie, nearly the size of Trundle's gruel pot, and wondered if he would ever stop growing. Just that morning he had asked her to hold him up to the turret window so he could watch the "scratchers" (squirrels). But when she tried to pick him up, she had tumbled backward and dropped him down four flights of curved stairs.

"I think it's time we give you a body," she said.

"I already have a body." Charlie rolled himself around in a proud little circle.

Nan returned the books to their shelf. "I mean a proper body with legs and arms so you can do things for yourself. You wait around all day for me to come home so I can fetch things for you or move you to high places. You're growing bigger anyway—so we might as well have a say in things."

Charlie considered this. "I think I would like that very much. What sort of body should I have?"

Nan thought about what sort of body might be useful. "You should definitely have a tail. And lots of legs. I'm thinking six or seven at least. And horns." She briefly considered wings but thought they might be too hard to manage.

"Can I have . . . fingers?" Charlie asked after much thought.

Fingers did not sound like much fun to Nan. "Are you sure you wouldn't rather have claws?"

·❖· ·❖· ·❖·

The next day, instead of selling her loose soot to Horace Nobbs, Nan brought it home. She emptied her sootbag on the cellar floor. The captain's cellar reminded her of Crudd's coal bin, only it was larger and didn't smell like unwashed children.

Charlie looked at the pile, which was many times larger than himself. "I . . . I'm not sure how to start."

"I found this in the study." Nan held up a large book with gold letters on the spine that said *The Illustrated Book of Beasts*. "This is called a 'bestiary,'" she explained. "It's a great big list of all the different kinds of monsters."

"But I am not a monster," Charlie said.

"Of course not." She opened the book. "You're more of a creature. A creature is anything that's not a proper person."

"Oh, yes," Charlie said. "I am *not* a proper person."

Nan turned the page. "What about this?" She showed him a picture of a winged cow with a snake's behind.

Charlie jumped back in fright. "I do *not* want to be that thing."

Nan shrugged. "Suit yourself." She continued browsing until she came upon something called a "questing beast." It had the body of a lion mixed with a leopard and a snake and something called a "hart," which she took to be a kind of stag. That looked just about right to her.

"Hold still," she said to Charlie. "This might hurt."

Nan took a handful of soot and mashed it against Charlie's side.

"Ow," he said.

"I told you it would hurt." Nan pinched the end to make it sharp. She was trying to make an antler.

Nan had thought that making Charlie a body would be like making a snowman. It was a bit like that, only the soot didn't hold together and Charlie kept wiggling. It also took an enormous amount of soot. After several hours, all she had to show for her work was a little stump on one side of Charlie's face. The stump was pointing off at the wrong angle, and it stopped him from being able to roll properly.

"It is a very nice antler," Charlie said. But Nan could tell he was just being polite.

"Tomorrow I'll make you one on the other side to balance you out," she said. She had already started to lose enthusiasm for the project. "At this rate, it will take months to finish all of you. Maybe we should cut back on a few of the legs?"

Charlie shifted his weight back and forth, as though trying and failing to get comfortable. "I wonder," he said in his smallest voice, "if I might try making me by myself?"

Nan looked at him. He was watching her with a fearful expression. "You don't like the antler?"

"It is very nice to be a questing beast," he replied. "But I think I would like to be a something else." His voice was full of fragile hope.

Nan knelt and touched Charlie's head. The end of the antler crumbled under her touch. "You couldn't do any worse than me," she said.

Charlie asked for privacy. Nan understood—even if it did make her a little sad. She left him with *The Illustrated Book of Beasts*. "Just in case," she said.

For the next week Charlie remained in the cellar, hard at work on his new body. Every so often he would call up for more soot. Nan swept chimneys as fast as she could during the day, selling only enough soot to keep herself fed. She found herself missing Charlie's company in the evening. She hoped he would finish soon.

Nan did not see Charlie in all that time. He asked that she dump the loose soot down the stairs, along with the occasional bucket of water. She tried her best to catch a glimpse of him in the shadows, but it was too dark. Once she heard him moving down there. He sounded frustrated. "Are you sure you don't want some help?" she called down.

"D–d–don't come in!" he shouted.

And so she was forced to wait and wonder. Charlie had the chance to become any sort of thing he wanted. Nan looked at her own skinny legs and stained fingers and thought about how she might change herself, if she could. But she didn't want to change. Not the way other girls her age changed. She did not want to "blossom." She would rather be a skinny weed than a stupid flower.

At long last Charlie finished himself. "You can come down now," he called up from below.

Nan was busy trying to get a model ship called the H.M.S. *Scop* out of a giant bottle. She dropped the bottle and raced down to the cellar.

She found the space dark but for a shaft of light from the high grated window. *The Illustrated Book of Beasts* lay open on the floor, just where she had left it the previous week.

"Charlie?" Nan said, peering down the unlit stairs. "Where are you?"

"I'm over here." Charlie was in the corner, hidden by shadows.

Nan could tell he was much larger now. Larger than her, even. "Let's have a look," she said.

"Promise me you won't laugh," Charlie said.

"I can't promise that," Nan said. "But if I do, I'll try my best to make it a nice laugh."

She saw him nod. He stepped out from the shadows. His steps were uneven. He was still learning to walk. "I didn't get all the parts right."

Nan put her hands over her mouth. "Oh, Charlie . . ."

Charlie's face was just as Nan knew it, only larger. He had the same fearful eyes. The same crooked mouth.

He had no neck to speak of. His head came out from his shoulders like a knoll. His body was uneven at the edges. He had two arms and legs like a person, but his legs were different sizes—even when standing straight, he looked as though he might fall over.

Nan stared at him, her hands still on her mouth. "Charlie . . . you're *enormous*." The thought that this was the same Charlie whom she had carried in her pocket only weeks before was too much to contemplate.

Charlie brought his hands together, twining his lumpy fingers—three on each hand. "You don't like it." It was strange to hear such a small voice from such a large creature.

Nan shook her head. She stepped closer to him. "Charlie . . ." She placed her hands on his chest, which was at her eye level. His chest was warm and crumbly. She wrapped both arms around him in a hug. Her fingers just barely touched on the other side. "You're *perfect.*"

⋅⊰ OBSOLESCENCE ⊱⋅

E ven though Charlie now had a body, the question remained. What was he? Nan thought that if she knew what sort of creature Charlie was, she might better understand why the Sweep had left him for her.

She spent the next day immersed in *The Illustrated Book of Beasts*, carefully studying each entry for hints about what sort of creature Charlie might be. He remained close by, ready to answer any questions that arose.

"Do you suppose your bite is venomous?" she called.

"I have no teeth," Charlie answered from inside the fireplace. He was making little puffs of smoke go up the chimney. Nan wasn't sure how someone as big as Charlie could still fit into the chimney, but he seemed to manage.

She turned to the next page. "You don't levitate under a full moon, do you?"

"I do not think I do that thing," Charlie replied. "But I can make my smoke go in shapes!" He moved his arms and formed some smoke into a ball. "Maybe I can teach you?"

"No time for games," Nan said, turning back to the book. "I'm working."

It was late into the afternoon before Nan had a breakthrough. "Charlie!" she cried, leaping from the floor. "I found it!"

Charlie brushed the ashes from his feet and ran to meet her. "What did you find?"

Nan pointed to an entry on a page right near the middle. "You tell me." She showed him a drawing on the page. It was a large, misshapen creature with dark eyes and huge shoulders.

"It's a Charlie," Charlie said.

Nan nodded. "It looks just like you . . . only it's made of some sort of stone."

Charlie touched his own belly, which crumbled and sprinkled to the floor. "What am I called?"

"The book says it's a 'golem.' " She read the entry aloud.

Golem: *Fabled monster in the Jewish tradition, a homunculus crafted from mud or clay and animated through Kabalistic ritual. Freq. in reference to a mindless servant or beast of burden, designed for obsolescence.* (ref. Psalm 139:16)

Nan very nearly read the word "monster" aloud but changed it to "creature" just in time. "What do you think?" she said.

Charlie looked at the book, his brow creased. "The golem is made of mud or clay," he said at last. "I am made of soot."

"Soot's pretty close to clay. It only means you're a different kind of golem. A *soot* golem."

"Soot golem." Charlie tried on the words. "What are obso-lessons?"

"No idea," Nan said. "But now that we know what you're called, we'll have an easier time learning more. I might know someone who could tell us about golems. I could ask him if you wanted."

Charlie pressed his fingers together. "I suppose that would be fine."

Nan could tell he didn't mean it. "I was just trying to help." She closed the book. "If you didn't want to know the answer, you shouldn't have asked the question."

Charlie nodded vaguely. "A soot golem may be a very nice crea-ture," he said slowly. "But I think I would rather be just Charlie."

Nan stared into his dark, unblinking eyes. She thought of all the times grown-up folks had called her "sweep" or "boy" or even meaner things. It made her feel as if they couldn't see her as her own person. Which, of course, they couldn't.

Charlie made another wispy smoke shape. "Are you very angry with me?"

Nan put the book aside and placed her hands on either side of his face. She stood on her toes and pressed her nose against the place where his nose might be.

"Just Charlie is plenty good enough for me."

·⊰ A TRIP TO THE EMPORIUM ⊱·

Charlie may not have wanted to know about golems, but Nan did. And that's how she found herself trudging along the cold banks of the Thames on a chilly Tuesday afternoon.

The south side of the river was lined with factories and stock-yards and more ships than she could count. Nan peered out across the docks. Even in the autumn cool, the river here smelled terrible. Folks called the Thames "the Queen's Chamber Pot." Most days she would gladly walk ten blocks out of her way to avoid the smell. But not today. Today she had business.

The river was at low tide, and all along the banks, children and old folks waded in the shallows, scavenging for trash. Nan traversed the rocks around the enormous stone pillars at the foot of Black-friars Bridge. She could hear horses grumbling and clip-clopping overhead, oblivious to the world beneath them.

Eeep!

A little white rat sniffed at her foot.

"Hello, Prospero," Nan said. "Is Toby around?"

The rat scurried past her and climbed up the shoulder of Toby Squall. The boy had just emerged from the water and was holding what looked to be part of a croquet mallet. His trousers were rolled up and his bare legs were muddy to the knees. He was wearing the most irritating grin in the world. "Hullo, Smudge." He dropped the mallet into his open bag. "I was wondering when you'd come around."

She wrinkled her nose. Toby smelled almost as bad as the river. "I find that hard to believe. I'm supposed to be dead."

Toby's smile got wider. "The boys all said you were burned up in that fire. City inspectors fined Crudd and everything. But I knew it wasn't true." He fed the rat on his shoulder something from his pocket. "Me and Prospero had a look at that school where they said you'd burned. Found a footprint, cake crumbs, and a broken window in a roost above the attic."

This surprised Nan. Toby was afraid of heights. He must have really wanted to know.

"Prospero thought you'd run off to Canada, but I told him you couldn't keep away from your dear old Toby." He tipped his cap. "To what do I owe the pleasure?"

"I come on business." Nan knew if she asked him about golems outright, he might figure things out. If Bonfire Night had taught her anything, it was that other folks were afraid of Charlie—and would be even more so now, given that he looked like an actual monster. *Not a monster*, she reminded herself. *A golem*. Whatever that was.

"On business, you say?" Toby clutched his heart. "The great Nan Sparrow wants to buy something from the emporium? After all these years of passing me by? Surely I'm dreaming! Someone pinch me."

Prospero nipped his toe.

Nan was beginning to regret she'd come. "If you're going to make fun of me, I'll just go somewhere else." She turned toward the bank. "Maybe Porky Dibbs over in Eastcheap. He's always offering me free gifts."

Porky Dibbs was a rag-and-bone man who had never offered Nan so much as a grommet. But Toby didn't know that.

"Now, hold up," Toby said, running in front of her. "I certainly can't leave my best girl to try her chances with the likes of Porky Dibbs." He gave her a smile. A real one. "I want to help, however I can."

Nan bit the inside of her cheek. "I don't need anything from the emporium," she said. "Or not exactly, anyway." She removed a yellowed piece of paper from her coat pocket. "I need you to make me one of these."

Toby took the paper, which Nan had torn from an old edition of *The Times*. He unfolded it and squinted at the tiny columns of tiny letters. His smile faded. "Smudge . . . You know I can't, um . . ." He shrugged. "Can you read it to me?"

Nan rolled her eyes and snatched the paper from him. "Here. At the bottom. There's an announcement." She read the beginning of the article.

> The Times *reports that Joseph Glass has been selected by the London Friendly Society for the Superseding of the Necessity of Climbing Boys as the winner of its £100 prize for the design of a mechanical brushing mechanism that allows sweeps to clean chimneys without the use of climbing boys . . .*

"You get the idea." Nan handed back the paper. "There's a drawing of the design beside it."

"Glass," Toby said. "Now, there's a name. . . ." He scratched his orange curls. "So they finally figured a way to clean chimneys without climbers. Master sweeps'll hate this."

"I don't think they're too worried. This clipping's more than fifty years old. Whoever this Glass fellow is, he's dead by now and his invention's forgotten. I found it while clearing out the captain's—" She caught herself. "It's none of your business where I found it."

"The *captain?*" Toby gave her one of his looks, as if she were a puzzle and he was one step away from putting her together. "What *is* my business, then?"

Nan shoved her hands in her pockets. "I want you to make one. For me." She could feel her cheeks flushing.

Toby's eyes went narrower, as though she'd just given him the last puzzle piece. "You're still sweeping? Even after what happened?"

"I got soot in my veins." Nan poked her toe in the mud. "Can you imagine if the Sweep comes back to find I've given up the trade? It's bad enough I lost his hat."

"The Sweep?" Toby gave Nan a look that she couldn't quite understand, but then he shrugged. "Soot or not, your climbing days are numbered. That's why you need this brush, isn't it? To go up the flue once you can't."

Nan shifted, looking away from him. Toby was right, and he knew it. She had split the seam in her trousers, and the sleeves of her coat were halfway to her elbows. Twice the previous week she had secured a job only to turn it down when she got to the house and saw the square nines. "So, you think you can make one?"

"Remember who you're talking to. Making things is in my blood." Toby liked to say he came from a long line of German tinkers. Nan liked to say he came from a long line of pests. He had been born in a town called Dresden. His folks had sent him to England when he was little because his home had been a bad place for people like him. His real name was Schaal. But when he came here, he changed it to Squall so that folks wouldn't give him trouble.

It didn't always work.

Nan had met Toby when she was still with the Sweep. They had come upon a pack of boys who were beating a smaller boy, calling him "Jew." The way they said it made it sound like a curse. Nan hadn't known what a Jew was at the time. She still wasn't entirely sure. The Sweep had rushed into the fray and chased off the bullies and given Toby what money he had. A few days later the Sweep was gone. Toby had followed Nan around like a stray puppy ever since.

Toby was still discussing the clipping with Prospero. "A pretty shoddy design." He rubbed his chin. "We'll need to make it sturdier. No use if it comes apart on the first job . . ."

"Do you know what a golem is?" Nan tried to keep her question offhand.

Toby glanced up. "Sure I do." He shrugged. "It's a . . . kind of pastry, right?"

Nan rolled her eyes. "Right." She was disappointed that the one Jewish person she knew in London didn't know any more about golems than she did. "I've changed my mind." She reached for the paper.

"Hang on," Toby said. "I think I can make it."

"Fine, keep it." She'd already gotten her real answer. "The design's probably rubbish anyway. Otherwise, we'd all have one already." She turned and walked toward the bank.

"Wait!" Toby called after her. "Hang the brush—Crudd's still looking for you. I need to know you're safe. Will you at least tell me where you're staying?" He clambered up the slope. *"Nan?"*

But she was already crossing over Blackfriars Bridge, stepping between hansoms and wagons, heading back toward the city. She thought she heard Toby call her name again. She didn't answer.

·❧ DEATH AND TAXES ❧·

One of the best parts about sweeping for herself was that Nan had enough money to buy her own food, and there was one food she preferred above all others.

"We're out of licorice," she called to Charlie from the turret window, which served as their front door. "I'm off to the sweets shop."

"Wait." Charlie's head poked out from the landing. "Can you get me some sugarplums?"

"Those are too expensive." She pulled her coat on and swung a leg out the window. "Besides, you don't eat people food."

"I do not," Charlie agreed. He drew a swirl on the wallpaper with his finger. "It is . . . for my friend."

Nan drew her leg back from the window. "Your *friend*?" She felt a clutch of panic in her stomach. Had someone else discovered Charlie? "What is your *friend's* name?" She tried to keep her voice calm.

Charlie took his hand away from the wall. "Not my friend," he said hastily. "I meant for my . . . *finger.*"

Nan closed the window. "You are the worst liar I've ever met."

Charlie nodded, a little proud. "Yes, I am."

She walked to him and set her hands on his shoulders. "I need you to tell me. Who is your friend?"

Charlie looked at the ceiling. He looked at the floor. He looked anywhere but at Nan. "My friend visits me in the Nothing Room. But only if I have food to share."

Nan shook her head. "I suppose that's where all my licorice has got to."

"My friend likes sweet things very much."

"I'll bet." Nan snatched a Grecian urn that hung from the wall and started down the hall. "Is your friend there now?" Whoever this "friend" was, she would make him sorry he'd trespassed in her home and eaten her licorice.

"Please don't be angry," Charlie called, clomping after her.

"I just want to meet him." She threw open the Nothing Room door and raised the urn over her head.

Eeep!

Crouched near the wall was a small rat with white fur. It was glaring at her with horrible red eyes.

Nan returned the glare with interest. "Hello, Prospero."

Charlie shuffled past her. He knelt down in front of the rat, who skittered into his hands. "My friend," he said. "I think his name is *Eeep*!"

Nan set the urn down. "I'm fetching licorice. When I get back, that *thing* had better be gone."

But she knew it was too late.

Wherever Prospero went, Toby was soon to follow.

✦ ✦ ✦

"Hullo, Smudge!" Toby was waiting for Nan when she returned. "Need a hand?"

Nan pulled herself onto the eave. She had picked up a jug of milk from the market, which made the whole climb a bit tricky. She couldn't use the front door on account of not wanting to be seen entering a supposedly abandoned house. Also, she didn't have the key. "I thought you were afraid of heights," she said.

"Deathly afraid," he admitted. She saw he was clutching some ship's rigging he had anchored to the finial. "But I thought you might need help getting things up and down, so I made this pulley." He worked one end of the rigging and pulleyed up a tattered sail whose ends had been gathered, making a giant sling. "I reckon it's just the thing for someone needing to haul goods from the street." Toby opened the sails to reveal his emporium. Prospero was sitting on top.

Nan scowled at the rat. "I suppose I have you to thank for this."

"Don't be sore at Prospero. We got no secrets, me and him. Tell each other everything. That's the way it is with best mates." He peered at the chimneys all around him. "When he told me you were holed up in the House of One Hundred Chimneys, I knew I had to see for myself. I'd tip my cap, if I wasn't terrified of falling."

Nan shrugged. "I just needed a place where no sweeps would come looking."

This made Toby laugh. "They are a superstitious lot. Did you know some of them actually believe that this place is *haunted*?" He said this as if it were the funniest thing he had ever heard.

Nan blinked at him. "Isn't it?"

Toby's eyes widened. "You really don't know why this house is empty, do you?"

Nan felt her cheeks go hot. "Are you going to tell me?"

Toby sat down on the gable, propping his feet on the gutter. "It's like I always say, the only sure things in life are death and taxes."

"I've never once heard you say that." She uncapped her jug of milk and took a sip.

She offered it to Toby, who took a long pull. "Taxes are the money that rich folks pay the queen so she can afford all her tea and gowns."

"I know what taxes are," Nan said.

"And the way Ol' Vickie tallies her taxes is by chimneys. The more chimneys a house has, the more money she gets. You can bet that a place like this buys her a *lot* of gowns. When the captain kicked off, all his family set to fighting over who would get the place. But none of them wanted to claim it outright, on account of having to pay for all the chimneys. But they also didn't want to let anyone *else* snatch it up. So they've all just been arguing over it for years and years. S'pose you're lucky they haven't just up and sold it."

Nan couldn't tell if he was teasing. "Do you think they'd do that?"

"Who's to say?" He shrugged. "But never you fear, there's always plenty 'o room under Blackfriars Bridge with me and Prospero!" He craned his neck toward the turret window. "Speaking of Prospero . . . he tells me you got something in this house with you. Something . . . *unusual*."

Nan moved to block his view. "Even if I do, it's none of your business." She folded her arms.

Toby shook his head. "Be that way, if you must. But if I figured it out, you can bet Crudd will, too. He's crafty, and dangerous."

"I'll be fine."

Toby tilted his head to one side. "You're really not going to show me, are you?" He pointed toward the winch. "After I made you a housewarming gift and everything."

Nan bit the inside of her cheek. Irritating though he was, she knew she could trust him. "Fine," she said. "But if I show you, you need to *promise* not to tell a soul."

Toby put two hands to his heart. "I will be a dais of discretion. The very picture of prudence. A fortress of forbearance—"

"I don't know what any of that means," Nan interrupted. "Just swear it like a normal human person."

"I swear it on the Thames." Toby nodded gravely. "And if I'm lying, I will let you hold my hand at the May Day parade."

Nan rolled her eyes. "Nice try." May Day was sacred for sweeps—they led a parade through the whole city, with thousands of folks watching and cheering. Toby had been trying to hold Nan's hand on May Day for as long as she'd known him. "I'll be boiled and plucked before I let you or anyone else hold my hand."

"All right, then." He removed his cap. "I swear it on the emporium and everything in it."

Nan hesitated. The bag was tattered and full of junk. But it was all he had in the world. She knew he would never risk losing it. She turned and climbed through the turret window. "Watch your head."

⊰ LIFE ⊱

Nan led Toby down the stairs. She was oddly self-conscious about the mess. "I wasn't planning on visitors," she muttered, kicking a pillow out of her path. It was as though Toby being there made her see the house with fresh eyes.

Toby gawked at the parlor, which had been cleared to build an enormous fortress out of furniture and bedding. "If the boys could see you now."

"They won't," Nan said. "Because you promised not to say anything."

Toby raised his hands. "Obviously."

Nan sighed and continued down the stairs. Soon they were outside the Banging-Pots-and-Pans Room on the ground floor. She stopped at the door and looked Toby dead in the eye. "Remember what you promised."

He seemed amused by her gravity. "Have you got a body in there?"

"You might say that." She opened the door. "This is Charlie."

Charlie was on the far side of the room, drawing. He had lately taken to drawing on the white plaster walls, which were easier for him because they did not rip. He had filled one entire wall with pictures of lumpy circles with eyes.

"Oh, hello," Charlie said, turning to greet them. "I am drawing a little me."

Toby was standing beside Nan. His mouth was slightly open. He had removed his cap, as if out of reverence. Prospero hopped down from Toby's shoulder and greeted Charlie with an eager *Eeep!*

Toby blinked, as if trying to wake from a dream. "You . . . ?" He turned toward Nan. "He . . . ?"

"Charlie is a golem," Nan said. "As you can see, a golem is *not* a kind of pastry." She was rather enjoying seeing Toby at a loss for words.

"A *soot* golem," Charlie added, pointing to the picture. "I used to be small like this. But that was a *very* long time ago."

"That was last week," Nan said.

Toby scratched the back of his neck and took a step closer. "What . . . Where did you come from?"

"I came from the Sweep's hat," Charlie said.

Nan explained. "You remember that clod of char the Sweep left me? The one that was always warm?"

Toby had learned about the Sweep's gift a few years back when Prospero had nosed around in her coat and tried to run off with it. "Sure I do," he said. "I tried to buy it off you, but you told me to go eat a boiled eel." It was eerie how well Toby recalled the things Nan told him.

"Well, that char was . . . Charlie." Nan turned over a giant pot in the middle of the room and sat on it. "It happened when I was trapped in the Devil's Nudge. The fire hatched him somehow. And now he's like this."

The crack along Charlie's face formed into a proud smile. "Nan said 'Help' and so I helped."

Toby snapped his fingers. "I *knew* it!" he said. "It's him that broke you out of that flue. He probably smashed right through it with those big arms."

"I did not have big arms then," Charlie said. "I used my head to push the bricks away. And then I helped in my Charlie way."

Nan was surprised to hear how clearly he remembered all this. He was usually quite forgetful. "What do you mean by your 'Charlie way'?" she asked.

The creature shrugged and looked down at his hands. "Um . . ." Loose soot crumbled from his fingers. "I made it wake up in you."

Nan shook her head. "Made *what* wake up?"

He looked up at her. "Your heart."

"You made my *heart* wake up?"

Charlie nodded. He drew a line on the floor with his foot.

Nan knew Charlie sometimes had odd ways of explaining things, but this was strange, even for him.

Toby marched up to Charlie and seized his hand in both of his own. "Allow me to shake the hand of the fellow that saved my best girl's life." He shook Charlie's hand vigorously. "My name's Toby Squall."

Charlie seemed rather to enjoy having his hand shaken. "Oh, yes," he said. "You are a giant pest."

Toby grinned. "So she's told you about me?"

Nan rolled her eyes.

⚜ ⚜ ⚜

Toby invited himself to supper, and Nan could tell that Charlie was happy to have the company, and so she allowed it. They didn't have much food in the larder, but Toby produced from his emporium a tin of herrings, which Nan fried up and served with day-old rolls and the rest of the milk. She had to admit it made a pretty good feast.

As they ate, Toby asked Charlie all sorts of questions—things that Nan felt foolish for not having thought of before.

"Are you soot all the way to the middle, or is there something else inside?"

"What happens if you get wet?"

"Can you breathe fire or just make yourself hot?"

"If your foot breaks off, will it wiggle around on its own?"

"Does Nan snore?"

Even when Charlie's answers didn't make exact sense—which was often—Toby would listen and respond as though he understood.

"Can Toby live with us?" Charlie asked, chewing on a piece of coal that Nan had brought up from the cellar.

"Absolutely not," Nan said.

Toby was one of those irritating people who got on with everyone. Wherever he walked, people would wish him a good day. And not just other children. She had even seen a policeman tip his hat once.

After supper, they all played a giant game of hide-and-go-seek. Prospero won by hiding inside a teakettle. It was late by the time Nan led Toby up to the turret window.

"It is very dark and cold outside," Charlie said. "You should probably just stay here and live with us."

"I've already told you, no," Nan said. "And if you ask again, I'll banish them from ever visiting."

Toby put on his cap. "It's nice of you to ask, Chuckles." He was already trying on nicknames for Charlie. "But even if Nan said yes, I could never live in a place like this." He stared out the window and released a dramatic sigh. "My roof is the open sky."

"Your roof is the underside of a bridge," Nan muttered.

Toby ignored her. "The whole of London is my home, Charlio. Every street, every steeple, every river, every park, every blade of grass. Mine to savor."

"Oh, yes," Charlie said. "I used to see those things when I was little. Only now I am big and I stay here."

Toby looked from Nan to Charlie and back to Nan. "He stays in here . . . *all day?*"

Nan shrugged. "It's not safe for him out there." She could still remember the horrified screams from Bonfire Night. She opened the turret window, and cold air rushed in from outside. "We're fine. We have a good life."

Toby stayed where he was. He lowered his voice. "Cooped up in a house day and night? Can you really call that a life?" He stepped out through the window.

Nan closed it behind him.

⊰ LEARNING TO READ ⊱

As the last days of November wore on, the demand for sweeps grew. Nan wanted to work as much as she could before the first frost. Sweeping was infinitely harder with frozen soot. She had spent the last four days sweeping every house that would have her. By the time she climbed through the turret and reached her bedroom that night, she was ready to collapse. "Today was terrible," she groaned. "You don't think fingertips can ache until your fingertips ache."

Charlie was sitting on the edge of her bed, just as she had left him that morning. For all she knew, he had been waiting in that spot the whole time. "Can you read me a story?"

He was holding a book of English tales, which included "Jack the Giant Killer," "Tom Thumb," and "The Wee Bannock." It was the only proper storybook in the house, and he had been asking

Nan to read it over and over for weeks. "The Wee Bannock" was his favorite, but it also troubled him. It was about a sort of cookie man who came to life and ran away to escape being eaten. Charlie was convinced that the Wee Bannock was a golem like him. "Why would all those animals and people want to hurt him?" he would always ask at the end.

"I'm tired of that book," Nan said, unwrapping her muffler. "And my hands are too sore to turn the pages."

"Oh," Charlie said. And then, "I will turn the pages for you. I will be very careful not to rip them."

Nan rolled over and looked at him. She wanted more than anything in the world to go to sleep. But there was something in Charlie's face that checked her response. She thought about Toby's question. What sort of life was she giving Charlie, cooped up in this empty house?

She pulled herself up. "I think it's time we taught you to read."

Charlie's eyes went wide. "Will it hurt very much?"

"Of course not." Then she added, "But it might give you a headache."

Nan and Charlie went to the study, which seemed like the right place for a lesson. "Just think, when we're done, you can read any of these books," she told him.

"I thought these books were dull," Charlie said.

"They are," Nan said. "But you can still read them."

She found some books filled with nautical charts, which she decided would make excellent scrap paper.

"Before you can read, I need to teach you to spell," she said.

"Oh, yes," Charlie said. "I know about spells. Spells are magic that witches and fairies do."

"Let's start with the letter *A*," Nan said. She took a bit of chalk and wrote *A* on a piece of paper. "Now you try it."

Charlie put his finger to another sheet of paper and traced out an *A* of his own. His lines were clumsy, and his first two tries ended in failure.

"It's okay," she said, giving him another sheet. "Take your time." This was what the Sweep had always said to her when she was learning something new. Most adults were impatient with children—snapping at them to hurry. But the Sweep had been different. He would say, "Take your time" over and over for as long as it took to get a thing done. He said it so much that you couldn't help but take your time.

At last Charlie finished an *A* that looked something like Nan's.

"The letter *A* makes the sound *Aaahhh*," she explained.

"It does?" Charlie's eyes went wide. "How wonderful!" He leaned very close to the paper and pressed the side of his head against it.

"What are you doing?" Nan asked.

"Shh," he said. "I want to hear it make the sound *Aaahhh*."

Nan tried to explain. "The letter doesn't make a real sound. You just hear the sound in your head when you look at it. The words happen inside of you."

"Now I understand," Charlie said, nodding. "Words are *feelings*."

Nan sighed. She wondered if it had been this hard for the Sweep when he taught her about letters for the first time. "Maybe we should try again in the morning."

When Toby heard that Charlie was learning his letters, he gave him a set of wooden blocks with a different letter carved into each side. It turned out to be just the thing Charlie needed to learn his alphabet. The blocks were sturdy enough that he would not break or tear them.

Instead of writing words, Charlie learned to *build* words.

They made a game out of it. Nan would make a little tower with some letters that spelled a certain word. Then she would make Charlie copy her tower. Only when he got all the letters right was he allowed to knock the towers down. (That was his favorite part.)

Once they had figured out the right way to teach, Charlie learned as fast as he learned everything. By the first frost, he could spell all the little words and a few useful bigger ones, including:

SPARROW

CHARLIE

CHIMNEY

SOOT

TOBY

PEST

KETTLE

POCKET

EAR WAX

He stacked up all the words he knew in a row.

"Look at you, Smokey!" Toby was still on the nicknames. "It's pretty as a poem. Before too long, *you'll* be the one telling *us* the stories."

"Toby is a very good teacher at reading," Charlie said.

Nan rolled her eyes. "How can he be a good teacher when he can't even read himself?"

Toby smiled, stacking up his own gibberish word. "Somebody sounds jealous."

Nan kicked over his tower and marched upstairs.

⊰ MISS BLOOM ⊱

Nan knew she could prove herself the better teacher, if only she had the right tools. That night she crept out of the house and traveled to Miss Mayhew's Seminary on Harley Street. Surely a school would have some sort of reading primer that could do the teaching for her.

Nan pulled herself onto the flat roof of the seminary and felt a flicker of terror as she approached the main chimney stack. This was the very same place she had nearly burned alive months before—if it weren't for Charlie, she would have died here.

The school library was on the top floor, and Nan had to travel only a few feet before touching down in the hearth. The ashes in the firebox were soft and warm beneath her bare feet—an hour dead, at most. It wouldn't do to leave tracks, so she dusted her soles off before stepping onto the floorboards.

The library was not a large room—much less grand than the

captain's study. It had one low bookshelf running along the inside wall. Nan crept along the shelves, trying her best to read the titles of books in the moonlight, which barely reached her through the windows.

The collection was not terribly inspiring. Most of the shelves contained sets of identical titles—so that every girl in class could have a copy of her own, she assumed. It seemed like a terrible waste. Why not let every person have a different book?

She found a book called *Bright Verses for Bright Minds*, which had a poem dedicated to each letter of the alphabet. She took the most worn copy from the shelf and turned back toward the chimney.

And that was when she noticed that there was someone else in the room.

Angled toward the fireplace was a large reading chair with a high back and stuffed arms. Nan had stepped past the chair without paying any attention to it, but now she saw that there was a woman there. She had an open book on her lap and the look of someone who had just woken up. She was staring straight at Nan.

"Am I dreaming?" the woman said.

Nan could see that it was the teacher, Miss Bloom. She must have fallen asleep while reading by the fire. "Yes, you're dreaming," she said. She slipped the primer behind her back.

The woman closed her book. "It's *you*," she said, rising from her chair. "The climbing girl." She walked around Nan in a slow circle, her eyes wide—as though at any moment Nan might vanish. "They told me you'd been caught in the crook of the flue. That you'd been . . ." She put her hands over her mouth as though unable to speak. "I heard you . . . I heard you *screaming*."

Nan recalled that Miss Bloom had been there when Roger struck the match. She and Newt had both tried to stop him. "Please don't tell them you saw me," Nan said. "It's better if they think I'm dead."

"Of course," the woman said. She shook her head, as if shaking off an unpleasant feeling. "When I asked them your name, they said it was Nan Sparrow."

Nan shrugged. "Still is." She liked that this woman had wanted to know who she was. Most grown-ups preferred to pretend that climbers didn't exist—doubly so when they died.

"It's a pleasure to meet you." She said this as if Nan were a person worth meeting. "I'm Miss Bloom." And then she added, almost hesitantly, "Esther."

"That's a pretty name" was all Nan could think to say. "Esther."

A sort of shadow flickered across the woman's face. "Not everyone thinks so." She looked down at the book she had been reading, still clasped in her hand.

"Is that a teacher book?" Nan asked. She tilted her head and tried to read the title but found she could not. "What are all those funny letters?"

The woman paused a moment before answering. "It's a *siddur*—a Jewish prayer book. My mother gave it to me when I was young. The 'funny letters' are Hebrew."

Nan's eyes widened. "You're Jewish?"

"I am . . . or I was, once." The woman raised a brow. "I see from your expression that our reputation precedes us." She said it like a joke, but Nan didn't think she was really joking. "Tell me what you have heard."

Nan shrugged. "Nothing." She shook her head. "Lots of things." The way some folks talked about Jews, it seemed as if all the pains of the world were because of what they had done. She knew that wasn't true, though; she'd suffered plenty at the hands of God-fearing Christians. "But I know it's all lies. I know another Jew named Toby, and he's harmless as a hamster." She wanted to add that she hated Toby's guts and wished she could throw him in the Thames, but she didn't think the woman would take it the right way. "Do the other teachers in the school know?"

Miss Bloom stiffened. "It's not as though I keep it a secret."

"Sure you do," Nan said. "That's why you're reading your Hebrew book while everyone else is asleep." She could tell from the woman's expression that she was right. She added, "I know a thing or two about keeping secrets." She thought of Charlie waiting for her back at the house. "What does the book say?"

Miss Bloom ran her thumb along the pages. "I couldn't tell you the exact words, though I do remember certain passages." She looked up. "In my family, girls were not taught to read Hebrew. They were scarcely taught to read at all. Girls were expected to keep the home until they could marry and keep another's home."

Nan shifted her weight. "Is that why you became a teacher? To help other girls like you?"

The woman made an incredulous face. "The girls at this school enjoy privilege and opportunity that we mortals can scarcely imagine." The way she said this, it was as though she saw herself as being apart from the school—an outsider looking in. "But they, too, are trapped by the expectations placed upon them." She smiled. "I daresay some of them might even envy the freedom of a chimney sweeper's life."

"Our *freedom*?" Nan felt a flush of anger. Did this woman really think her life was one to be envied? "They don't know a thing about us."

The woman seemed to understand. "No, they do not." She shook her head. "And neither do I. Forgive me."

Nan wasn't sure she'd ever had a grown-up ask her forgiveness before. She wasn't sure how to reply. She said, "Why are you looking at a book you can't read?"

"A fair question." Miss Bloom looked down and smiled.

"Tonight is the first night of Chanukah, the Jewish Festival of Lights. I suppose I am feeling . . ." She searched for a word. "Sentimental." She tucked the book into the folds of her skirt.

Nan could tell that the woman had finished with the topic. But she still had one question. "Miss Bloom?" she said. "Do you know anything about golems?"

"*Golems?*" She gave a sort of chuckle. "I haven't thought about golems since I was a little girl."

"So they're real?" Nan said.

"They are not." She folded her hands together. "You will some-day learn that many of the things you believe to be real as a little girl prove not to be." She gave Nan a searching look. "But tell me. Why does a climbing girl want to know about golems?"

Nan shifted, uncomfortable. She knew better than to tell this woman about Charlie. Toby already knew about him, and that was bad enough. "I just heard the word and was curious is all."

The woman did not quite look as if she believed this. "Did your friend Toby tell you about them?"

"He's not my friend," Nan snapped. "He told me they were some kind of pastry. But he's ignorant. He can't even read. Not like you and me." She liked the idea that she and this woman were the same in some way.

Miss Bloom nodded and sat back. "Golems are monsters formed from clay."

"Monsters?" Nan said. "Are you certain?"

The woman misread Nan's tone for fear. "Not all monsters are frightening." She gave a reassuring smile. "Most golems are protectors."

Nan screwed up her mouth. Thinking of Charlie as a protector didn't quite sound right. If anything, *she* spent her time protecting *him*. "Do you have any books on golems in this library?"

"There are no books about golems that I'm aware of," Miss Bloom said. "But I do know a story of one. It's a story my mother used to tell me when I was a little girl."

"Could you maybe tell it to me?" Nan said.

"I might be persuaded." The woman rose from her chair. "But first, perhaps you'd like to tell me about that book you've got behind your back?"

Nan felt her cheeks go hot. "I'm not a thief," she said. "I was only going to borrow it." She drew out the book of poems and gave it to Miss Bloom, who examined the title. "I was hoping to use it to teach someone to read."

Miss Bloom looked up with a teasing smile. "This *someone* wouldn't by any chance be named Toby, would he?"

Nan felt the burning spread to her ears. "If you're going to make fun of me, I'd just as soon be off."

"Wait," Miss Bloom said. "If you want to teach someone to read, you'll need better tools than this tripe." She tossed *Bright Verses for*

Bright Minds over her shoulder—right onto the floor! "The best way to inspire a love of reading is to read something *you* love . . . even if it is difficult." Nan followed her as she walked along the shelves and removed a slender volume with a gilded spine. "Take this." She offered it to Nan. "I think your pupil will find it much more diverting."

Nan turned the book over in her hand. "*Songs of Innocence*," she read. "What does that even mean?"

Miss Bloom smiled. "Once you've read it, maybe you can tell me." Somewhere outside, a church bell struck the hour. "It is late. I'm afraid we shall have to talk of golems another time."

Nan understood that she was being asked to leave. She nodded her thanks and turned toward the hearth. "Just tell me this," she said. "The golems—can some of them be . . . messengers?" She was thinking of the words Charlie had told her on Bonfire Night, that he was meant to tell her something about the Sweep.

"I suppose they can be made for whatever need arises."

"I read something about them in a bestiary. It said golems are made for something called *obsolescence*."

Miss Bloom nodded. "*To every thing there is a season, and a time to every purpose . . .*" She looked down at the prayer book, still in her hand. " 'Obsolescence' is a form of the word 'obsolete'."

Nan swallowed. "What does that mean?"

Her gaze met Nan's. "It means that once a golem has fulfilled its purpose, it must die."

·⇥ WONDER ⇤·

*T*he girl owned very few things. She had her tuggery and her brush and her pail and her sootbag. Someday, when she was old enough, she would have the Sweep's hat. And she had the doll.

The doll had brilliant green eyes—green as emeralds. The girl had seen it in a curiosity shop. The doll's hair was missing in patches. It had a delicate crack along its porcelain cheek. The doll was perfect.

The girl would stand at the window and talk to the doll for hours. She believed that the doll could hear her. The girl was very young. She had never had a friend before.

The Sweep had very little money. He swept half the shire to afford her that doll. And when the girl took the doll into her arms, she felt her heart grow larger. She named the doll Charlotte. She promised Charlotte that she would black her dress and teach her how to be a proper sweep and that they would be together always.

The girl carried Charlotte on her shoulders, as the Sweep had once carried the girl on his. She told Charlotte stories, and they played games.

"Why is that filthy boy playing with a doll?"

The question came from a young lady, who was standing in a row of other young ladies. They were all wearing matching dresses and matching bows, and they held matching books in their arms. The girl would later learn that this meant they were from a thing called a "school."

The Sweep was busy finishing work, and the girl was alone. The girl told the young lady that that she was a girl like them and that this was her doll Charlotte.

The young ladies in matching dresses began to tease the girl. They danced in a circle around her and called her mean words. One of the young ladies snatched Charlotte and waved her in the air.

The girl pleaded for her to return the doll. She was afraid that Charlotte would be frightened to be so high above the ground. "Give her back!" she begged. "Give her back!"

The young lady said, "Here she is!" and threw the doll—

up

up

up

into the air.

The doll circled and spun and then struck the ground with a sickening CRACK!

The young ladies retreated with their books, and the girl was left with her doll—whose porcelain face had shattered into a hundred pieces.

The girl wept bitterly. She tried to fit the pieces together, but they would not go. The girl was very young. She had never lost a friend before.

"Girl, why are you crying?"

It was the Sweep. He had returned from his work.

The girl held up the pieces of her shattered friend. "I have lost my doll. Some mean children tried to steal her, and now she is dead."

The Sweep knelt beside the girl. "Those fools. They left the best part." He reached into the pile of shattered Charlotte and removed a single doll's eye. Green as an emerald. "You see this eye—it's a magic eye, and it can see wonders hidden to the rest of the world."

The Sweep held the eye up to his own, as though peering through it. He gasped. "You see that woman with the large bustle?" He pointed to a spinster hailing a cab. "She's wearing the bustle to hide her tail."

"She is not," the girl said, sniffing. "That's just the fashion."

The Sweep seemed not to hear her. "Look! I saw it just now when she stepped into her carriage! A long, bushy thing with spines on the end— probably poisonous. See for yourself."

He handed the eye to the girl, who squinted as though looking through it. "I think I see it!" she exclaimed. "A big, ugly tail. And if you chop it off, I bet a hundred more will grow in its place. And if you chop those off, a hundred more, and a hundred more after that, and on and on forever!"

The Sweep helped the girl to her feet. "Let's get out of here before she comes after us!" He pointed down the way. "Look in that alley, and see if you can't find a fairy door we can escape through."

The girl and her Sweep spent the rest of the afternoon looking through the doll's eye—beholding wonders all around them.

⊹⊱ FIRST SNOW ⊰⊹

It was the first week of December and the city was still. Nan and Charlie walked along the frosty rooftops. Dark streets beneath them, darker sky above. The last leaves had fallen from the trees. Cold air wrapped around everything like a shroud. Nan was thinking about Miss Bloom, whose parting words had haunted her ever since—

Once a golem has fulfilled its purpose, it must die.

Nan glanced at Charlie, walking beside her. Steam rose off his shoulders, drifting behind him like a white shadow. Nan had wondered a hundred times what Charlie's purpose might be—why the Sweep had given him to her. But now that wondering came with a fear.

"Thank you for letting us visit the outside," Charlie said.

"Thank Toby," Nan said. It was because of him that she had started letting Charlie explore the neighborhood after dark. Windows glowed golden and warm along the road—illuminating little scenes of people preparing for bed. Somewhere below, Nan could hear the hiss and snap of the lamplighter, setting spark to the gaslights along the street.

Nan recalled a dream she had recently had about the Sweep— it was something that had happened when she was very small. In a moment of terrible heartbreak, he had taught her to see wonder. Charlie had stopped walking and was peering up. "Look," he said, pointing. "A falling star."

Nan stood next to him and looked where he pointed. The sky before her was starless and black.

Except for one speck of white.

"There it is," Charlie said. "It's coming to visit."

The speck swirled

and spun

and drifted

closer to them.

Charlie opened his hands and the little speck landed softly in his black palms. The moment it touched his palm, it fizzled and shrank into a little drop of water.

"Oh, no," Charlie said. "I melted the star."

"That wasn't a star," Nan said. "It was *snow*."

"What is snow?" Charlie asked.

"Snow is . . ." Nan stared up at the pregnant sky. "You'll find out tomorrow."

⊹ ⊹ ⊹

Nan woke to the sound of Charlie bumping into her side table. "Is it morning yet?" he whispered, feeling his way through the predawn darkness. "I heard bells."

Nan sat up and listened for chimes—they sounded different than usual, softer. "Meet me on the roof." She threw off her covers. "And cover your eyes!"

She pulled on her trousers and coat as quickly as she could. She didn't have a proper hat but didn't think it would matter.

The sun was rising by the time she reached the turret window. Snow was still falling—fat, lazy flakes drifting slowly down from the sky in a way that made her dizzy. Charlie was waiting for her on the back roof. "The snows are tickling me," he said. "Can I open my eyes yet?" Steam billowed off him like a furnace.

"Not yet," Nan said, shivering. She faced him out toward the sun. "Now."

Charlie opened his eyes.

Spread out before them was London—only it was a London transformed. The endless rooftops were now glittering and white against the sun. The streets were coated so thick you couldn't make out gutters or potholes. Not even boot prints marred the expanse of whiteness.

Nan watched Charlie watching the world. "Where . . . where did everything go?" he said at last.

She leaned close, tucking her arm under his. His warmth spread over her. "It's still right there," she said. She knelt down and picked up a handful of fresh snow. It was so light it spilled from her fingers as she raised it. "Only now it's covered in snow."

Charlie stared at the handful of snow, his face carved in wonder.

He reached out to touch it, but it stained black and melted instantly. "I broke the snow!"

"You didn't break it," Nan said. "You turned it into water. Snow is frozen rain, and if it touches something warm, it will melt back into water."

Consider the fact that Charlie had never seen or even heard of ice, and you can imagine how confused this left him. "So I can't touch the snow?" he said. Already a pool of black slush had formed around his feet and was dripping off the edge of the roof.

Nan shrugged. "I'm sorry."

"I don't mind," Charlie said. He lunged ahead and stamped across the roof, steam hissing from his footsteps, kicking up slush in every direction.

Nan watched him playing with such perfect abandon. She

thought again of Miss Bloom's words and felt a flicker of worry cloud her mind. What if Charlie's first snow was also his last?

Her thoughts were interrupted by a cry from the rainspout. "Hullo, Smudge!"

Toby's hand appeared over the gable and he pulled himself up onto the roof. His cheeks were pink from the cold. "River's froze up, so there's no treasure to be found." He worked one end of the pulley, bringing up his emporium after him. "I thought I'd pay a visit to my best girl and my best golem."

"And you are my best Toby," Charlie said.

"That goes without saying." Toby removed his bag and tossed it onto the roof. It hit the snow with a satisfying crunch. "I brought a gift for you."

Nan folded her arms. "I don't want any gifts from you."

Toby gave an amused smile. "I meant for *Charlie*."

"I am a gift from the Sweep," Charlie said. "Did you bring me a golem?"

"Nothing so grand." He opened his bag and rummaged inside. "I was thinking about how warm you are and how that might make it tricky to play in the snow." He emerged holding two enormous leather gloves that might have once been used by a smithy. "Just the thing for a soot golem, I'd wager."

Toby slipped the two gloves onto Charlie's steaming hands.

They didn't fit exactly right, on account of Charlie having the wrong number of fingers, but they fit well enough.

"Go on," Toby said. "Give it a try."

Charlie crouched down and timidly poked a pile of snow with his gloved hands. He scooped up the snow. "It's not breaking!" he said. He was slushing back and forth with giddy little steps. He threw the snow up into the air and let it fall onto his head.

"What did I tell you?" Toby said. "Just the thing."

Nan had to admit that it was a pretty thoughtful idea. She showed her approval by throwing a snowball at Toby's head.

The three of them spent the next hour in a glorious snowball fight, traveling from roof to roof along the block. After that, they made snowmen together on the flat roof of the Foundling Hospital. Nan and Toby rolled the snowballs, and then Charlie stacked them up. "Look," Charlie said proudly after several failed attempts. "I made a snow Nan and a snow Charlie."

"A perfect likeness if I've ever seen it," Toby said. "I can hardly tell it from the genuine article!"

The play was broken by cries from the street below.

Sweep!

Sweep O!

Sweep for your soot!

Nan looked up. She recognized the voices. "It's the boys," she said.

Charlie dropped his snowball. "Really?" Nan had told him all about her life with Crudd, and he had expressed many times that he wished he could meet them. "Can we do a snow fight with them?"

"Best not," Toby said. "Wherever the boys are, Roger is close to follow."

Nan and Charlie and Toby crept to the edge of the roof and looked down into the street. Whittles, Shilling-Tom, and Newt were rounding the corner, trudging through the black slush.

The boys looked even more miserable than Nan remembered. Their bodies were deathly thin, their faces red and chapped. They were shivering, even as they walked.

Newt looked worst of all.

He was carrying his own brush and bag now. Gone was the innocent child fearful of his first climb. His feet looked frostbitten. His eyes had the furtive, twitching look of an animal expecting to be struck down.

Nan heard a small whimper as he slipped and collapsed in a snowbank, spilling his sootbag.

Toby nudged Nan, and she looked to the end of the line, to another climber who had just rounded the corner—Roger.

"Get up, you lazy maggot!" he shouted. "That's my soot you're spilling!" He stomped up to Newt and struck him hard with the butt end of his broom.

Newt cried out in pain and scrambled to retrieve the spilled soot, already soaking into the blackening snow.

Nan couldn't take her eyes off Roger. Apparently he had been promoted in Nan's absence. He was wearing the blacks of a proper apprentice now—full trousers and a long coat with tails. New boots, polished to a shine. And perched atop his head was a black top hat.

"That's . . . *my* hat," Nan whispered.

Toby shrugged. "You weren't around, so Crudd made Roger apprentice."

"No," Nan said. "That hat is *mine*."

She looked hard at Toby, and he seemed to understand. "He must have swiped it after the nudge," he said.

Charlie smiled. "I remember that hat," he said. "That was my first pocket."

Roger had Newt up by the arm now and was dragging him back to the others.

"I'm going to murder him," Nan muttered. Before she knew what she was doing, she had packed a ball of snow in her cold fingers—packed it hard as a stone.

"Nan," Toby whispered. "Don't be rash—"

Nan leaped up from her perch. "You're a stinking *thief*!" She hurled the snowball with all her might.

Perhaps it was her form, or perhaps it was her ire, but the snowball hit Roger with such force that the boy was knocked right off his feet and landed—*splat*—in the slushy gutter.

Whittles and Shilling-Tom, who had turned to behold the commotion, set to clapping. "Bravo!" Whittles called. "A spectacular performance."

Shilling-Tom whistled with two fingers. "Encore!"

Roger meanwhile was sputtering curses and struggling to right himself. "*Who threw that?*" he shouted, spinning around.

"Get back!" Nan felt Toby snatch her collar and pull her away from the eave. "Get to the house, before he sees you!"

Nan, Charlie, and Toby raced along the rooftops, careful to avoid being seen from the streets below.

"That was incredibly stupid," Toby said when they were safely inside. He threw his cap down and pushed a hand through his wet hair. "I told you, Crudd's still looking for you." He was breathing hard.

"They didn't see me," Nan said, pulling off her coat.

"You don't know what they saw!" Toby was staring at her, his face flushed. "Don't think Roger won't look on that roof. Let's just hope there's enough snowfall to cover our tracks."

Nan had never seen him like this before. She didn't like it. "Let him," she muttered. "Then I can get my hat back."

"Hang your hat!" he shouted. "If Roger figures out you're alive, you can be sure Crudd will hear about it. And if Crudd finds you, then all of *this*"—he gestured to the house, to himself, to Charlie—"will be destroyed."

Nan folded her arms. How had such a wonderful morning turned into all this yelling? "Why do you even care?"

Toby glared at her, his jaw tense. "Sometimes I ask myself the same question." He grabbed his bag and marched back out into the cold.

·❧ THE CHIMNEY SWEEPER ❧·

After her encounter with Roger, Nan decided to heed Toby's advice and stay inside for the next few days. The thought of Crudd intruding on her new life filled her with dread beyond words. And if he did find her, what would become of Charlie?

She tried her best to put these things out of her mind by throwing herself into Charlie's education. She was relieved to learn that *Songs of Innocence* contained no songs. It was a collection of poems with pretty decorations around the edges. The pictures were strange and dreamy—they looked as if they were made from painted water and might disappear if you touched them. Nothing like the hard black lines in most books.

The poems were not printed in regular type but had been hand-drawn to match the pictures. The writer was someone named William Blake, but Nan liked to think that Miss Bloom was the actual writer. And that she had made the book just for Nan.

She took Miss Bloom's advice and decided to focus on reading. Charlie had trouble sitting still, even for a poem, and so Nan let him draw on scraps of paper while she read to him. She sat by the crackling fire, reading him poems about shepherds and lambs and blossoms and other nice-to-think-about things. Charlie always asked to see the pictures in the book so he could draw them right, but Nan wouldn't let him.

"I'd rather you did pictures of your own," she would tell him. Charlie's drawings were beautiful in their own smudgy way.

Nan enjoyed the poems well enough—certainly more than the pictures—though she couldn't quite determine whether they were meant *for* children or merely *about* them.

She learned the truth soon enough.

"Aha," she said upon turning the page.

Charlie, who had been drawing a picture of a lamb with three legs and a spiked tail, looked up from his work. "What's 'aha'?"

" 'Aha' means 'I've learned the truth!' It's something inventors and explorers say when they make a discovery."

"Did you make a discovery?"

"I did." Nan showed him the book. "This next poem is called 'The Chimney Sweeper.' " Surely this was why Miss Bloom had chosen the book for Nan.

"The Chimney Sweeper?" Charlie's eyes widened. She could

almost see him putting thoughts together. "It's a poem about Nan?"
He leaned toward the book, but Nan kept it out of view. "No
peeking," she said, and then she read the poem aloud.

> When my mother died I was very young,
> And my father sold me while yet my tongue,
> Could scarcely cry weep weep weep weep.
> So your chimneys I sweep and in soot I sleep.

> Theres little Tom Dacre, who cried when his head
> That curl'd like a lambs back, was shav'd, so I said.
> Hush Tom never mind it, for when your head's bare,
> You know that the soot cannot spoil your white hair.

> And so he was quiet, and that very night,
> As Tom was a sleeping he had such a sight,
> That thousands of sweepers Dick, Joe, Ned and Jack,
> Were all of them lock'd up in coffins of black.

> And by came an Angel who had a bright key,
> And he open'd the coffins and set them all free.
> Then down a green plain leaping laughing they run,
> And wash in a river and shine in the Sun.

Then naked and white, all their bags left behind,
They rise upon clouds, and sport in the wind.
And the Angel told Tom if he'd be a good boy,
He'd have God for his father and never want joy.

And so Tom awoke and we rose in the dark
And got with our bags and our brushes to work.
Tho' the morning was cold, Tom was happy and warm,
So if all do their duty, they need not fear harm.

Nan was silent for a long moment. The fire crackled in the hearth. She had too many things to say but no words to say them.

The poem was confusing. That was sometimes the way of poems. But there were other parts that she thought she understood all too well.

"Those boys sound very happy to be in the clouds," Charlie said.

"They sure do," Nan said. Her jaw was set. She could feel her pulse throbbing in her temple. Was this really what Miss Bloom thought of climbers? That they were happy little angels, eager to climb up into cramped chimneys? Was she really that blind?

She thought of Newt in the slush—cold and hungry and scared. Then she looked at the picture beneath the poem: a parade of little naked children with shining curls and plump cheeks prancing up to

Heaven. Nan had known hundreds of real climbers, and a few dead ones. None of them had shining curls or plump cheeks.

Charlie apparently agreed. "Who are all those little people with no clothes?" he asked, peeking over her shoulder. "Are they sweeps?"

"No," Nan said. "They're not."

"What are they?"

Nan snapped the book shut. "They are rubbish."

"Aha," Charlie said. "Maybe we should put it in the Rubbish Room?"

"I've got a better idea." Nan tossed the book into the crackling hearth.

And that was the last of *Songs of Innocence*.

⊰ THE GREAT CHRISTMAS CAPER ⊱

Who is Mary Christmas?"

Charlie asked this one morning during breakfast. He had heard people calling this woman's name on the streets all week and had become quite worried. "I hope they find her."

Nan was eating cabbage stew—her favorite breakfast—from a cracked teacup. "Not *Mary* Christmas," she said through slurpy mouthfuls. "*Merry* Christmas. 'Merry' means happy. It's what folks say to each other when the baby Jesus is born every year—that's Christmas."

"Every year? I thought born only happens once?" This was all too confusing for Charlie.

So Nan told Charlie about the whole thing. How the baby Jesus was born in a basket and how a wicked king tried to kidnap him but then a big bearded angel named Father Christmas fought the king. "And then he tossed the baby Jesus down the chimney of a girl named Mary, and that was the first Christmas present." Nan had never set foot in a church, so you can forgive her for not knowing better. "Now, every year in winter, Father Christmas spends one night bringing presents down the chimneys of all the good boys and girls in the whole world."

"Is that true or a story?"

"It's in the Bible," Nan said, wiping stew from her chin.

Truthfully, Nan had her doubts. If there were a fat giant hopping down chimneys once a year, she would probably have spotted him . . . or at least heard him stomping on the roof. Chimneys were her business, after all.

"I'm *merry* that Father Christmas saved the baby," Charlie said, pressing his fingers together. "Only I'm not sure I'd want to find him inside our chimney. Is he very frightening?"

"Oh, he's terrifying. Dressed all in red, with long white whiskers. And big fat hands like a pair of bear claws."

Charlie nodded vaguely. "How does he fit inside the chimney?" he said.

"Same as you, I'll bet." Nan slid down from her stool. "He just squeezes himself in there. I suppose he has to tuck his whiskers in his belt so they don't catch fire."

Charlie drew a little rabbit onto the table with the tip of his finger. "Will . . . will Father Christmas come to *our* chimney?"

"If he did, I'd tell him a thing or two," Nan said. "He only gives presents to rich children who already got more than enough. I've worked in rich houses the day after he's come. You wouldn't believe all the heaps of toys and sweets and new clothes—more than any one kid could ever want for. But do you think he comes by Crudd's and gives so much as a handshake to the climbers who clean the chimneys for him? Never once. Doesn't seem fair to me."

Charlie stared at the icy window, and Nan could tell his brain was working hard. "If Father Christmas won't give presents to the climbers," he said slowly. "Maybe we should do it for him."

And that was how the Great Christmas Caper was born.

Nan and Charlie made a list of the people who deserved presents. They included Newt, Whittles, Shilling-Tom, and Miss Bloom. She even thought of a "present" for Roger.

"What about Toby?" Charlie said. "Do you think he would like a present?"

"*Not* Toby."

"What about Prospero?"

Nan rolled her eyes. "Fine."

They spent the rest of the day collecting things that might pass for presents. Charlie went slowly from room to room, determined to find just the right gift for each person. "Folks should be good and grateful for whatever they get," Nan said, putting a fresh horse apple she had collected from some nearby stables into a pretty little box—the perfect present for Roger. "Just pick something already."

Charlie wanted a Father Christmas disguise, and so he and Nan made beards for themselves out of dander taken from the inside of a throw pillow that had split open during a pillow fight. They stuck the dander onto cut-out paper with gum paste and then tied the paper around their ears with twine.

When they were done, they bowed to each other.

"Ho-ho-ho, Father Nan," Charlie said.

"Ho-ho-ho, Father Charlie," Nan said.

Miss Bloom was the first stop. Nan remembered the woman saying something about a "Festival of Lights." She found a book in the captain's study called *Into the Holy Land* that said Jewish people celebrated the festival by lighting a magic candlestick that had nine arms. She decided to give her a pair of candelabra from the captain's dining hall. Each candelabrum only had four arms, so she had Charlie fuse them together to make eight, which seemed like plenty.

Miss Bloom's room was on an upper floor of the school, and so Nan had little trouble reaching her window from the roof. She carefully pried the window open. She set the candelabrum on Miss Bloom's bed stand and lit the eight candles. Then, quickly, before the woman stirred, she closed her window and slipped away.

After that was Prospero. Nan led Charlie across the river. They found Toby sleeping, nestled beneath Blackfriars Bridge, Prospero curled up next to him. She was alarmed to see Toby—muddy, shivering, his cheeks gaunt in the moonlight. It was hard to imagine that this was the same smiling boy she knew in the daylight. She wondered if he was still cross with her after their argument over Roger.

Nan hadn't been sure what sort of thing a rat might like as a gift. Charlie came up with the idea of giving him a little ember from his own body that might keep him warm all through the winter. Nan resisted at first, but Charlie was firm. "Just a little bit of my elbow or tummy."

They decided he could afford to lose some tummy, and so he carved a small piece out of himself, and Nan buried it beneath a loose stone, right near where Toby's head lay. The snow on that spot melted right away, and Nan could feel Charlie's warmth emanating up from the ground.

"How long will that spark last?" Nan asked, wiping her wet hands on her false whiskers. A few feathers came off. "Forever?"

Charlie lowered his head, as though he were suddenly ashamed. He tightened his grip on the sack of presents. "Not forever."

Nan pretended not to hear this. "Next stop, Tower Hamlets." They crossed back over the river and headed into the East End. It was slow going, traveling by rooftop wherever possible. She remembered Toby's warning and needed to be certain that no one spotted her. Eventually they reached Crudd's rooftop. Charlie looked out past her, his eyes fixed on St. Florian's Church. She wondered how much he remembered of Bonfire Night.

"I should go down without you," Nan said, taking the bag of presents. "We can't afford to make too much noise."

She quickly found herself in the coal cellar that had been her home for five long years. It was even danker than she remembered. The hearth was a bit warm, and she supposed that Crudd had let them make a small fire that night—just enough to keep them from freezing to death.

She scratched under her false whiskers while she let her eyes adjust to the darkness. Newt and the others were huddled together, no doubt to keep warm. She picked her way across the floor and set to delivering her gifts.

Whittles was the easiest. She gave him a penknife from the captain's arsenal; it had a real mother-of-pearl handle.

Shilling-Tom got an empty billfold for all his future riches.

Nan had wrapped the horse apple for Roger, but Roger was not in the bin. Part of the reason she had agreed to doing Christmas was the thought she might be able to swipe her hat back—but no luck. She put the wrapped horse apple in Roger's spot under the stairs so it would be waiting for him when he returned.

Newt was last. Nan had found a fur cap with a bushy striped tail in back—she had no idea what animal it might have come from.

She knew how sad Newt had been when Crudd shaved off his curls. Now, at least, his head would be warm. She crept close to him and carefully placed the wrapped gift in his arms.

She must not have been careful enough, because Newt opened his eyes. He broke into a sleepy grin.

"Nan," he whispered. And then, "Why've you got feathers stuck to your face?"

Nan shoved a finger under his nose. "I'm Father Christmas," she said. "If you tell anyone you saw me, I'll come back here and slit your throat."

Newt didn't seem to get the message, because he kept on smiling. "You brought me a present," he said, already tearing open the package in his hands.

Nan slipped back into the chimney. She didn't want to be there when he opened his gift. When she reached the roof, she found Charlie waiting for her. He was still looking at the church. "Did you get your hat back?"

"Roger wasn't there." She tore off her beard, which had begun to itch. "We should get out of here in case he comes back and spots us."

"I wish we could be there when they all wake up," Charlie said, following behind her. "Do you think they will like their presents very much?"

"Don't matter what I think." She was already on to the next rooftop. "Gifts are meant to be left behind, not waved under a person's nose like a boast. It's a very private thing to open a present, and a person deserves to do it in his own way." Nan had actually never received a Christmas gift before, but she imagined that if she did get one, she would like to open it without anyone looking over her shoulder to make sure she smiled or said thank you the right way.

"Maybe Father Christmas thinks that, too," Charlie said. "And that's why no one sees him."

"Or because he's a fairy tale," Nan said. "We've been out here for hours and not seen so much as a stray footprint."

The Christmas Eve air was still and quiet and had a pleasant bite to it when Nan took it in her lungs. Even the fog seemed to know the season, and she could almost make out stars overhead. Nan remembered growing up with the Sweep—how some nights they would lie on their backs and tell stories about the constellations. She wondered now if the stars had really been visible through the fog.

Perhaps the Sweep had just made her believe.

⊰ AULD LANG SYNE ⊱

The following week brought New Year's Eve.

Toby came to celebrate with them. "It's bad luck to cross a threshold without gifts." Toby opened his tattered emporium and producing three crowns made from golden paper. "Just the thing for a Hogmanay celebration!"

"Oh, yes," Charlie said. "That is a holly-day with *many* hogs."

"If only!" Toby took a crown and perched it on Charlie's head for him. "Hogmanay is how the Scots celebrate the new year. Old Queen Vickie's gone dotty for the day. It's one last chance to say farewell to *auld lang syne*."

Nan sniffed her crown. The points were crumpled, and it smelled like food. "Where did you find these? Digging through rubbish bins after someone's Christmas dinner?"

"Don't worry about where I got them." Toby scraped a daub of what looked very much like dried pudding from his. "It's very important that we're properly dressed for the last day of the year."

"Very important," Charlie said. "What is a year?"

"A year is a bunch of days put together," Nan said.

"Oh, it's much more than that!" Toby perched himself in front of Charlie. "A year is a little lifetime. A year is how long it takes for the world to dance around the sun. A year is how long it takes to build a house. A year is how long it takes to grow proper whiskers. A year is how long it takes for a baby to learn to walk. A year—"

"A year is how long it takes Toby to explain things," Nan said.

She scrounged some food from the larder, and they made a picnic on the roof. Ordinarily it would be much too cold for a picnic, but Charlie kept them warm. The three of them watched the revelry in the streets. Men and women in coats and hats came calling on friends and relations, bearing gifts and glad tidings.

"Why is everyone awake?" Charlie asked, snuggling himself against Nan. "Isn't this sleeping time?" He was very fond of sleeping time.

"It's different on New Year's Eve," Nan explained. "In order to properly celebrate, you're supposed to be awake at the exact moment when the bells toll midnight."

"The secret is to not let yourself yawn," Toby said. "Once you yawn, it's the beginning of the end."

"I will keep all my yawns in my mouth," Charlie said. "I am very excited to stay awake until midnight."

⁜ ⁜ ⁜

Charlie was asleep by ten o'clock.

Nan was determined to make it to midnight. She had never understood the point of it before. But tonight it felt different.

Charlie was slumped over on the gable. His body radiated warmth against her back. "Why is it that when I want to sleep, I can't?" she said through a yawn. "But when I want to stay up, I feel sleepy."

Toby shrugged. "You are an enigma, Nan Sparrow."

"Enigma?" She considered the word. "Think I'd take that over most of the other things you try to call me."

"See what I mean?" Toby said. "The only compliment you'll accept is one meant in jest."

"That's because the rest is rubbish," Nan said. "Why can't you just treat me like a normal person?"

Toby gave her one of his looks. "Now, what would be the fun in that?"

"Fun for you, maybe." She turned away from him and rested her head against Charlie's shoulder and closed her eyes. She could feel him breathing beneath her. The sounds of celebration wafted up from homes below. She thought about how nice it might feel to fall asleep like this.

Toby broke the quiet. "He asked me to watch you, you know."

Nan opened her eyes. "Who asked you? Crudd?"

"Not Crudd." Toby was staring into the horizon. He released a breath of steam. "The Sweep."

Nan sat up. "The Sweep?" She knew that Toby had met the Sweep once before—she'd been there, too. But this sounded like something else. "When? How?"

Toby looked her right in the eye. "He made me promise not to tell you." He lowered his head. "I was six years old. All alone. I didn't even speak English." He blinked into the distance, as though trying to remember things he would rather not.

"The Sweep found me sleeping under the bridge. I recognized him as the man who had helped me days before. '*Du bist alleine*,' he said." Toby shook his head. "He spoke *Deutsch* like me. They were the first kind words I'd heard since I had lost *meine eltern*—my parents." He pressed his lips together, and Nan realized that he must miss them as bad as she missed the Sweep.

"What did he tell you?" Nan said.

"He told me his name was *Spatz*—Sparrow. He told me there was a girl asleep on a roof near St. Florian's churchyard. He said she would soon wake up and find herself alone. He said she was special. And that I needed to keep an eye on her."

"Why would you do that?" she said. "Did he pay you?"

"He said he didn't have money," Toby said. "All he had was his empty sootbag." His gaze slid to the ledge beside him.

Nan looked past him to the battered and patched bag that Toby carried everywhere. "The emporium?" she said. "That was *his*?" She wondered at how she had failed to recognize it—looking at it now, she could see he was telling the truth. She could picture it draped over the Sweep's shoulder.

"He told me it was lucky," Toby said. "That it would be *just the thing*." He shook his head. "I still don't know if I believe him . . . but I'll tell you what: Everything I find that goes into that bag turns out to be *just the thing* for someone in need."

Nan nodded. "The Sweep's like that." She sighed, thinking of what he had left for her. "All these years of waiting for him to come back, and I still don't understand it. Why did he just disappear like that? Why didn't he take me with him?"

Toby shrugged. "He couldn't take you with him. Not where he was going."

Nan shook her head. "What are you talking about?"

He watched her for a long moment. "He was dying, Nan."

Nan pulled back. "That's a wicked thing to say!" She drew her arms tight around her chest.

He scooted closer to her. "Is it any more wicked than letting yourself believe in something you *know* isn't true?"

Nan opened her mouth but said nothing.

"You know I'm right. You've always known."

Nan took a deep breath. When she pulled memories of the

Sweep, she could sometimes see through the stories and smiles. She could see a man with hollow cheeks and hollower eyes. A man with a limp that would not go away. She could see him coughing up phlegm as black as soot. She could see a man wasting away.

Nan closed her eyes. She felt warm tears run down her cheeks. "Soot wart," she whispered.

"It was a mercy, what he did," Toby said. "He didn't want you to wake to find him . . . like that. And so he left you. You and Charlie. Only something went wrong, and Charlie wasn't born right away, like he was supposed to be."

"I held on too tight," Nan said. "He probably figured I would get cold and burn the soot to keep warm. But I didn't."

"No harm in the end," Toby said. "All it took was being burned alive in a chimney to fix your mistake." This was a joke, but neither of them laughed.

"Why wouldn't he want you to tell?" she said. "Why keep it a secret from me?"

"I'm not sure it was about you." He gave a tight smile. "I think he was trying to save *me*."

"By giving you the bag?"

"No, dummy," Toby said. "By giving me a *purpose*. From that moment on, I had to stay alive—no matter how bad things got. Because if I died, then there would be no one to keep an eye out for Nan Sparrow." He looked up at the sky. It was just clear enough to make out the faint glimmer of moonlight. "That's how it works, doesn't it? We are saved by saving others."

Nan wiped her nose with the back of her hand. She looked down at Charlie's face. He was sleeping peacefully on the roof beside her. Had she saved Charlie? Or had Charlie saved her?

"I think it's almost time," Toby said. He was facing the sky. "You can feel it in the air. Like all creation is holding her breath."

The bells of churches across London struck midnight. Front doors all along the street were flung open, and the sounds of cheering filled the air. There was a New Year's tradition to throw sticky rum cakes out the open doors. They said it ensured a full larder for the year to come. Nan saw figures scurrying from the shadows—beggars running to collect the wasted food.

All across the city, Nan could hear singing.

> *Should auld acquaintance be forgot,*
> *And never brought to mind?*
> *Should auld acquaintance be forgot,*
> *And auld lang syne?*
>
> *For auld lang syne, my dear,*
> *For auld lang syne,*
> *We'll take a cup of kindness yet,*
> *For auld lang syne.*

Nan shivered. "What do you think it means—*auld lang syne*?" She brushed a strand of hair from her eyes.

Toby examined a dead leaf that he'd found in the gutter box. "It means 'days long ago.' The song's about whether we should remember what's behind us."

"Of course we should," Nan said. "What's happened to us is who we are."

"I suppose so." He let the breeze take the leaf from his fingers. "But if you're always looking back, you might not see what's in front of you."

She shrugged. "I guess it's another enigma."

"You know what they say about Hogmanay?" Toby said. "Whatever you're doing at the stroke of midnight is what you'll be doing all through the new year."

Nan considered this. Sitting on a rooftop. Charlie on one side. Toby on the other. A clear sky above. The whole world below. She hugged her knees against her chest. "I could do worse."

⊰ PART TWO ⊱
EXPERIENCE

·⊰ THE BESPOKE MAN ⊱·

I was wondering if I would see you again."

Miss Bloom slid open the frosty dormer window for Nan to enter. "It's dreadful out there. Haven't you any boots?"

Nan dropped to the floor and wiped the slush from her feet. "Not sure I've use for them." She breathed into her fist. "Boots and rooftops don't mix. I prefer cold toes to a broken neck." She had been avoiding the library ever since she had tossed *Songs of Innocence* into the fire. She had regretted burning the book immediately and had even tried visiting some bookstalls to buy a replacement. She was afraid of making Miss Bloom upset, but she also knew she needed to return. There were things she still needed to know about Charlie.

If Miss Bloom remembered the book, she chose not to mention it. "Warm yourself by the fire." She indicated a seat opposite the hearth. "I seem to have brought up more cakes than I can eat. It would be a kindness if you finished what was left."

The cakes looked as if they hadn't been touched. Nan wondered if Miss Bloom had actually set them out for her specifically. She noticed that the chair had a blanket laid over its back to protect it from soot. "Thank you, ma'am." She tried a cake, which tasted of anise and ginger.

"Cakes are the least I can give in return for the handsome menorah you left on my bed stand." The woman smiled. "That *was* you, wasn't it?"

Nan bowed her head and concentrated on her cake. Now that she took regular baths, it was much easier to catch her in a blush. "Did you like it?"

"I did." Miss Bloom folded her hands. "It made me think of holidays past." Her gaze settled on the crackling fire. "It made me think of home."

Nan settled herself deeper into the chair. Her feet barely touched the floor. "Is home very far away?" She thought she could detect a hint of accent in Miss Bloom's voice.

The woman shook her head. "I was born on Brick Lane."

"In Spitalfields?" Nan wrinkled her nose. "That's hardly an hour's walk from here."

"It is not far. And yet . . . it is a world apart. My family is quite traditional. They live by different rules than their gentile neighbors." Miss Bloom gave an apologetic smile. "The last time I saw my parents, I was scarcely older than yourself. I fear they would not recognize me today. Neither would they welcome one who has strayed so far from their ways." Her smile tightened into a wince. "But I think you did not come here to interrogate me about my history."

This was true. Ever since talking to Toby on New Year's, Nan had felt a growing urgency to understand what Charlie was—and why the Sweep had left him with her. If she could discover his purpose, perhaps she could avoid fulfilling it. "The first time you found me up here," Nan said, "do you remember our conversation?"

"How could I not?" she said. "A ghost come back from the grave to steal a reading primer."

"I asked you if you knew about golems, and you promised that you would tell me if I returned."

Miss Bloom sat back. "I wondered if you had forgotten about that."

"Can you tell me now?"

"Golems are not something easily studied. After you asked, I did a little searching at Hatchard's Bookshop. I could find no books about true golems, though echoes of such creatures appear in many stories." She handed Nan a book, which Nan opened to the title page.

FRANKENSTEIN;

or,

The Modern Prometheus

And then, beneath the title, an inscription from something called *Paradise Lost*:

> *Did I request thee, Maker, from my clay*
> *To mould me man? Did I solicit thee*
> *From darkness to promote me?—*

"What's a Frankenstein?" Nan stared at the word. "Is that a sort of monster?"

"Frankenstein is not the monster. Or perhaps he is. You can tell me after you've read it."

"Thank you." Nan closed the book. She ran her thumb over the ridges on the spine. She wished she could talk about Charlie, but it was impossible. "I know it's an odd thing, asking about golems. All I can tell you is that it's important."

"You needn't justify yourself, not to me." Miss Bloom looked at the fire. "I can tell you what my mother and father told me when I was a little girl." She paused a moment, and Nan thought she might be remembering what it was to have her mother and father with her still. "A golem is a 'bespoke man.'"

" 'Bespoke'?" Nan shook her head. "I'm afraid I don't know that word."

This made Miss Bloom smile. "I've always admired a person who can admit to not knowing something. Most people smile and nod and pretend they know everything for fear of being caught out. But those people only ensure their ignorance." She shook her head and answered more plainly. " 'Bespoke' means a thing has been custom-made. It is a one-of-a-kind treasure created for just one person."

"How is a golem made?"

"A sage or rabbi—that is, a Jewish priest—forms a body out of mud or clay and then brings that creature to life with a sort of magic word called a *shem*."

Nan wondered if the Sweep himself had been Jewish. She knew he had come from a kingdom far away—a place where chimney sweeping was an honorable trade, respected by all. "This *shem*," she asked, "is it some kind of spell?"

"More like a spark," the woman said. "Some say the word is the true name of God." She smiled as if she were almost embarrassed to talk of such things. "The maker might carve the word into the golem's forehead or stitch it into his heart or whisper it into his ear. It is that word that gives the golem life."

Nan thought of Charlie. He had no word on his forehead. She tried to imagine the Sweep bringing Charlie to life. For some reason, she pictured it the same way she pictured story soup—dropping ingredients into his hat. She wondered what words he might have said to bring those ingredients to life. "In your stories, why did the rabbi make his golem?"

"Why does a person create anything? Out of necessity." Miss Bloom leaned closer. "The golem is made to help people who fear for their lives. For reasons that have never quite made sense to me, Jewish people are despised and attacked the world over. Their need is great."

"Golems are protectors," Nan said, remembering what the woman had told her the last time they talked.

"That is the idea, yes."

She knew from the way Miss Bloom was speaking that she did not believe in golems. She tried to imagine what Miss Bloom would do if she met Charlie. "I remember you saying that golems live until they have fulfilled their purpose. And after that they must die."

"You remember very well."

Nan shifted, leaning closer. "But what if they don't want to die? Or if someone else doesn't want them to die? Is there some way to stop it?"

Miss Bloom seemed to understand that Nan's question was a serious one. "There are stories in which, once the golems have done their work, they try to keep living. They resist the will of their creator." She shook her head. "I suppose we should not blame them. Who among us would not do the same?"

"Does it work?" Nan's throat felt dry. "Do the stories ever have a happy ending?"

"Things sometimes do end well for the people—they are delivered from danger or blessed with riches. But not so for the golem. For the golem"—Miss Bloom took a breath—"there is no happy ending."

·ℋ A BAD DAY ℋ·

I t was cold, and the larder was bare.

Nan stared at the empty shelves, as though staring might make food appear. The icy stone floor was covered with opened tins that she hadn't bothered to dispose of. The smell was not pleasant.

"Charlie!" she called. Even indoors, her breath came out as steam. "What did you do with the loaf of bread I got last week?"

"I gave it to Prospero." He stumped into the kitchen with a birdcage full of yarn. "It had green fur on it—that part is his favorite."

"You should tell me when we're out of food."

"Oh, yes," Charlie said. "Nan, we are out of food."

She rolled her eyes and closed the larder door. This was her fault. She had stayed inside for most of the week, which meant she had earned no money. And now it was Sunday—a day when almost no one hired sweeps—and she had nothing to eat.

Nan felt a sort of anxious gnawing inside her gut. She told

herself it must be hunger, but it did not feel like hunger. She had spent the past three days devouring the book that Miss Bloom had given her. *Frankenstein* was unlike anything she had ever read. There was arctic adventure and a vain inventor and mobs of angry people and murder. The story had not angered Nan the way "The Chimney Sweeper" had. Instead, it had unsettled her. As had Miss Bloom's final words:

For the golem, there is no happy ending.

Thinking about this made the gnawing in her gut stronger. "I'm going to get some work," she said, climbing upstairs to her room.

Nan's room had once been her favorite place in the world. But today she hated the sight of it. There were cobwebs in the corners and clutter on the floor. A layer of black soot covered every surface that Charlie had touched. "Can't you do anything without ruining it?" she muttered.

Almost every room within the House of One Hundred Chimneys looked like a rubbish heap. Most of the furniture had been broken apart to make firewood. An icy wind slid through a cracked window, carrying tiny motes of snow into the room. Nan clenched her teeth to stop them from chattering. She had once been so excited to show snow to Charlie, but at the moment it was hard to fathom how she had ever felt fondly toward the stuff.

She pulled on the warmest trousers she could find. They were mottled with patches. She found they barely covered her knees. She thought of Miss Bloom's students at the seminary, all prettied up in wool coats and fur mufflers and high boots.

She told herself she wasn't jealous. And she wasn't. But still, it was hard not to envy those girls whose only job was to learn from Miss Bloom all day. She recalled how Miss Bloom had petitioned the headmistress to help her. What if some rich patron paid for Nan to join the school? But that imagining was ruined by another thought—

Charlie.

Even if that impossible opportunity did appear, Nan would have to refuse it. Because Charlie needed her.

Nan heard a clatter below as he knocked over something in the Inventing Room. "I told you to stay out of there!" she shouted. She had been trying to make herself a mechanical brush with things she'd scavenged around the house. But the effort had proved fruitless, and she hadn't touched it in more than a month.

She felt the gnawing grow. It was in her chest now.

Charlie appeared in the doorway holding a book. "Can you read me a story?"

"Not today." She took up her brush.

"Oh," he said. "Can *I* read *you* a story?"

"No." She walked past him into the hall.

Charlie followed after her. "Can you tell me about the Sweep?"

"No."

"Can we play skittles?"

"No."

"Can we build a fort?"

"No."

With each question, Nan felt the gnawing more keenly. She wanted Charlie to stop asking questions—she wanted everything to stop.

"Can we build a snow Charlie?"

"No."

"Can we be Father Christmas?"

"No."

"Can we visit Toby?"

"No."

"Can we visit Prospero?"

"No."

"Can we—?"

Nan spun around. "NO!" she shouted. "NO! NO! NO!"

Charlie blinked. He looked like he was about to cry. "Why are you shouting at me?" he asked.

Nan rubbed the bridge of her nose, as if she could massage out the gnawing. "I'm not shouting." She released a tense breath and forced herself to smile. "Today's just a bad day."

"A bad day?" Charlie's eyes went wide. "Is that a kind of holly-day?"

Nan sighed and opened the window. "I'm going out."

A gust of snowy air swept into the room. "It is very cold outside," Charlie said. "If I went with you, I could keep you warm."

Nan closed her eyes and balled up her fists until her hands hurt. She was afraid of saying something she might regret. She released a slow breath, and again heard the words:

For the golem, there is no happy ending.

"Please just stay here." She climbed through the window and into the cold.

✦ ✦ ✦

It was freezing outside—the sort of cold that makes your temples throb and your lungs sting. Even though it was Sunday and the factories were closed, the fog was thick as gruel. Only the most desperate were outside on a day like this. Unlike Charlie, Nan needed to eat. And unlike Charlie, she needed privacy.

Why had she been so short with him?

She gripped her brush and pushed her chin into her chest. She wished she had taken the time to grab a turban or busby from the Dress-Up Room—better foolish than frostbit. The streets were mostly bare. Those who were out of doors moved quickly, as though they might freeze into statues if they stopped. Nan tried to imagine what that would look like. Then she imagined pushing the statues over.

Nan tried to sing for work, like she usually did, but the words caught in her throat. She spotted a housemaid on the corner of Bury and Hart. From the marks in the snow, Nan could tell the girl had been pacing in that spot for some time—a good sign that she was on the job.

"Looking for a sweep?" Nan said through chattering teeth.

The housemaid turned toward Nan. She had red hair and a pinched, mousey face. Her cheeks were filthy with freckles. "Oh! Tell me I'm seeing things."

"You're seeing a sweep," Nan said. She breathed into her fist. "Do you need your chimneys cleaned or not?" She was cold and in no mood.

"Tell me truly: Were you the girl who swept the Lofting house up on Dover Street? And the apartments over in Cavendish Square?"

Nan inched back. She did not like the idea that people were talking about her. "Who's asking?"

This seemed answer enough for the housemaid. "Oh, thank the good Lord up in Heaven and all His angels!" She clasped her hands together. "I've been across half o' London looking for you. Last week my master was having Missus Lofting over for tea, and she started going on about this sweet little girl who did her chimbleys. Well, my master heard that and *insisted* I find the same girl to do his chimbleys, on the double. *And Betsy*, my master said to me, *if you don't find her, I'll turn you out on your ear!*"

That sounded about right from what Nan knew of masters.

"Three hours I've been out here, frozen up to my shins." The housemaid put her hands to her heart. "I'd just about given up hope when you came straight up to me, plain as you please. Like an angel fallen from the sky."

Nan eyed the girl. Something about her story didn't make sense. Nan had spoken to thousands of maids in her life, and every one of them had talked to her as if she were nothing. And here was this "Betsy," with her smiles and clasped hands and her angels in Heaven. "I charge two shillings," Nan said, naming double what she normally did.

"Oh, that won't be a problem," the maid said. "And you can believe that the cook will be finding a cake or two with your name on it before you're done."

That was all Nan needed to hear. She followed after Betsy, who was already deep in another rapturous retelling of her ordeal. Nan wondered if the maid might harbor a secret passion for the stage.

They walked south and were soon heading through the twisting, maze-like alleyways of the rookery in St. Giles. This was a neighborhood where even the most seasoned traveler could get lost. Most of the folks in this area were poor, and even the few middle-class homes were not nearly as splendid as the other mansions in the West End. Nan was surprised to think that Mrs. Lofting would have tea in such a place.

"Here we are," Betsy said, unlocking a door of a modest home with no lights in the windows. "The master will be pleased as punch to hear you've come. I wouldn't be surprised if he pays you an extra penny just for the trouble."

Nan kicked the slush from her feet and followed the girl, who led her to a drawing room on the ground floor. A fire crackled in the hearth. Nan stepped through the doorway and peered into the otherwise unlit room. The windows were shuttered, and the furniture was all under tarpaulins. It did not look like a lived-in house, nor one that wanted its chimneys swept.

Nan inched backward. "What did you say your master's name was again?"

"She didn't," said a voice in the corner.

Nan started as a man stepped out from behind a privacy screen. He had shiny boots and an impeccably clean coat.

"It's Crudd," the man said. "Wilkie Crudd."

·❊ TRAPPED ❊·

Nan stared at the man before her. He looked just as he always had. The same immaculate dress. The same expression of icy calculation. "Crudd?" she whispered, inching back.

"It has been a while." He removed his top hat and put it over his heart. "I'm touched you remember me."

Nan turned to run, but the housemaid grabbed her roughly by the shoulders and shoved her back into a chair. "Easy now," she said. "You just got here."

"You . . . tricked me!" Nan said.

The housemaid gave a sneer. "Don't you start playing the lamb." She turned to Crudd. "You shoulda seen her out there, Wilkie. Her eyes got big as saucers when I mentioned extra pay." She gave a sort of braying laugh. "Greedy little snipe—she'd have believed anything I told her."

"Thank you, Betsy," Crudd said. He drew a half crown from his waistcoat and pressed it into the girl's open hand. His fingers lingered on her palm for a moment too long. "You are a true marvel."

Betsy gave Crudd a sort of lewd wink and then walked to the hall doors. "The house staff's all in the country with the missus. You got the place to yourself." She drew the doors apart and stepped into the hall.

"No!" Nan leaped to her feet and ran after her. "Wait—!"

Whap!

The door slid shut—nearly taking Nan's fingers off. She heard a *clack* as the lock turned into place. She strained against one pull and then the other, but it was no use.

She was trapped.

Crudd had seated himself in one of the covered chairs beside the crackling hearth. He studied her with the unhurried satisfaction of a cat who has cornered a mouse. "You're looking very well. Considering you're supposed to be dead."

Nan looked past him toward the window. Perhaps she could unlatch the shutters and break through the glass before he grabbed her? "How long have you known?" she said, inching along the wall.

"I never *didn't* know." Crudd examined his fingernails in the firelight. "Nan Sparrow, felled by the Devil's Nudge?" He shook his head. "Maybe another climber, but not you. When the brickmasons failed to discover your remains, I knew for certain: You had escaped the burning flue and left me to handle the mess." He leaned forward, and Nan saw a flicker of cold anger in his eyes. "And what a mess it was."

She took another half step toward the window. "I'm sorry."

Crudd either did not hear or did not care for her apology. "The Board of Works fined me ten pounds for trade malpractice and endangerment. Ten pounds! I could keep a dozen climbers for that sum." He shook his head. "But the fine was nothing compared to how news of your death sullied my reputation. Servants talk. I can't very well call myself 'the Clean Sweep' if I'm leaving dead children in people's chimneys, can I?"

"That's why you needed me back?" Nan had to keep him distracted. "To clear your name?" She took another half step backward. Her hand touched the rail along the wall.

"I knew if I was patient, you would make yourself known. All I needed was a way to draw you into the open." Crudd ran his finger along the brim of the hat perched on his knee—the Sweep's hat.

"The hat," Nan said. She dropped her hand from the wall. "You had Roger wear it on purpose. You *knew* I would see it."

"And see it you did," Crudd said. "You can't imagine my delight when he reported that you'd assaulted him with a snowball on Great Ormond Street. An early Christmas present."

Nan closed her eyes. Toby had been right. How could she have been so reckless?

"That hat doesn't belong to you," she said through grit teeth.

"Not anymore." He stood, and with a flick of his wrist tossed it into the fire. A cloud of sparks floated up from the coals as flames took the silk.

"No!"

Crudd stepped aside, laughing as Nan flew past him and fell to her knees before the hearth. She plunged her hand into the flames and grabbed the hat. She beat it against the floor to put out the fire. But it was too late. The crown was already warped and split. One side of the brim had burned away completely. Her hand throbbed where she had burned herself, the skin raw and blistered.

"Why?" A bitter sob escaped her throat. "You didn't need to burn it . . ."

"After five long years, at last she cries." He was standing over her, smiling. "I had begun to think you didn't have the capacity."

"You . . . *monster*." Every muscle tensed with defeat and rage. Her gaze fell upon an iron poker propped against the mantel. She wondered if she could smash his skull in with it.

Crudd must have noticed, for he gently took the poker and set it out of reach. "Easy, child," he said. "I've use for you yet."

Crudd clasped both hands behind his back—so little was his

fear of her. "Your first step will be reporting your deception to the Board of Works so that I might have my ten pounds restored to my coffers." He paced the length of the room. "And then you will return to Tower Hamlets and sweep for me as you have done these many years."

"I don't understand. All this work . . . just to take back one climber?"

Crudd wheeled around. "It's the principle of the thing. News travels—never faster than along the gutters. All across London, climbers whisper of the girl who escaped her master. If Nan Sparrow could manage it, then why not them?" He shuddered at the thought. "No, I need you back so that I might make an example of you."

Nan pulled herself to her feet, wiping her cheeks. "And if I refuse?" The pain in her hand was overwhelming.

"Then I must make a different example." He shook his head and stepped toward her. "I had hoped it wouldn't come to this." He sounded disappointed in her.

"Come to what?"

Crudd tilted his head. "The Board of Works does not need your testimony to remit my ten pounds. They only need to see that you escaped *that* particular chimney." He took another step toward her. "They only need to find your body . . . somewhere else."

Nan's eyes widened. "You wouldn't . . ." But she knew he would. She'd seen him buy and break a dozen climbers over the years without so much as a sniff.

"Watch me," he said.

Nan leaped past him—scrambling to the window. "Help!" She pounded at the shutters. "Help, someone—!"

"Silence!" Crudd grabbed her wrist and pulled her from the window. "For a ghost, you make entirely too much noise." He dragged her across the floor toward the fire burning in the hearth.

"NO!" Nan screamed, twisting to get free. "Let GO!"

He held her by the back of the neck and forced her to her knees. Nan could feel the flames—blistering hot against her skin. "Would you care to change your answer?" He pushed her face closer.

"Charlie!" Nan screamed into the flames. "Charlie, help!"

She did not know why she had called his name. She knew he was half a city away.

But the words had barely escaped her lips when she felt a flash of heat as something very large hurtled down the length of the flue and crashed into the hearth in a burst of sparks and smoke and hot brick.

Nan and Crudd were both thrown backward across the floor. White smoke filled the room.

Hacking, gasping, Nan pulled herself to her knees. Through the haze, she saw a figure step from the charred ruins of the fireplace—hulking and huge.

The figure was crackling red like an ember. Smoke billowed off its gigantic shoulders. It stepped closer, and its two black eyes narrowed into deadly slits.

Nan stared up at the smoldering creature above her.

"Charlie?" she whispered.

⊰ THE PROTECTOR ⊱

I f Nan was shocked to see Charlie standing above her, that must
have been nothing compared to what Crudd felt. The man scuttled backward, his mouth wide, eyes wider. "Wh–wh–what . . . ?"
He was unable to form the sentence.

Nan drew herself up, clutching her burning hand to her chest.
"This is Charlie," she said. "And he is very angry."

Charlie had not moved from the front of the hearth, but somehow he seemed even bigger than he had a moment before. The
smoke spilling off his shoulders had choked the small room. The rug
beneath his feet had caught fire and was burning beneath him.

"M–m–monster!" Crudd clambered to his feet and snatched
the iron poker, which had been knocked across the room. "S–s–stay
back!" he shrieked. "I'm warning you!" He swiped the poker
through the air.

Charlie stepped toward Crudd. "Leave . . . her . . . alone."

"Charlie." Nan rushed to him. "I'm safe." She tried to grab his arm, but he was too hot to touch. "Let's go."

Charlie did not seem to hear her. "Leave . . . her . . . alone." He took another step.

"We need to go!" Nan cried. "Now!" She was sure that the maid Betsy had heard the chimney crash. Who knew how many other people had heard it, too?

Crudd gave a feral cry and lunged at Charlie, swinging the poker at his head. It connected with a dull crunch. Bits of sooty rubble fell to the floor.

Charlie grabbed the end of the poker and ripped it from Crudd's hands. He flung it to the floor and then seized the man's head in one hand, as one might take an apple.

Crudd screamed at the scorching touch. The room filled with the acrid smell of burning hair, burning flesh. Charlie hoisted the man up and hurled him through the air. "Leave . . . her . . . ALONE!"

Crudd's body smashed clear through the shuttered windows and into the frozen street.

"Charlie!" Nan ran to the window. Debris covered the street outside. The defenestrated man was sprawled on the snow. His clothes were charred and shredded.

"Oh, Charlie," Nan whispered, stepping back. "What did you do?"

Crudd moaned in agony. "I am not done with you, Nan Sparrow!" he snarled, drawing himself to his knees. Nan saw blood streaming from his lowered face, staining the snow. "I will make you pay!"

He fixed his eyes on hers, and Nan gasped at the sight of him.

Wilkie Crudd was now a man disfigured. His golden hair had been burned along the side of his head where Charlie had grabbed him. His nose was swollen purple and streaming blood. Three of his front teeth were missing.

"N–N–Nan?" Charlie was behind her, but he was not looking out the window. He was staring at his open hands, a look of pain and confusion on his face. "I was following you. I was afraid you might get cold. What . . . what happened?" He looked as though he had just woken from a trance.

Outside, Crudd staggered to his feet. "Monster!" he howled into the cold air. "*Monster!*"

Shouts echoed from houses up and down the way. A few people emerged from their front doors and raced to the scene.

Charlie stepped back from the window, shaking his head. "Nan?" he whispered. "Did I do something . . . bad?"

Nan picked up the Sweep's charred hat. "You saved me."

Someone spotted Charlie in the window and screamed. More cries of "Monster!" and "Police!" rang out. Somewhere in the distance, a whistle sounded.

Nan took Charlie's hand in her own. It was hot but no longer burning. It was the hand of her Charlie.

Charlie looked at her. "Wh–wh–what do we do?"

"We run."

◆ ◆ ◆

They traveled by rooftop. The journey home was tense, and it wasn't until they were safely inside the captain's parlor that Nan felt she could breathe. The pain in her hand had subsided, and she was relieved to see that the burns were not nearly as severe as she had thought.

The sky outside had turned dark. Charlie usually slept in the Nothing Room hearth. But tonight he asked to stay in Nan's room.

Nan sang the Sweep's song to him and then told him a story about the Sweep. It was a good, long tale that she made up, about how the Sweep had once been hired to clean out the inside of a volcano, and how that was where the Sweep had learned the language of smoke. "And that's why every sweep ever since knows when it's safe to climb a flue."

"Nan?" Charlie whispered. He was twining his crumbly fingers. "Did . . . did I do bad things to that man?"

She nodded. "Yes."

He looked up at her. His face was etched with pain. "*Why* did I do those things?"

Nan took a long breath. "I think you did those things because you are a golem . . . and you were made to protect me." And then she told him everything she had learned about golems from Miss Bloom.

Almost everything.

When she finished, Charlie just stared into the darkness. "So when I hurt that man," he said slowly, "I was doing *protecting*?"

"Crudd was going to kill me, and you stopped him." Nan worked her hand along the brim of the Sweep's hat. It was burned beyond repair. "That's what golems are for. Their job is to protect people. Or sometimes just one person."

Nan thought she could almost see him smile. "Just one person— like Nan?"

She leaned close. "And did you ever."

"Did I ever," Charlie said.

She shook her head, remembering the sight of Crudd's battered face. However handsome he may have once been, he would never be so again. "I don't think there'll be too many more weddings in the Clean Sweep's future." She said it in a way to let him know she was proud. "I think it's fitting. Folks ought to look the way on the outside that they are on the inside."

"Nan?" Charlie said. "Do I look on the outside the way I am on the inside?"

Nan hesitated. She knew what Charlie looked like. And the way he had looked in front of Crudd—smoldering and huge. If he hadn't been a monster before, he was then. "Actually, I think I was wrong to say what I just said. My whole life, folks have treated me like I was nothing—just because of how I looked. And maybe *that's* the problem. If we all could just ignore the way other people looked, then we could see who they really were."

Charlie nodded. "He called me a monster. Just like those other people." He looked down, kneading his thick fingers. "I tried reading about golems in our book of beasts. I saw the word 'monster' there, too."

Nan put her hand on his. His fingers were warm and crumbly and just the right size. As though they had been made for her. "So what if you are a monster?" She squeezed his hand. "I wouldn't have it any other way."

·❧ THE CHIMNEY SWEEPER ❧·

Nan continued to worry about Charlie. He seemed to have returned to his sweet, Charlie self, but anytime she looked at him, she couldn't help but recall the vision of him standing over Crudd. She made Charlie promise to stay inside the house. "No more rooftop walks," she told him. "Even after dark."

Charlie seemed disappointed, but he did not argue.

In the weeks that followed, Nan made a habit of visiting Miss Bloom's library. She and the teacher had devised a system. Miss Bloom would leave a lamp burning in the window as a way to let Nan know it was safe.

Every time Nan came, she brought back whatever book she had borrowed from the library and Miss Bloom would give her a new book to read.

The teacher would ask Nan all sorts of questions about her life as a climber. And the way she listened, it was as though she *really* wanted to hear the answers. Nan told her whatever she could, except for a few things. She never said anything about Charlie. And she never said anything about the Sweep.

She made a point of reading and returning the books as quickly as time would allow. The bigger the book, the faster she read it. She could see how impressed Miss Bloom was when she returned a book like *Great Expectations* or *The Pilgrim's Progress* in only a few days' time. Miss Bloom would ask Nan questions about the story. She seemed interested in Nan's opinions, but Nan thought the questions might also be a way of testing to see if Nan had actually read the books. She was a teacher, after all.

"My goodness," Miss Bloom said one night when Nan appeared with her copy of *Robinson Crusoe*, which she had read aloud to Charlie over the course of a single rainy Wednesday. "No sooner do I lend you a book than it is back in my hand."

"It's not hard when the stories are good," Nan said. "And I figure you might need them for your real students."

Miss Bloom tilted her head and held Nan's gaze. "I can't help but notice that there is *one book* that you have not returned."

Nan felt her heart sink. She had been dreading this question. "The poems," she said.

"*Songs of Innocence,* by William Blake." Miss Bloom gave a patient smile. "Am I to assume you are still reading it?"

Nan dug her toe into the tassels of the rug. "I did read it—well, most of it. But then I . . . misplaced it." This was not an exact lie. Nan had misplaced it. In a burning hearth.

The woman raised an eyebrow. "You are usually so careful with the books I give you. Would you like another copy to read?"

Nan chewed the inside of her cheek. "That's very kind, but . . . I'm not sure I like that William Blake fellow very much. His poems are pretty, but it seems to me he doesn't know much about the world the way it really is."

Miss Bloom nodded. "I think I can guess which poem gave you that impression." There was a hint of a smile on her face. "Did something happen to the book?"

Nan released a slow breath. "I may have . . . dropped it . . . in the fireplace."

Miss Bloom's expression changed. "You should not have done that." She sounded more like a teacher than she usually did. "No good has ever come from destroying a book."

Nan felt her cheeks grow hot. "I couldn't help it! All that stuff about happy little sweeps doing their happy little jobs! And folks like you believe it. Because it's easier to think that than to face what's really going on, how bad it really is." She could feel her eyes welling up. "I thought you were different than the rest of them. I thought you *understood*."

Miss Bloom released a deep breath. "I understand that I cannot possibly understand." She shivered, as though warding off a chill, and walked across the room.

Nan followed. "Are you very upset with me?"

"A little surprised. But surprising me seems to be one of your talents." The woman knelt down and perused the shelf. "There is a lesson here. Just because a book makes you *feel* bad does not mean it *is* bad." She removed a small book and offered it to Nan. "You might discover that Mister Blake is more sympathetic to your plight than you first thought."

Nan took the book from her hand. It looked just like the other book of poetry. The title, however, was different. "*Songs of . . . Experience?*" Nan said.

"Blake meant them to be read together—first *Innocence*, then *Experience*. The twin stages of life. I suspect you'll find this collection a bit more accurate." She gestured for Nan to sit. "Take a look."

"Now?" Nan had her doubts. She was pretty certain that anything this man had to say she didn't want to hear.

Miss Bloom nodded, so Nan sat down in her chair by the fire. She opened the book. It had tiny decorations around the edges, just like the other book. Only these pictures were different. The characters in them did not look so sweet or so happy. Nan turned the pages and stopped at a poem in the middle.

"The Chimney Sweeper," she said aloud. "This poem was in the other book." Only now that she looked more closely, she could see that it was not the same poem. It was shorter and began differently. "He wrote two poems with the same name," she said. "Why would he do that?"

"Read it," Miss Bloom said.

Nan read it.

> *A little black thing among the snow;*
> *Crying weep! weep! in notes of woe!*
> *Where are thy father and mother? Say!—*
> *They are both gone up to the church to pray.*

Her voice caught in her throat. This poem felt different. She could see the steeple towering over the child. She could see the stream of well-dressed ladies and gentlemen filing through the gates—could see them stepping right over the crying child, a tat-tered bundle in the snow.

> *Because I was happy upon the heath,*
> *And smiled among the winter's snow:*
> *They clothed me in the clothes of death,*
> *And taught me to sing the notes of woe.*

Nan could see her own ragged clothes, drenched by sleet, covered in holes. She could hear the cries of Whittles and Shilling-Tom, desperately calling for work.

> *And because I am happy, and dance and sing,*
> *They think they have done me no injury:*
> *And are gone to praise God and his Priest and King*
> *Who make up a heaven of our misery.*

Nan blinked, and she felt tears burning in her eyes. She was angry. But not at the poem. At the way that the poem felt like her own true life. The anger twisted inside her like a knot.

She felt Miss Bloom's hand on her shoulder. "Some of us *do* see," the woman whispered.

Nan put the book down. "What does seeing do?" She brushed a tear from her cheek. "We're still out there. Getting shoved into flues. Burning, falling, starving, dying."

She stood up, feeling the angry knot tighten. "Do you know what I found in an old newspaper? There was some inventor fellow who made a mechanical brush that could go up a chimney all on its own—no climber needed. That was ages ago, but no one even knows about it. Why? Because the life of a boy or girl is worth less than a few rods of steel." She sniffed, brushing the wet from her cheeks. "The truth is folks don't help us because they *need* us.

Because keeping themselves warm is more important than keeping us alive." She gestured to the hearth, which even now was crackling and warm. "Children are *dying* so folks like you can have a cozy read by the fire!"

Miss Bloom did not respond in anger. "There are people who want to change that world. Ever since your incident—"

"You mean ever since I was almost *burned alive*?"

Miss Bloom nodded. ". . . I have begun to wonder what can be done. And I think I might have an idea."

Nan could tell she was serious. "What kind of idea?"

"Tell me." Miss Bloom folded her hands. "What do you know of 'friendly societies'?"

THE MAYHEW MOTHERS
FRIENDLY SOCIETY

What is a friendly society?" Charlie asked the day after Nan's visit with Miss Bloom. "I think it must have very many friends."

"Nothing so exciting." Nan wrung water from her dripping hair. "A friendly society is just a room full of rich ladies who want to help the poor."

"Oh, yes," Charlie said. "That is very nice of those ladies."

Miss Bloom had given Nan a special kind of hair soap called "shampoo" that made an enormous quantity of bubbles. Charlie was using the leftover bubbles from Nan's bath to make himself a nose and ears. The white suds crackled and turned black at his touch.

" 'Nice' is one word for it." Nan tossed her towel aside. This particular friendly society was composed of mothers of the students at Miss Mayhew's Seminary for Young Ladies. Miss Bloom had told the mothers about Nan, and they very much wanted to meet her and hear her testimonial. "Miss Bloom seemed to think these ladies might be able to help climbers." She glared at the dress strewn across the bench. "But I'm not sure it's worth the price."

Miss Bloom had given her a pink dress along with a wool coat and pair of boots. She wanted Nan to wear them when she talked to the friendly society. "We need these women to see past the soot," Miss Bloom had said. "We need to show them the smart, strong little girl that you are. The *real* you."

Nan didn't much care for the "real" her. She had already scrubbed her face and hands raw. Her hair reeked of shampoo. The sweet smell made her want to retch and sneeze at the same time— like someone flicking her in the nostrils each time she breathed.

She picked up the dress the way one might pick up a soiled handkerchief. "I don't even know which end is the top." She held it up to the mirror and tried to imagine what she would look like inside it. The skirt seemed to be made of endless frills. "If Miss Bloom thinks I'm wearing this thing without trousers, she'll be disappointed."

Toby's voice rang out from the hall. "You sure you can trust this teacher lady not to tell them who you are?" Toby was at the house for some reason. Nan had made him wait outside while she changed; she felt silly enough about the dress without him mocking her. He went on, "Crudd's still got it out for you—doubly so after what happened with him and Charlie. I heard he's offering six crowns to anyone who turns you in."

"I trust Miss Bloom," Nan said. "It's the other ladies I'm not sure about." She tried to step into the dress through the neck like a pair of trousers. That didn't work. She pulled the whole thing over her head like a shirt. The fabric was scratchy and stiff. "How do people *wear* things like this?" she muttered, smoothing her skirt in front of the mirror.

"Your bottom is much bigger now," Charlie said. "And very colorful."

Nan looked at her face, which did not look like her face at all. Her hair, which she had let grow through the winter, was a tangled mess. "Maybe some ribbons will help." She took up a bit of hair ribbon that Miss Bloom had given her.

"Are you done yet?" Toby called. "Let's have a look!"

"Toby, no!" Nan shouted, turning around.

But it was too late. Toby pushed through the door and then stopped dead in his tracks. "Oh, Smudge," he whispered, removing his cap.

"I . . . I didn't get the ribbon tied." Nan felt her cheeks burn. "What do you think?" She kept her eyes on the floor. She couldn't bear to look at him.

"Isn't she very colorful?" Charlie said from the tub.

Toby just stared at her, his eyes wide as saucers. "You . . ." He shook his head. "You look . . . *ridiculous*."

Nan snatched her wet towel and threw it at him. Toby stepped to dodge it but slipped on a soapy puddle. "Whaaa!" He tumbled backward over the rim of the tub and hit the water with a terrific splash.

His head emerged a moment later, sputtering and soaked.

Nan pulled the ribbon from her hair. "Now who looks ridiculous?" She took up her shirt and trousers and marched toward the hall.

"What about the friendly society?" Toby called.

"I've got a better idea," she said, and slammed the door.

Nan knew she wasn't the right person to address the friendly society. Miss Bloom needed someone who knew how to talk to rich folks. Someone who had once been rich himself.

"Hello, Newt," she said. "Got a minute?"

Newt was sweeping a house in Hackney. When he heard Nan's voice, he startled and very nearly fell down an open chimney. "I knew it!" he said as hopped down from the stack. He gave Nan a hug, which surprised her. "I just knew you'd come back! I told the boys that it was you and not Father Christmas who gave us those presents, but they wouldn't believe me." He stepped back, shaking his head. "You should have seen Roger's face when he opened his box to find a ripe horse apple. He looked about ready to cry."

Nan smiled. "Now *that* I wish I'd seen." She opened the flap of her bag and sat down on the roof. "I brought food." She pulled out a half a loaf of bread.

The boy grabbed the food from her hands and began eating. Nan watched his face. His cheeks were hollow, his eyes sunk deep in their sockets. He had burns and scrapes on his shaved head. He looked nothing like the sweet-faced innocent she had known only a few months earlier.

"I suppose you're wondering why I'm here," she said.

Newt didn't answer. He just kept eating. He looked as if he was afraid Nan might snatch the bread from his tiny hands.

"I've come here because I need you to do me a favor," she said.

Newt slowed his chewing. "I don't want trouble."

"Trust me." Nan took an envelope from her pocket and handed it to him. "You'll go to twenty-seven Eaton Street at six o'clock tonight. Don't tell *anybody* where you're going—especially not Crudd or Roger. When you get there, give this letter to a woman named Miss Bloom. She'll explain everything."

Newt couldn't read, but he studied the envelope all the same. "What am I meant to do there?" he said. "Is it a sweeping job?" He suddenly looked excited. "Is it a sweeping job with you?"

"It's not a sweeping job," Nan said. "Miss Bloom will take you to some very nice people—rich ladies who want to meet a climber.

Not a sweep but a *climber*. You need to tell them about your life—about the job. I need you to tell them the truth—the real truth of what it's like." She met his eye. "And you need to tell them about Before."

Newt blinked at her. "B–B–Before?" Nan thought for a moment that he might have truly forgotten. Most climbers did, sooner or later. He hung his head. "I'm not sure I can," he said. "I might start to cry." Already his little lip was quivering.

"That's the point." Nan put her hands over his. "These people will see you cry and want to help you. And," she added, "there will be food."

That clinched it.

Newt promised to do as she'd asked. As Nan turned to leave, he caught her arm. "Why me?" he said. "You could have picked Whittles or Shilling–Tom. Why me?"

Nan wasn't sure of how to answer. Whittles and Shilling–Tom were best mates. And whatever happened, they would have each other. It was the same with her and Charlie. Newt was alone. "Remember how you used to beg me to hear about the Sweep before bed?"

He nodded. "Feels like ages ago."

"I think that little boy is still inside you. Somewhere. It's him these ladies need to meet."

Newt kicked his bare foot against the stack. "I miss the dreams," he said. "After you left, they stopped." This made sense; when Nan left, she had taken Charlie with her. "I miss the Sweep," he said.

Nan looked past him to St. Florian's Church in the distance. "I do, too."

She turned and walked away.

⇥ WAITING FOR SPRING ⇤

February ended with an unseasonably warm wind from the east. The air was still cold, and there were mountains of gray slush in the streets. But even so, there was a sweet smell in the air that carried the promise of things to come.

Nan decided that she should skip sweeping in favor of a snow fight. A mild day in winter was too good to waste. The weather would make the snowballs heavier, which meant they would hold together and hurt just enough to be fun. Plus, she couldn't be sure how much longer the snow might stick around.

"Charlie, get your mitts!" she called into the hall. "It's time for a snow battle. Come on!" She took up her coat and the boots that Miss Bloom had insisted she keep. The boots were stiff and felt strange on her feet. Nan had not spoken to Miss Bloom since sending Newt in her stead. She hoped the woman would understand. She hoped the friendly society could help.

Charlie startled her when his head appeared in the fireplace. He was upside down and smoldering with excitement. "Is a water-baby the one with wings?" he said.

Nan looked up from her boots. "No, that's fairies," she said. She had been reading him a book called *The Water Babies*, which Miss Bloom had given them. It was about a little climbing boy who fell down a chimney and landed in a magical underwater world full of fairies. Charlie loved it, and he had made Nan read it a second time. That is the sign that you really love a book.

Charlie said, "I think there is a fairy in the Nothing Room. I heard sounds up there. And when I looked in, I saw a fairy in the, um . . ." He gestured with his hands. ". . . in the roof branches." Charlie sometimes forgot words when he got excited.

"Do you mean the *rafters*?"

"Yes," Charlie said. "There is a fairy in the *rafters*."

Nan was pretty sure fairies were make-believe. But then, so were golems. She cinched the laces on her boots. "I'll fetch a net." If there *was* a fairy, she didn't want to miss it.

Charlie was waiting in the Nothing Room when Nan arrived with a butterfly net. "It's still here," Charlie whispered. He pointed at the rafters near the window.

Nan crept close with her net and peered up at the spot.

"That's not a fairy," she said. "It's just a bird." She tried hard to not sound disappointed.

Charlie's eyes widened. "What kind of thing is a bird?" He inched behind her. "Are they very dangerous?"

"Only if you're a worm." Nan shot him a look. "You've seen birds before—loads of times. They were everywhere before winter."

"Oh, yes . . ." Charlie grimaced, straining to recall. He shook his head. "That was a very long time ago."

"I suppose it was to you." Nan wondered what else Charlie had forgotten about those early months. Did he remember her carrying him in her pocket?

"Maybe you could just remind me about birds a little bit?" he said.

Nan tried to think about how to explain a bird to someone who had never seen one before. "Birds have feathers and beaks, and they can sing."

Charlie's face lit up. "Could we ask it to sing 'Oranges and Lemons'?" This was a song that Toby had taught them. Charlie's favorite bit was the end when they sang:

Here comes a candle to light you to bed,
Here comes a chopper to chop off your head!

"Birds don't sing proper songs," Nan said. "They sing like this." She whistled a few notes. To her surprise, the bird looked down at her and whistled back. It sounded very much like the tune of "Oranges and Lemons."

Charlie was amazed. He tried to whistle, but it didn't work.

"Don't worry," Nan said. "Whistling takes practice. This sort of bird is called a 'robin redbreast,' because of the color on its breast. It must be home early from its winter travels." Nan wasn't exactly sure where birds went every winter. She figured they hibernated in the mud, like toads—only that didn't sound quite right. "This must be a mother bird making a nest. Soon she'll have a little egg, I bet."

"Oh, yes," Charlie said. "And then she will eat breakfast."

"No, this is a different kind of egg. It's alive. It has a baby bird inside it. And when the bird gets big enough, the egg will crack open and the baby bird will come out."

Charlie's eyes widened. "A *bird* will come out of the egg?"

"It will," Nan said. "That's when we'll know spring is here."

Charlie blinked at her. "What is a spring?"

Sometimes Nan forgot how much Charlie didn't know. It could be exhausting. "Spring is when the whole world comes back to life," she said. "The sun gets warm, trees sprout green leaves, there's the smell of flowers and fresh dirt, little insects and baby animals come up from the ground. If we're lucky, we might even get to see a rainbow." It was hard not to get excited when imagining it. "And don't forget May Day—that's the most important holiday of the year. Every climber in London parades through the streets with the Green Man. There's music and dancing and lucky pennies. The whole city comes to cheer us on. It's the one day of the year when folks are happy to see us climbers." Nan tried not to think of whether she would be able to attend this year's parade—Crudd would certainly be on the lookout, and she could only imagine what he might do if he found her.

The robin cheeped at them and flapped its wings. "We should give her some privacy," Nan said, and they crept out of the room.

The cold weather returned the following week and brought with it another blanket of snow. But up in the attic, Nan and Charlie had their robin and her nest—a promise that spring was near.

⫸ MENDING ⫷

*T*he girl sat with the Sweep on a rooftop. He was mending a hole
that had appeared in her coat—she had snagged it on a brick while
sweeping. "There's no art so important as that of thread and needle," he
told her, drawing the thread tight. "It's taking what's rended and making
it whole."

The girl watched his fingers, quick and delicate. The thimble was her
favorite. It had the white shine of scoured moonlight. The Sweep had told
her it was made of tin, but she knew the truth. She knew it was silver.

The thread was soot-black, like his fingers, like her coat. As he sewed,
the hole in her coat seemed to disappear. The girl could scarcely believe that
it had ever been torn. "Where did you get the thread to match so perfectly?"
she asked.

The Sweep pulled at the stitching to test it. "It's a magic needle," he
said, and bit the string off with his good tooth. "It draws the thread from
the air."

The girl was not sure if he was teasing or telling a truth. The Sweep could be tricky that way. She felt pretty certain that if anything was magic, it should be the silver thimble. She looked at the Sweep's coat, draped over his crossed legs. It was covered with holes, and one of the tails seemed shorter than the other. "Why don't you mend yours?" she asked him.

He smiled at her and covered his coat with his hand. "I prefer to feel a breeze when I work."

"Doesn't it make you shiver?" She was fairly sure she had caught him shivering before.

"I love a good shiver," he told her. "The secret to being cozy is always to let one tiny part of yourself feel cold. If every part of you is toasty warm, it's too much and you'll feel stifled."

The girl was not so sure. She wished she could be every part toasty warm. The Sweep put away his magic needle, put away his silver thimble. He gave the girl her coat, which was now better than new. The place where it had ripped was stronger than before—like the tissue of a scar.

The Sweep donned his own coat—so tattered and thin, so full of breeze.

"Are you certain you're not cold?" the girl asked.

"Someday you will understand," the Sweep said, which was something he said often.

They took up their brushes and set off for work. The girl was not certain, but she thought she noticed a hole over his breast that had not been there before.

·≼ DENT ≽·

N an woke from a dream about the Sweep. He had been mending her coat, as he often did, and she had noticed something about his own clothes—how worn and tattered they had become. With every stitch he gave her, he had lost one of his own.

Warm light shone through the curtains. Nan yawned, stretching like a cat. Outside she could hear wagons and sellers and the faint chirrup of newborn birds.

Nan's eyes snapped open. "Birds?"

She jumped from her bed. "Charlie!" She ran to the window and pulled back the curtain. There was no frost on the windowpanes. The icicles on the eave were glistening and wet. The whole city looked as if it had been washed clean.

"It's happened!" she called. "It's *spring*!"

For weeks now Charlie had talked of nothing but spring. Just as Nan had predicted, the robin in the Nothing Room had laid an egg, and Charlie was desperate to see it hatch. "Easy, Charles," Toby had warned him. "A watched bean never sprouts."

Nan finally made Charlie promise not to go up there until the first thaw—she was afraid he might scare off the mother.

But now, at last, the day had come.

Nan cupped her hands and shouted into the hearth. "Charlieeeeee!" But Charlie did not answer.

Nan found him in the Nothing Room. She supposed she should have looked there first. He was kneeling on the floor, hunched over something small. Next to him was an open pot of paste and torn-up paper. He had made a mess all over the floor. There was no sign of the robin.

"I've been calling for you," Nan said, catching her breath. "It's spring!"

Charlie looked up at her. His face was twisted in pain. He did not seem to care that it was spring. "It . . . won't go back together," he said.

Nan stepped closer. She saw what was at his feet. It was the robin's egg, speckled and blue. But it was not an egg anymore. It was shattered in a dozen places, as if someone had dropped it from the roof.

"Oh, Charlie. What did you do?"

"I saw it move in the nest. I—I—I wanted to hold it," Charlie stammered. "I didn't know it would break." He closed his eyes as if he were crying. But golems have no tears. And his face remained dry. "I didn't know . . ."

Nan knelt and took the broken egg in her hands. It was heavier than she expected. The outside was sticky. One end had been completely crushed.

"I tried to put it back," Charlie said. "But the pieces are too small." He held up his crude, misshapen hands. They were covered with paste and little bits of blackened paper.

Nan stared at the egg in her palm. Through one crack, she saw a matted tuft of down. It twitched with every slowing heartbeat. She pictured the baby bird inside—crushed, gasping. It would die before it had even lived. Nan had seen dead things before. But Charlie had not. "You didn't mean to break it," she said. "It was an *accident*."

"Yes." Charlie nodded slowly. "Only . . . an accident still feels very bad."

"In some ways, accidents feel even worse than if you'd done them on purpose," Nan said.

Charlie shifted on his knees. "Can I . . . hold my accident?" He wasn't looking at Nan but at the egg. Nan eyed his large, clumsy fingers—still sticky with paste. She feared he might break it even more. "Here," she said, and gave him the egg.

He held it in his open hands, gently. So gently. "I'm sorry," Charlie whispered, and he closed his eyes.

Nan couldn't bear to look at him, but she also could not look away. She knew it was worse for Charlie. He was hunched over the broken egg—his accident—silently sobbing. She had never seen him like this. She desperately wanted to fix it, to fix him. But some things could not be repaired.

And then, a change in the air.

First was the smell—a flinty spark, as though someone had struck a match. Nan looked at Charlie—at his hands—and saw that they were smoldering. His dark fingers crackled and began to glow red and then white. Smoke billowed from his open hands. Holding the egg in one open palm, he stroked the shattered egg with the thumb of his other hand.

"Charlie," Nan said, shielding her face from the heat. "What are you doing?" She would have grabbed his arm but was afraid of hurting herself, of hurting the egg. "Stop—you'll burn the house down. CHARLIE!"

Charlie started as if woken from a dream. "Wh-wh-where are we?" His hands were dark again, cupped over the egg—smoke trailing from his fingers. The air in the room had cooled.

Nan knelt beside him. "You started burning up." She put a hand on his shoulder, which was warm and crumbly. "Why?"

Charlie met her gaze and shook his head. "I . . . I don't know." He looked down at his hands, still cupped around the egg, and pulled them apart to reveal the cracked shell. There was a black scorch mark where his thumb had touched it.

And then Nan saw something that snatched the breath from her breast—

The egg moved.

It was only a small movement. But it had happened. She knew it. A moment later, the egg moved again, rocking to one side.

"Charlie," she whispered, very quietly. Like someone afraid to break a spell. "The egg . . . it's *moving*."

It *was* moving. Twitching slightly from side to side, as if something inside it was fighting to get out. The egg rolled to one side and then—*Crack!* A little chip of shell broke away to reveal a tiny black beak. The beak pecked at the morning air and then—

Cheep!

Charlie jumped so high he nearly dropped the egg.

"Come on," Nan whispered. "You can do it." She clutched Charlie's arm, and together they watched the tiny bird push its head free.

Cheep! Cheep!

The bird was ugly. Babies always are. It had matted tufts of wet down and a pink body. Its eyes were swollen shut. But it was also beautiful.

"It's a miracle," Nan said.

The bird cheeped again as it shook itself free of the shell and stretched its wings. One wing was twisted and wouldn't open right. But the bird was alive.

It half hopped, half fell along Charlie's open palm. Charlie raised his hand to his face, and the bird pecked at his chin.

"I think you have a new friend," Nan said. She blinked and found she was crying. She had seen countless birds in her life and never once thought of them. But this bird was different. This bird was *Charlie's*.

"Hello, new friend," Charlie said.

Cheep! the bird said.

Nan sat down next to him. "What are you going to name it?"

Charlie peered closely at the bird, who peered right back. "He is my Accident. I will call him that."

"That's not a proper name." Nan thought for a moment. "What about just 'Dent'?"

Charlie held the bird up. "Do you want to be called 'Dent'?"

Cheep!

Charlie and Nan spent the rest of the day caring for Dent. Charlie had ruined Dent's old nest, and so they made a new home out of crumpled paper and a tureen. Charlie fed him sips of water from a thimble.

There was something Nan did not notice until later in the day.

All the time they worked on Dent's nest, Charlie kept one hand down at his side. And later that evening, when Nan happened to brush against the thumb of that hand, she noticed that it felt different. It wasn't crumbly and warm. It was cold and hard . . . like a dead stone.

⊰ PROMISES ⊱

Nan could not stop thinking about what had happened in the Nothing Room. The egg had been crushed beyond repair. She had held it in her hands, had felt the bird's final, trembling heartbeat.

And yet Dent was alive.

He had two eyes that blinked and wings that flapped and feet that hopped. Charlie remained in the attic day and night, tending to his new friend. Dent's mother—frightened off by Charlie—never returned to the house. But that was fine. Dent had a new mother: He had Charlie.

Dent's right wing was malformed, and it soon became clear that he would never fly the way a bird was meant to. "If he cannot fly, I will make him a home here in the Nothing Room," Charlie declared. "So he will be happy."

"I'm not sure that's the right thing to do," Nan explained. "Birds need sunlight and trees and dirt. An attic is no place for a bird. We should leave him in the park—I bet he'd love it there." It is possible she was jealous.

"A bigger animal might find him and hurt him," Charlie said. "He belongs here with us."

And so Charlie set to making a home for Dent. Nan knew he would soon learn how hard it was to keep a wild creature.

But Charlie did not give up. He spent days in the attic, making a "garden" for Dent to play. Every so often he would request that Nan bring him new supplies—a bucket of soil, some fallen leaves, a bundle of twigs from the park, a handful of soft moss.

"It's no use being glum," Toby said, shaking black mud from his arm. Nan had come by to pick up some fresh worms for Dent. "That's just the way of it when you've got a new chum. You want to spend all your time with them, and the rest of the world can go hang itself."

Toby filled an old cigar box with dozens of squiggling worms. The look of them made Nan's stomach twitch. "Think of how little Newt must have felt when you ran off to live with Charlie." He hopped up, carrying the worms with him. "Speaking of Newt, did you hear the news?"

"Is he all right?"

"Seems a certain *friendly society* had him over for tea. When he told them about climbing with Crudd, they were so moved that one old lady offered to adopt him on the spot."

Nan caught her breath. "Newt's . . . getting *adopted*?"

Toby nodded. "Some old biddy named 'Lady Wilde.' She sent a solicitor straightaway to Crudd to negotiate his release. He'll be little Lord Newt before May Day."

"A *lord*?" Nan imagined Newt, his curly hair grown out, wearing a blue satin suit. A train rumbled above them. "That's wonderful." She wiped a speck of ash from her eye.

"Like something from a story." Toby gave her a look. "Though I wouldn't blame you for wondering what might have happened if *you'd* gone instead."

Nan imagined herself in the home of this Lady Wilde—with carriages and balls and private tutors and not another day of work for the rest of her life. "What's to wonder?" she said. "I doubt a lady would take kindly to a golem moving in with her." She reached for the box of worms. "And don't get me started on the dresses."

Toby held the box fast. "It was a good thing you did, sending him there." He was looking at her without any trace of a smile. It was the same way he had looked on New Year's when he had told her about the Sweep. "You probably saved his life."

Nan held the box under her arm as she walked back to Bloomsbury. She tried not to think about Newt—about what she had possibly given up by helping him. Again she reminded herself that Charlie needed her. But lately he had been so consumed with caring for

Dent that she had hardly seen him. Perhaps he needed her less than she thought.

When she got to the captain's house, she found a notice posted on the front door.

> ~ *Metropolitan Board of Works* ~
> *The Honourable Jas. Higgens, Chairman of the Office of Building, as commissioned by Her Majesty Queen Victoria, hereby identifies that the property at 111 Runcible Street shall be posted for public auction after a three-week holding period. All parties* . . .

Nan didn't bother reading the rest. It was a notice of auction for the captain's house. Apparently his relations had given up squabbling and were resolved to sell it. She wondered what would happen then—where could she and Charlie live where they would be safe from Crudd? Safe from the world?

Nan decided that she should at least nail the front door shut, just in case anyone came snooping. She tore down the notice and crumpled it into a ball.

"Charlie!" she called when she reached the turret window. "I got worms!"

Charlie poked his head out of the Nothing Room door. "Did you bring the stretchy ones? Dent likes the stretchy ones best."

Nan gave him the box. "They're slimy and gross—that's all I know." Charlie went to close the door, but Nan caught it. "May I come in and see the garden?"

Charlie shifted slightly. He drew his stone thumb across the lid of the box. "It's . . . not finished yet." He stepped back from the door, limping slightly.

Nan stepped into the Nothing Room. What she saw made her gasp.

Charlie said, "Do you like it?"

Nan had no words. In just a few days, the attic had been utterly transformed. There were flowering bushes along the walls and soft moss on the floor. Ivy crept along the rafters. There were even three sapling trees—nearly as tall as the roof. Dent hopped happily from a mossy stump to the branch of a bush. *Cheep!*

"You grew all of this?" Nan reached for his arm.

Charlie moved away. "Yes." He shuffled over to Dent and opened the lid of the box. The bird cheeped again and hopped close. He thrust his beak into the mass and pulled out an unlucky worm. Charlie watched him for a moment and then turned away. He didn't like seeing things die. Not even worms.

"That's not a good enough answer," Nan said. "Folks don't just grow gardens in attics. It's not natural." Gardens are, of course, quite natural. But she had a point.

Charlie shrugged. "I woke it up. In my Charlie way"

"Show me," Nan said. "Please?"

Charlie nodded and moved to a corner of the room. Nan noticed something strange about the way he moved. His steps seemed heavier, more uncertain. She watched him dig through a pile of old sticks and leaves. He found a single acorn in the pile. "I will show you."

He held the acorn in his open hands and closed his eyes. Nan felt a shift in the air—as if she were suddenly inside a warm chimney. There was a smell of crackling embers. Charlie's hands began to smolder, just as they had done with Dent's egg. His hands turned red and then white. The acorn was glowing, too.

And then it began to *grow*.

Nan watched as the top of the acorn popped off. A tiny sprig pushed its way out of the shell and stretched up into the air. Green leaves sprouted from the end of the sprig, stretching into branches. The branches stretched higher and higher. The acorn was completely gone now. Twisting roots spilled out over Charlie's open hands until they touched the floor.

The tree grew taller still. Branches upon branches upon branches. Its trunk was thick as Charlie's body now and went all the way to the floor. He kept his hands on either side of the trunk as it stretched up to the rafters. A canopy of green leaves filled the attic. Nan could hear a groaning sound as they strained against the roof and then—

Crack! the tree broke through.

"Stop!" Nan cried.

Charlie pulled his hands away from the trunk. He opened his eyes and blinked at the tree standing before him. "This one is very big." He sounded a little frightened.

Dent was hopping excitedly around the base of the tree, flapping his wings. *Cheep! Cheep!*

The highest branch had broken through the roof, and warm sunlight shone down through the leaves. Nan looked at the tree, which had not been there a moment before. "You made all this grow?" She looked at Dent. "Just like you made him grow?"

Charlie nodded. "Are you very upset with me?"

"Upset?" Nan's face broke into a smile. "It's incredible!"

She reached out to touch Charlie's hand, but he pulled back.

"What's wrong?" Nan said.

"I don't want to say." He was holding one hand behind his back. It was the same hand whose thumb Nan had grazed the week before.

Nan stepped closer. "Show me."

Charlie nodded and held out his right hand. It looked different from the rest of him. And not just the thumb. The whole hand was lighter in color, a sort of ashy gray that went almost to the bend in his arm. Nan touched his fingers, and they felt cold. They did not bend. They did not crumble. It was like touching a statue.

"What's happened to it?" Nan said.

Charlie pulled his hand away. He stared down at it. "I don't know."

"Will it change back?"

He shook his head. "I do not think so." He massaged his stone elbow. "I did not mean to give it so much." He was looking at the tree.

Nan stared at the flowers, the moss, the tree, Dent. "You made all this *life* . . ." They were all pieces of Charlie. She remembered how Charlie had said he had saved her after the Devil's Nudge. Had he given a part of himself to heal her burns? "If you keep making things grow, what would happen?"

He looked at her. "I think I would have nothing left."

At these words, Nan felt a chill. "Charlie . . ." She clasped his hands—one cold, one warm. "You have to promise me you will stop making your garden."

Charlie nodded. "I promise."

Nan held him tighter. "You have to promise me, no matter what happens, that you will *never* give away any piece of yourself. No matter how much you want to."

Charlie looked at her. For a moment, his face was filled with sadness. He drew his hands away from her.

"I cannot promise that."

·⚹· PASSOVER ⚹·

I t was the first week of April, and the cherry blossoms had begun to bloom.

After such a bitter winter, the whole city seemed determined to live every moment out of doors. Everywhere Nan walked, she could smell fresh flowers and fried kippers. Old women sold painted eggs on the corners. Bakers pushed carts full of steaming wares, singing—

> *Hot cross buns!*
> *Hot cross buns!*
> *One a penny, two a penny—*
> *Hot cross buns!*

Nan cut through Russell Square, which was abuzz with Easter preparations. Farmers had put out boxes of spring chicks to sell as pets to children. She always wondered what happened to those pet chicks once they grew bigger and became ugly. She wondered if they even lived that long.

With the holiday fast approaching, the girls in Miss Mayhew's Seminary had all gone home to their families. This meant Nan was able to spend a day at the school with Miss Bloom. "It's strange not to be sneaking through chimneys or windows," she said as Miss Bloom met her at the door.

The woman took Nan up to her room on the third floor. "This day is different from all other days. I've prepared a bit of a picnic for us." Laid out on the writing table were bowls of chicken soup and several pieces of very flat bread. In the middle sat a larger platter with little dishes arranged in a circle.

"What is this?" Nan sniffed a shallow bowl of apple relish. It smelled like cinnamon.

"It is called *charoset*," Miss Bloom said. "Or at least an approximation. When I was a little girl, my mother would prepare it to remember *Pesach*—Passover."

Miss Bloom pointed to each of the things on the plate and explained that they were all part of a holy meal called a "seder." "The Jewish people eat these things to remember when God delivered us from slavery in Egypt." Whenever Miss Bloom talked about these traditions, she usually spoke as though they did not apply to her.

But not today.

"Why do they call it Passover?" Nan asked, nibbling the corner of a very flat biscuit.

"Before the Jews escaped from Egypt, God sent an angel of death to the city. The angel visited the homes of the Egyptians and killed every firstborn child as they slept. It was punishment for the wickedness of their parents. The angel *passed over* the homes of the Jews and spared their children."

"That's horrible," Nan said. She imagined it happening—not as some story but as a real event. She imagined parents waking to the screams of dying children. She imagined blood. "Those children didn't deserve that."

"Children seldom deserve what befalls them. But there was grace in the slaughter. It was in the wake of this horror that the Jews were able to escape to freedom." Miss Bloom shook her head. "I despised that story as a girl. It haunts me still."

"I thought you didn't believe in religion."

"It is not exactly a question of belief," Miss Bloom said. "But for the first time in many years, I am finding myself wanting to remember." She looked at Nan. "Your question about golems has made me recall my own life at your age. It has made me realize that there are worse fates for a girl than feeling stifled by her family." She ran her hand along the edge of the plate.

Nan felt once again the desire to tell Miss Bloom about Charlie. Especially the things she had learned about him recently. Even now, the thought of his cold-stone hand filled her with a gnawing dread.

Miss Bloom took a fork and cut into a boiled egg. "I suppose I am remembering Passover as a way to remind myself that the struggle for freedom is as old as time. That there are always others who yet need to be delivered."

"You mean like climbers."

Nan tried a bit of something Miss Bloom had called *maror* but quickly spit it back onto her spoon. "How is Newt? Is he happy living with Lady Wilde?"

Miss Bloom looked at her with something like alarm. "William . . . is still climbing. I assumed you knew."

Nan shook her head. "I didn't." She had been so caught up with worry about Charlie and Dent that she hadn't thought to check up on him. "What happened?"

"Nothing. And that's the exact problem." Miss Bloom sat back and released a long breath. "Lady Wilde's solicitor was discreet— he posed as a carpenter looking for an apprentice. But somehow Mister Crudd discovered his true intentions. Now he is demanding an extortionate—a very large sum of money for the boy."

Nan caught her breath. "Can't the friendly society do something? Can't they force Crudd to give him up?" She thought of how bad Newt had looked the last time they met. She wasn't sure how much longer he could survive the work.

Miss Bloom gave a disconsolate shrug. "There are legal measures, yes, but courts are slow. And Mister Crudd has a legitimate claim on the boy in the form of an indentured service contract that was signed by William's guardian."

Nan knew the contract that Miss Bloom was talking about. She had signed one herself long ago. "Crudd won't let him go." She sipped her drink, which was sweet and dark. "You don't know him—what he's willing to do." She could still remember his hand on her neck, forcing her toward the blazing hearth.

"We are trying our best, and that is all we can do." Miss Bloom sighed. "But so long as Mister Crudd holds that contract, we are helpless."

Nan set down her cup. "I have to go."

-⊀ SIX CROWNS ⊁-

Nan knew if she could find and destroy Newt's contract, then Crudd would lose his claim on the boy. She supposed she could sneak into Crudd's house and look for it, but she hadn't the faintest idea where it was hidden. Not to mention the fact that Crudd wanted her dead.

Nan needed an accomplice.

More than that, she needed an *apprentice*.

Nan knew Roger hated her, but she also knew he hated Crudd even more. Roger had spent his entire life trying to earn the love of a man who paid out only scorn. She hoped this hatred would be great enough to convince him to betray Crudd. And if that didn't work, the promise of a reward from Lady Wilde might do the trick.

First she needed to get him alone. Nan had lived with Roger for five years, and in that time she had learned of one mysterious habit. Two nights a year—on Christmas and Easter—Roger snuck out of the coal bin without a word. None of the boys ever knew where he went or why. The one time Whittles tried asking, Roger had bloodied his nose.

Nan caught sight of Roger as he slipped out from Crudd's front door. She followed him past the Matchstick and across London Bridge, keeping herself hidden behind the few carriages and pedestrians rushing to get home for Easter.

The factories in Southwark were dark, their smokestacks black against the setting sun. Roger cut a path eastward toward Lambeth, Nan trailing at a distance. The twisting streets were muddy and unlit, but the boy moved quickly without getting lost. It was clear he had traveled this way many times before.

The houses here were all built on top of one another and very narrow. Nan thought they might be called "humble"—which was what people said when a place was poor but not dangerous.

The street was quiet. The sun had set. Most people were home, celebrating Easter with family. Nan could smell roast lamb and steamed oysters somewhere close by.

She spied Roger in the shadows of a narrow alley. He was staring at a house directly across the way, his hands jammed deep in his pockets. He was staring so intently that he didn't even notice when she walked up behind him.

"Taking up housebreaking?" she said. "I'd pick a better neighborhood."

Roger gave a twitch of alarm. She saw that his face was red around the eyes. "I was wondering when you'd turn up." He sniffed, wiping his nose. "S'pose you're here to do to me the same thing you did to Crudd? You and your pet monster?"

Nan shifted back. "Crudd told you about Charlie?"

"You named it *Charlie*?" He gave a humorless snort. "Crudd said a burning monster tried to murder him. Everyone else just laughed, but not me. Why would he lie? It only makes him look a fool. Plus, I saw proof. On the day you threw that snowball from the Foundling Hospital, I went up on the roof. You were long gone. But I saw footprints bigger than any man's." He peered into the alley behind her. "Is it here now?" He sounded as if he might rather enjoy being murdered by a monster.

Nan shook her head. "It . . . Charlie isn't a monster." The last thing she needed was Roger to be afraid for his life. "He was just trying to protect me from Crudd. He gets confused easily. He's like a child."

"Some child." Roger snorted again. "Did you see what it did to Crudd's face?"

Nan remembered the night Charlie rescued her. She remembered the odor of burned flesh. She remembered blood on the snow. "Is it bad?"

"It's worse than bad. I don't know what your 'Charlie' did to him, but Crudd's ugly as a pail of cat sick. And anyone who asks or stares too long gets a hiding to remember. There's no customers. No weddings. Even Trundle moved on."

"Is that what you're doing out here?" Nan said. "Moving on? Looking for a new master?"

Roger pushed his hands deeper in his pockets. "Why I'm here is none of your business."

Nan shrugged. "You're probably right." She glanced at the house across the way—the house Roger had been watching. The windows were lit. Inside a man and woman were settling in for supper at a square table. The home looked very poor, but it was clean and cozy. There were Easter decorations cut from newspapers on the window. The man set down wooden plates. He kissed the heavy-set woman as she placed a steaming crock of stew in the middle of the table. "Who are they?" Nan asked.

Roger made a scoffing sound. "You don't see the resemblance?"

She looked from the window to Roger. Her eyes widened as she made the connection. "They're . . . your *parents*."

He gave a bitter smile. "They *were*, at least."

All these years Nan had thought Roger was an orphan, like the rest of them. But no. He had parents. Living not four miles off. "I don't understand."

"Ain't much to understand, is there?" He turned back toward

the window. "They were poor. Stuck with a child they couldn't feed. It was a cold winter. We were one bad day from being put out in the streets. I remember them fighting about food—about not having any." He swallowed. "And that's when Crudd showed up."

Nan looked at Roger's face and understood at once what he was telling her. "They sold you."

"The answer to their prayers." Roger shook his head. He pushed a pebble through the mud with the side of his foot. "I still remember it. This tall man in nice clothes at the door. His boots were so shiny. I thought he must be a lord or a prince. He takes out his purse and counts out six crowns. I see them fall right into my father's hands. I remember being so excited to see the money, I begged Father to let me hold one."

"Oh, Roger . . ."

"He wouldn't even look at me. None of them would." Roger shook his head, and Nan saw fresh tears filling his eyes. "Crudd just picked me up under one arm and carried me away. They didn't even say goodbye." He closed his eyes.

Nan stared at him. She wanted to hold him, to say or do something, tell him that she knew what it felt like to be abandoned. But she couldn't. However much heartbreak the Sweep had caused, it was nothing like this.

She heard a voice from the house. The woman—Roger's mother—called for supper. There were shrieks of delight as three small children stampeded into the room and pushed and fought to take seats at the table, which had been set for five. They all sat down and prayed before eating.

"And now look at them," Roger said, wiping his cheeks. "A family."

Nan felt like her heart had sunk to the pit of her stomach. "Every Christmas and Easter . . . you come here to watch them."

Roger nodded his head. "It's a family tradition."

Nan thought of what Miss Bloom had told her about the angel of death—choosing some children to live and others to die. Crudd was like that angel. He could have knocked on any door in the city. But he chose Roger's.

"Do they know?" Nan stepped closer to him. "Do your parents know you're still alive?"

Roger looked at her as though she were daft. "I doubt they remember I ever lived at all. And if they did know, I'm sure they wouldn't like it. They've got all the family they want." He spit into the mud. "So, is that it? You came all this way just to mock me?"

Nan shook her head. "Newt needs your help. Crudd won't let him go, and he's . . . Newt's not like us. He can't survive."

She could tell from Roger's expression that he knew all about Lady Wilde. "You always were a soft touch for hopeless causes." He sniffed and turned back to the house. "Why should he get a family when none of us do?"

Nan watched the family eating in their cozy little home. She tried to picture it. Roger knocking on the door. The mother opening it. At first she doesn't recognize him. But then she *sees* it. And in a single moment, all of the hurt and regret melts away and Roger is swallowed into that home. The lost child returned to them.

"You have to tell them," Nan said. "You have to try."

Roger took a deep breath. Perhaps he was trying to imagine the same thing as Nan. "I'll tell them," he said. "But not yet. I'm an apprentice now. And in a few more years I'll become my own master. I'll work hard, work my crew harder, and soon I'll have a bit of real money. Enough to buy that house there from the landlord."

Nan thought he meant to make it as a gift to them. "And then you'll tell them?"

"No." His jaw tensed. "First I'll raise the rent. Raise it so high they're put out in the street. And wherever they end up next, I'll buy that place, too. I will follow after them like a black cloud, taking every farthing they have. Until there's nothing left. No stew in the pot. No oil in the lamp. No shoes on their feet." Tears ran down his cheeks as he spoke. He ignored them. "And *that* is when I will come back to them." A bitter smile crept across his face. "Only they won't recognize me. I'll be a grown man. In a fine suit. And shiny boots. And with six crowns in my purse . . ."

Nan stared at this boy who had spent five years tormenting her. How many times had she longed to see him cry? But looking at his face now, she knew there was no help to be found in him. He was already too far gone.

Nan said, "Happy Easter, Roger."

What else could she say?

She turned around and started the long journey back home.

·≼ THE QUEEN OF ICES ≽·

Nan spent the remainder of the month working. She knew they would need the money once the captain's house sold. She still had no idea where they would live—no idea where Charlie would be safe.

She cut through Regent's Park with an empty sootbag on her shoulder. Dappled sunlight shone through the cherry blossoms and danced on the surface of the lake. The trees made her think of Charlie, and what he'd shown her in the Nothing Room. It made her think of the promise he wouldn't make.

Nan heard shouts from the gates of St. John's Wood cemetery. It looked like the groundskeeper was yelling at a beggar boy. She ignored the commotion and continued toward the Baker Street Bazaar. It was a house of wax figures some French woman had brought to the city. Out in front were mannequins—perfect likenesses of queens and pirates made from wax—their faces frozen in time. They made her think of golems.

A voice rang in her ear. "Hullo, Smudge!"

Toby was behind her, cheeks flushed and out of breath. He was holding his emporium with both hands.

"What are you doing up in Camden?" Nan said.

"Looking for you." He glanced over Nan's shoulder and adjusted his feet. "Charlie said you were out sweeping." He nodded at Nan's empty sootbag. "Business is slow, I see."

Nan shrugged. "I figured I'd take the day off." The truth was, she had taken a job that morning. But when the maid showed her the first flue—a square eleven—she burked it and ran.

"Oi! You!" an angry voice shouted. It was the groundskeeper from the cemetery. He was waving a rake over his head. "Get back here!" He was headed straight for them.

Nan looked at Toby. "Is he yelling at *us*?"

"Let's not stay and find out." He adjusted his emporium, which looked fuller than usual, and hopped off the curb. "Follow me!"

Nan stayed where she was. "Where are we going?"

Toby wagged his eyebrows. "I'm taking you to meet the Queen."

Toby made Nan follow him down Tottenham Court Road. The warm weather seemed to have brought out all of London—everywhere she looked were phaetons and parasols.

"Better hop aboard if we want to beat the mob," Toby called, grabbing on to the back of an omnibus. He crouched low so the driver wouldn't notice him.

Nan and Toby rode the omnibus all the way to Charing Cross Station. "There she is," he said, dropping back to the street. He pointed at a food stall parked at the front of the station. Well-dressed men, women, and children were in a queue that went clear around the block. They were all eagerly chattering to one another.

"Looks like the mob beat us here," Nan said.

"You forget who you're with," Toby said. He took Nan's hand and led her to the stall. A banner hung from the top:

The World–Renowned Mrs. Agnes Marshall
"The Queen of Ices"
Scoops ~ Pints ~ Penny Licks

Working behind the stall was a plump woman with a striped apron and pinned sleeves. Her spectacles looked as if they would slip from her nose at any moment. She had three girls assisting her. They were all busily passing out shallow tin dishes of something that looked like colored cream.

Nan wrinkled her nose. "That doesn't look anything like ice."

Toby removed his cap and bowed. "Hullo, Aggie!"

The Queen looked up from her work. Her face broke into a

smile. "Toby Squall!" She took off her apron and marched out to meet them. "I was wondering if you mightn't come by today." Despite operating a food stall, there was something refined about her—she really did seem like a queen.

Toby took her hand and kissed the back of it. "How could I resist?"

The Queen turned toward Nan. "And this must be the famous Nan Sparrow!"

Nan shifted her weight. "Pleased to meet you . . . um . . . Your Highness." She gave a sort of curtsy.

The Queen laughed. It was a hearty, infectious laugh. "She is every bit as lovely as you promised!" She put a hand around each of them and led them to the cart—right to the front of the line. A few customers made sounds of obvious indignation.

"Ignore them," the Queen said, donning her apron. "Now, what flavor would you like?" There were several tubs behind the counter, each a different bright color. They were named strange things like Pistachio Bliss and Star Anise.

"I haven't a penny," Nan whispered to Toby.

"Never you fear." He set down his emporium and opened the top. "We're guests of the Queen!" He produced an enormous bouquet of flowers—roses, honeysuckle, lemon blossoms, and lavender. The smell was overpowering.

The woman took up the flowers. "Lovely as always, Toby. These will be *just the thing* for my recipes." She handed the flowers to an assistant.

It was clear to Nan that those flowers had *not* come from the Thames. She remembered the groundskeeper at St. John's Wood. "Did you *steal* those?" she whispered.

Toby pretended not to hear her. "Two amarettos, please." He nudged Nan. "That's the best flavor—and I've had 'em all."

The Queen took two dishes and filled them with a sort of whitish ice. Nan watched her work. She was clearly wealthy, but also not afraid to get her hands messy. Nan liked that.

Soon she found herself in possession of a tin bowl filled with amaretto cream ice. She was a little disappointed not to get one of the brightly colored flavors. The outside of the bowl was frosty, and it stuck to her fingers when she adjusted her grip. She sniffed the ice. The dish had the tangy smell of hammered metal, but beyond that, she caught the faint aroma of almonds. She stuck out her tongue to taste it.

"Stop," Toby said. "You can't eat it yet."

"But won't it melt?" Nan said.

"Not if we hurry!" They hopped onto the back of another omnibus, which carried them down Piccadilly. Soon they were standing at a giant house facing Hyde Park. The walls were made of red brick, with tall pillars. The windows along the facade were round and grand. It looked like a miniature fortress.

Climbing with a dish of ice was tricky, but Nan was soon sitting up on the roof overlooking the park. "You've gotten much better with heights," she said, scooting over to make room for Toby.

"I've had some practice." The boy reached into his bag and removed a pair of spoons with long handles. "*Now* you can try it."

Nan took a spoon and dipped it into the ice. The whole thing felt like a prank. She put the spoon into her mouth. The taste was very much like cream—smooth and rich—only so much sweeter. She had eaten ice and snow before, but this was different. As the cream melted and spread across her tongue, it sent a shiver right down her spine. She made a sort of involuntary murmur.

Toby gave an amused smile. "I take that to mean you like it?"

Nan felt her face flush, which somehow made it taste even better. She did not want to be impressed, but her face betrayed her. The muscles in her jaw clenched, and her mouth twitched into a pursed smile. She couldn't help it. "I do," she said.

"You could have this every day, if you wanted." Toby rapped his spoon on the edge of his dish. "Of course, you'll have to come with me if you want to skip the line."

Nan put her spoon down. "You can't do things like that— swiping flowers from graves. It's horrid."

Toby laughed. "I don't think anyone will miss them."

"That groundskeeper could have caught you, and then what?" She shook her head. "Someday, you're going to find yourself in trouble, Toby, and you won't be able to smile your way out of it."

Toby's smile soured. "We don't all have magic protectors." Nan's thoughts went back to Christmas Eve, when she'd seen Toby asleep under the bridge—so cold, so alone. However hard life with Crudd had been, at least she had the other climbers. Toby had no one.

"Besides"—he clinked the edge of Nan's bowl with his spoon— "take another bite and tell me it wasn't worth it."

She took another bite. And another. She worked the bit of cream in her mouth as if it were a piece of mutton. "It's terrifying to think this existed without me knowing it," she said, scraping up the last of her ice and licking the dish clean. "Makes me wonder what else I've been missing that's right in front of me."

"Indeed." Toby offered her his dish. "Do you want this one, too?"

Nan hated herself for accepting, but accept she did. "Thank you," she said, spooning ice into her mouth.

Toby did her the kindness of not watching her eat. He leaned against a chimneystack, staring out at the park—grass and trees stretching clear to Kensington Gardens. "If this weather keeps, it'll be a perfect May Day."

"I'm still not holding your hand, if that's what all this is about." Nan took another bite.

"It's never about that," Toby said. "But there *is* a reason I brought you here, to this rooftop." He tapped his knuckles against a slate. "This place is called 'Chesterfield House.' It's one of the finest in London. It was built a long time ago by a fellow named Isaac Ware."

For as much time as Nan spent climbing up and over houses, she didn't give much thought to the men who made them. "What's so special about him?"

"There's nothing special about him. And that's the point." He widened his eyes. "The story goes that Isaac Ware was a climbing boy, just like any other. No learning. No family. One day some famous building-maker sees him out on the street in front of a church—face black, barefoot, in rags. The boy is drawing a picture of the church on the wall with some chalk. He's getting every window and turret just right. The builder is so impressed with the drawing that he hires the boy and trains him as an assistant. Ware grows up to become one of the greatest builders in all England."

Nan could tell that Toby wanted her to be impressed. "Good for him." She tried to savor the last bite of ice. "What's your point?"

Toby shook his head as though she'd said something funny. "You're like Isaac Ware. Miss Bloom sees it. That's why she's taken a shine to you. I've known it my whole life." He was looking right at her. "You are destined for something great, Nan Sparrow."

Nan tapped her spoon against the bottom of her dish. "I'm just trying to keep alive."

"Keeping alive isn't enough. You have to live *for* something. You need purpose."

Nan shuddered. "Maybe you do, but not me." She was thinking about Charlie. About Miss Bloom's story. About everything.

She could feel Toby watching her. "Before I found you at the park, I swung by the house," he said. "You've got a tree sticking out of the roof. And also, I noticed something different about Charlie. His arm . . . It was—it had changed."

"Stone," Nan lowered her head. "It's turned to stone."

"There something you want to tell me?"

"No." Nan wiped a speck from her eye. "I don't know." And before she knew it, she was telling him the whole story. What Miss Bloom had told her about golems. What had happened when Charlie saved her from Crudd. What had happened with Dent.

"That's quite a tale," Toby said when she had finished.

"I'm afraid," Nan said. "Afraid he . . . afraid I . . ." She shook her head. "What if I can't protect him?"

"That's what it is to care for a person," Toby said. There was not even a hint of mocking in his voice. "If you're not afraid, you're not doing it right."

⤜ GOODBYE THINGS ⤛

It was the last week of April. May Day was just around the bend, and all through the city preparations were being made. Coal pies cooled on racks. Flower garlands filled market stalls. Banners hung between lampposts.

Nan and Charlie were at the house, enjoying an afternoon together, just the two of them.

"Goodbye . . . cat?" Charlie said.

"We don't have a cat," Nan said. "Guess again."

"Oh, yes," Charlie said. "Only I thought we maybe had a secret cat." He peered around the room. "Goodbye . . . *kitten?*"

"That's the same as a cat," Nan said. "Guess again."

They were playing a round of Goodbye Things. This was a game that Charlie and Nan had invented. One person would look around the room and try to remember everything that was in it. Then that person would close his or her eyes and count as high as possible. (Nan would count to fifty; Charlie would count to purple.) While that happened, the other person would take something from the room and make it disappear.

Then the counting person would open his or her eyes, look round the room, and try to guess what had gone away—making guesses by saying, "Goodbye, pillow with the yellow stitching" or "Goodbye, framed print of the Virgin Islands" or (in Charlie's case) "Goodbye, cat."

Nan usually won, because she could see where Charlie had been from his footprints. Charlie never won because he only guessed animals.

Nan was figuring out how to remove a suit of armor without making noise when she heard a pounding at the front window.

"Nan!" a voice shouted. "Nan!"

"That sounds like Toby," Charlie said. "Maybe he will want to play."

Nan ran to the foyer and drew back the curtains. Toby was still pounding against the glass. "Open . . . up . . . ," he said through gasps of air.

Nan unlatched the window. "You know you're not supposed to approach the front of the house. Someone might see—"

Toby grabbed her arm and started to pull her through the

window. "You have to follow me!" he said in a hoarse voice. "Bring Charlie!"

Nan pulled back. There was something in his face that she'd never seen before. "Are you mad? We can't take Charlie outside in broad daylight."

Toby ignored her. "It's Newt." His eyes were wide. "There's been an accident."

❖   ❖   ❖

Moments later, Nan was sitting with Charlie and Toby inside a rattling cab. "Miss Bloom gave me fare for the ride. When the boys told me what had happened, I knew I needed to get you—both of you." Toby closed a gap in the curtain, keeping Charlie hidden from view. "Don't worry about Desmond," he said, nodding to the driver, who had not said a word. "He's a friend."

"Where are we going?" Nan had never been inside a carriage before and found the movement slightly nauseating. She gripped Charlie's stone arm. "What happened to Newt?"

"Miss Bloom is having him taken to London Hospital. Crudd had him sweeping a stack in an iron mill over in Southwark."

"Was Roger with him?" She braced herself against the door as the cab turned onto Oxford Street.

"I think he'd been sent up on his own," Toby said. "Now that

Crudd's on the outs with the gentry, he's taking any job that comes along."

Nan could not believe what she was hearing. "Newt did a factory *alone*?" Factory stacks were too wide to scale the regular way. Climbers had to be lowered down on ropes—it was a two-climber job, at the very least. "How did he manage the rigging?"

"There was no rigging," Toby said. "He slipped and took a nasty tumble."

Nan peered out the carriage curtain toward the factories across the river. She could see giant brick stacks as tall as steeples belching black smoke into the sky. "How far did he fall?"

Toby looked at her, his face pale. "It's bad, Nan."

After what felt like an eternity, the carriage rattled to a stop in back of London Hospital. Nan and Charlie followed Toby through a service door that had been propped open. Inside, the hallways were broad and empty. "Miss Bloom had the nurses put Newt in a room where folks wouldn't bother us," Toby said, running up a stairwell. "They're still building this wing." He was peering into open doorways as he ran.

Nan felt Charlie take her hand. "I do not like this place," he whispered.

She squeezed his hand. She didn't like it, either. The whole place smelled like gin and bile. It smelled like sickness.

Toby motioned to a door at the end of the hall. "He's in here."

Nan followed Toby into a dark room lined with beds. The curtains were drawn. There were no doctors or nurses present. Miss Bloom stood in the corner. Whittles and Shilling-Tom were with her. They were all holding hands.

Whittles caught sight of her, and his eyes widened. "Nan?"

Nan ran toward them. "Where is he?"

Miss Bloom turned and met her. "Nan. I'm sorry . . ." Her eyes were rimmed red.

Nan ran past her to a bed in the corner. At first she thought the bed was empty—his body was that small. But now she could see that Newt was lying beneath the white sheet. Little Newt with the tiny dark eyes and the tiny little voice. Little Newt, who had begged her for stories about the girl and her Sweep. Little Newt, broken from the fall.

"We're here," Nan whispered. "I brought help."

She pulled the sheet back from Newt's face. His skin was wet with perspiration. His eyes were closed. "I brought someone who can help you." She grabbed his cool hand. "Charlie!" she called. "We need you!"

Charlie was still in the doorway, half-hidden behind Toby. He looked afraid. Toby led him into the room. Nan heard murmurs as Miss Bloom and the boys stepped back from the bed.

"W–w–what is . . . ?" Miss Bloom whispered.

"This is Charlie," Nan said, glancing up. "He's a golem."

The woman looked from Nan to Charlie and then back to Nan. Her mouth was open, but no words came from it. Nan thought of all the times she had pictured Miss Bloom meeting Charlie. None of them were like this.

Toby led Charlie to the bed. Charlie seemed confused. "Where is Newt?" he said, looking at the faces—all of them staring at him. Nan wondered who among them was the most frightened.

Nan nodded at Newt's bed. "That's him."

Charlie peered at the bed for a moment. Then realization dawned on his face. "He is very small." His voice was shaking. "Is . . . is he an *accident*?"

Nan took Charlie's hands in her own. One soot. One stone. "Charlie. Listen to me. I know what I told you about . . . about *helping*. But right now you have to try." Tears stung and blurred her eyes. "You have to save him. Do you understand?"

Charlie nodded and looked at Newt. "You want me to . . . wake him?"

"Please." Nan let go of his hands and stepped back. She forced herself not to think about what would happen to Charlie. How much of him she might lose.

Miss Bloom moved close to Nan. "What is it doing—?"

"Shh," Nan said. "Just wait."

Nan watched, hardly breathing, as Charlie leaned close to Newt. The golem placed his crumbling gray hand on Newt's pale, clammy hand. Charlie closed his eyes and breathed slowly. Nan could feel the heat kindling inside Charlie's breath. It warmed the room. His hand smoldered and began to glow.

"Come back, Newt," she whispered. "Come back."

Charlie strained his face, and his hand burned brighter. But nothing happened. At last, the golem opened his eyes. "He won't . . . I can't help him. . . ." He let go of Newt's hand. It fell limp on the bed.

"No," Nan said. "You have to try harder. You have to help him. Charlie!"

Nan felt Miss Bloom's hand on her shoulder. "I tried to tell you, Nan," she said gently. "William died in the carriage on the way to the hospital."

Nan looked at her. She looked at the faces of Whittles and Shilling-Tom. They had fresh tears in their eyes. "Dead?" She felt her chin quiver. She felt as if her legs might give way beneath the weight of it all. Newt wasn't supposed to die. He *couldn't* die. He had to live with Lady Wilde. He had to survive and be happy and be a little boy.

"I am sorry." Charlie lowered his head. "I wanted to help him."

Nan realized that for all his gifts, this was one thing Charlie could not do. He could not bring back the dead.

Nan put her arms around Charlie. She could feel him trembling. She buried her face in his chest. She held him with everything she had. "I know you tried," she whispered.

"Goodbye, Newt?" he said.

"Goodbye, Newt," she said.

·¾ ARRANGEMENTS ·¾

Nan brought the others to the captain's house.

Miss Bloom couldn't get in through the turret, and so she had Charlie force open the front door, which Nan had barricaded with nails and spare wood.

Nan led them all to the study, which was the room with the most chairs. Toby quickly made himself useful by making a pot of something he called "boiled chocolate," using a jar of sweet powder from his emporium. He understood that this was not the time for jokes or stories.

Charlie had not spoken since the hospital. He sat in the fireplace, knees hugged to his chest, staring at the floor. Even when Dent hopped over and pecked his foot, he did not respond.

"So this is where you've been living all this time?" Miss Bloom said. Even though she was speaking to Nan, she kept glancing at Charlie.

Nan knew Miss Bloom must have a hundred questions about Charlie. She was grateful that the woman did not ask them.

Whittles and Shilling-Tom were both standing by the book-shelves. Whittles had his penknife open, clenched tight in his hand. "So . . . how long have you had a pet monster?"

Nan glanced at Charlie, who did not seem to have heard the remark. "He's not a pet," she said. "He's my protector. The Sweep left him for me. He used to be much smaller. Small enough to fit in my pocket. Just a little lump of char."

Comprehension dawned on his face. "Your lucky char? That was . . . *that*?"

Nan nodded, sipping her mug of chocolate.

Whittles clapped his knee. "Now that's a real corker. And just like the Sweep, too! Wait until I tell . . ." He stopped short, lowering his head. "I was going to say wait until I tell Newt."

Shilling-Tom put a hand on his shoulder.

"So . . . what's next?" Nan asked. She was talking to Miss Bloom.

The woman cleared her throat. "We'll need to make arrangements for the . . . for William's body." She sounded very much like a person determined not to cry. Like a person determined to be the grown-up.

"It's the least he deserves," Shilling-Tom said. "Guess I know what I'll be spending this on." He was holding something between his thumb and forefinger—

A battered silver coin.

Nan's eyes got wide. "Tom, your shilling . . ." In all her years of knowing Shilling-Tom, she had never actually *seen* the fabled coin. Roger had searched him countless times, even checking in his mouth, but never had the coin appeared. She had begun to think the coin was a myth. "Where did you hide it?"

Shilling-Tom took his brush off his shoulder and offered it to her. "Whittles carved a little hideaway in the handle."

Nan looked at the worn wooden handle. She could see a notch in the base just large enough to hold a coin. "That's brilliant."

Whittles tipped his cap with the point of his knife. "Isn't it, though?"

Shilling-Tom looked at the coin. "I know it's not much, but it should be enough to get us a pine box, at least." He gave a tight smile. "Guess you'll be calling me Plain-Old-Tom after this?"

"Oh, no," Miss Bloom said, standing. She opened her small purse. "The ladies of the friendly society will insist on paying—"

"No," Tom said, firm. "Newt was one of us. It's only right that we see him off proper."

Miss Bloom looked as if she wanted to object, but Nan caught her eye. "Very good," she said quietly, and sat back down.

Nan turned to Toby, who was clearing the empty mugs. "Toby, do you know someone who could get us a box? Nothing fancy."

Toby nodded and took the coin. "I'll take care of it," he said, and slipped into the hall.

"Wilkie Crudd will pay for this," Miss Bloom whispered. She wiped her eyes. "The friendly society has connections—influence, power. They will make sure that he rots in a cell for what he's done to that boy." She looked up. "To all of you."

Nan looked at Whittles and Shilling-Tom, who did not seem comforted by this declaration. Whittles scratched the back of his neck. "No offense to your friendly society, but what good'll that do *us*?"

"Aye," Shilling-Tom said. "Even if you lock Crudd up for all eternity, he'll just sell us off to Martin Grimes or Ned Tookley, and we'll be back at it before May Day's through. You'll see."

Miss Bloom shook her head. "Obviously we won't allow that. When I tell the friendly society about both of you, I assure you, they'll—"

Nan put a hand on her shoulder. "That's not what they mean, Miss Bloom," she said. "Even if you save Whittles and Tom, there're still thousands more out there just like them." She felt odd talking to Miss Bloom like this, but she needed to make her understand. "You *can't* save them all."

Miss Bloom shook her head, defiant. "But we must do *something*. We must show people the true cost."

"It ain't going to happen, ma'am," Whittles said. "We're inside their houses every day—right under their noses. It's been this way for hundreds of years. Some folk are very good at not seeing things they don't want to see."

Nan glanced outside—at the flower garlands draped over the gaslights. "That's true," she said, stepping to the window. "Except for *one day* a year." She looked back at the boys who joined her side.

All three of them stared at the street. Flowers. Banners. Coal pies. "One day a year," Whittles said.

Shilling-Tom chuckled. "That's brilliant."

Miss Bloom was looking between them, clearly confused. "I'm afraid I don't follow. . . ."

"May Day." Nan turned around, the hint of a smile playing on her lips. "The whole city comes out to cheer for the sweeps. So let's show them what they're really cheering for."

·⊰ A COUNCIL OF CLIMBERS ⊱·

Nan and the others had an idea, but they wouldn't be able to pull it off alone.

By the next morning, their company had grown to include Finn O'Gready, Lucky John, the Twins, Ham-n-Eggs, Sticky Fingers, and a dozen more of the most senior climbers in London. They had all been pulled away from their traditional May Day preparations in order to hear about the plan.

Nan tried to explain what she and the others had come up with the previous night. The boys listened as best they could, only occasionally sneaking glances at Charlie, who had busied himself with making smoke shapes in the corner.

"Let me get this straight," said Lucky John after Nan had walked them through everything. "You want us to *cancel* May Day?"

"No, not cancel," Whittles said. "We'll do the march. Only this time we'll be marching *for* something."

"We already do march for somethin'," Ham-n-Eggs said. "Coal pies and pennies. And that's plenty enough for me!"

"Coal pies, my ear." Lucky John ribbed another boy with his elbow. "Hammie's just hopin' to get a kiss from the flower girl on Hastings!"

"Oi! You shut your mouth!" Ham-n-Eggs shoved him, and the two boys set to wrestling. Soon the rest of them had joined in on the fun.

Nan rubbed her temple. May Day was the next day, and they had already wasted half the morning trying to explain even the most basic parts of the plan. "It's hopeless," she said to Miss Bloom. "They're barbarians."

"Perhaps I can help?" The woman rose from her chair. "I am a teacher, after all."

"By all means," Nan said.

The woman approached the scrum, hands clasped in front of her. "That's quite enough tomfoolery," she said in a stern tone. "Hands in your laps, eyes on me. Spit-spot."

The boys in the pile looked up at her.

"Do I need to repeat myself?" she said.

Without a word of grumbling the boys disentangled themselves and sat in a circle around her. It was as though they were hypnotized.

"That's better," Miss Bloom said, her voice softening. "Now . . . who can tell me what a law is?"

Nan listened as Miss Bloom walked the boys through the plan. It wasn't anything too complicated. They would turn the May Day parade into a protest march. They would use this moment to reveal to all of London the truth about their lives. A few of the boys were resistant—climbers spent all year looking forward to the parade. There was meant to be music and dancing, not gloomy protests.

"We'll need all the climbers in London," Miss Bloom insisted. "It won't work if it's just a handful. That's why we brought you here—your teams respect you, and we'll need all of you to get them on board."

"That won't be a problem," Lucky John said. "When we tell 'em that Nan Sparrow's alive and marching with us—you can bet they'll come running." He, like many of the boys, was a little sweet on Nan.

Nan felt a flicker of apprehension. "Best not to mention my name." After so many months living as a ghost, she wasn't sure she was ready to re-enter the world of the living. "This isn't about me, it's about *us*."

"One last question," said Sticky Fingers. He was maybe the smartest of the bunch and hadn't said a word all morning. "Even if we do all this and it goes off without a hitch, what's to say it'll really change anything? Folks will still need their chimneys cleaned."

"Sticky's got a point," one of the Twins said. "So long as there's fires in the hearths, there'll be climbers in the flues." A few other boys murmured in agreement.

"They're right, Smudge." Toby walked across the room to his emporium. "In order for this plan to work, you'll need to show folks that there's another way to get the job done." He opened his bag. "And it so happens, I have *just the thing*."

Toby drew out a bundle of bamboo reeds with a long cord running through the middle. At the top was a ring of stiff bristles.

"The mechanical brush!" Nan said. "You actually finished it."

"I didn't want to show it to you until it was perfect. You'll notice I made a few improvements on the design." He pulled the cord tight and the bristles extended with a *snap*. The boys stared in awe.

"So . . . you can clean a whole chimney without climbing up inside?" Ham-n-Eggs asked.

"And in half the time," Toby replied. "All that's left for you is to scoop up what sprinkles down." He showed them how the poles fit into one another and could bend around even the sharpest shuttle flue.

Miss Bloom was looking from Nan to Toby. "And you two invented this all on your own?"

"Not exactly," Nan said. "I just found a diagram in an old newspaper. Toby did the real work." She shoved him with her elbow.

Toby doffed his cap. "Not bad for a mudlark."

Sticky Fingers had the brush in his dirty hands. He collapsed the head with a *snap*. "Who cares about coal pies and flower girls." He stood up, facing the others. "It ain't just Newt we're marching for. Every one of us has seen ten Newts on the job—maimed or kilt or taken ill. We're doing this for every one of them." He raised the brush. "Brooms up?"

Every boy in the room leaped to his feet. "BROOMS UP!"

⊰ SIGNS AND WONDERS ⊱

Whittles and Shilling-Tom volunteered to help spread the word to climbers across the city. It wouldn't take long. Sweeps traveled a hidden network along the rooftops. They needed only to whisper the word into open chimney caps and the whole of climbing London would hear.

"Whatever you do," Toby warned them, "don't let your masters hear a word of it." The boys looked at one another, perhaps realizing for the first time how much trouble they would be in if their masters knew what they were plotting.

"What about the parade?" Lucky John said. "Old Grimes will surely see us. And he won't be none too happy." He climbed for Martin Grimes, who was notorious for his beatings.

"We'll be safe," Nan said. "We'll have Charlie to protect us."

The boys looked over at Charlie, who was in the middle of playing Catch-the-Feather with Prospero and Dent.

"Terrifying," Whittles said.

Nan didn't let herself worry. "You've seen what he did to Crudd."

The next question was how to best get their message across to the crowds. Miss Bloom suggested that they follow the example of the suffragists and employ painted signs. "The written word carries authority—it commands respect."

Nan seconded the idea. "Miss Bloom and I can do the letters."

The boys looked visibly relieved to learn that they wouldn't have to be responsible for that part. "That's settled, but what should the signs say?" Sticky Fingers asked.

They discussed at length what sort of message might make the best impact. Should every sign say the same thing? Should they use clever slogans? "No, nothing clever," Miss Bloom insisted. "That will give people permission to laugh. Remember, these signs are not for your benefit. They are for the benefit of those watching. The ladies of the friendly society will have brought members of Parliament with them, including Lord Shaftesbury, who is sympathetic to our cause. He has been trying to effect change for years. It is them we need to consider."

They needed something that couldn't be disputed or ignored. In the end it was Whittles who came up with exactly the right words.

⁜ ⁜ ⁜

Nan and Miss Bloom stayed up through the night working on the signs.

They raided the captain's map collection and painted the backs of as many as they could manage—more than a hundred in all. "All those boys, and not one can spell his own name," Miss Bloom said, shaking her head. "To live in poverty is one thing, but to live in ignorance . . . It breaks my heart. They deserve more."

"Maybe your friendly society can help with that?"

"Maybe so." Miss Bloom dipped her brush into the pot. "I was myself a beneficiary of a friendly society. After I left my family, I was taken in by a charity school for girls. I don't know what I would have done without it."

Nan set her brush down. "I still don't understand. You had a family. You still do. How could you leave them behind—just because they were *strict*?" Nan nodded to Whittles and Tom, who were sleeping on the hearth beside Charlie. "Do you know what those two would give for strict parents?"

Miss Bloom looked at Nan. "And if I had stayed in my home, I would never have met a curious little climbing girl who could answer riddles."

Nan wiped paint from her hands. "I think about that riddle sometimes," she said. "I found a copy of it in one of the books you gave to me." She got up and removed the book from a stack. She opened it to a page in the middle.

Feathers and bone without and within,
I am that and this and that once again.
Borne aloft among the winds,
I encircle new life within my limbs,
I bear the seed that bears the seed—
And by spring's end, small mouths I'll feed!
What am I?

She ran her hand along the page. "I read that on the slate, and I thought I knew the answer."

"*I am an egg.*" Miss Bloom smiled. "How could I forget?"

"Only I'm not sure that's the real answer." Nan handed her the book. "When I read it now, I see a different answer. The riddle isn't about an egg. It's about a bird."

Miss Bloom's smile deepened. She looked proud. "Perhaps it is both," she suggested. "Perhaps we are each of us an egg that becomes a bird . . . children who become parents. When I first met you, you were a child in need of care. And now you are caring for others."

Nan looked over at Charlie, who was stirring in the hearth. "Nan?" he said through a yawn.

"Yes, Charlie?"

"Can the . . . Green Man have . . . long whiskers?"

"Yes," Nan said. "Go back to sleep."

Charlie nodded. "And a tail and . . ." His voice drifted off as he fell back to sleep.

Nan turned back to Miss Bloom, whose eyes were still on the golem. "You've not said a word about him."

"I . . . don't know what to say." The woman shook her head. "What . . . ? How . . . ?"

Nan told her everything. And not just about Charlie. About the Sweep. About the little lump of char she had carried all those years. About the chimney and the fire and the moment when Charlie first opened his little eyes.

"I know that the Sweep left him to protect me," Nan said. "But I also think there was some other reason—some *meaning* behind it all."

"You ask of meaning?" Miss Bloom released a deep sigh. "What does it *mean* for a Jewish schoolteacher who has left her faith behind to meet a golem?"

"Do you think it's a sign?" Nan scooted closer. "Does it make you believe in God?"

Miss Bloom stared at Charlie for a long moment. "It makes me believe that the world is full of wonders that I can scarcely imagine. Perhaps that is the same thing."

"That's the way the Sweep made me feel when I was little," she said. "Like every day was a miracle." She lowered her head. "Until it wasn't."

"There is an old proverb from my childhood. *Say not in grief 'He is no more,' but live in the thankfulness that he was.*" She shrugged. "Easier said than done, I suppose."

Nan nodded. Another dark thought flitted across her mind. "Those things you told me about what happens to golems—do you know if they are going to happen to Charlie?"

Miss Bloom looked at her for a long moment. "You should rest," she said, standing. "We've got a big day tomorrow."

Nan got up. She could have gone up to her bed, but instead she walked to the hearth and curled up beside Charlie—his warmth covering her like a blanket. Whittles was on one side, Shilling-Tom on the other. Dent nestled himself under her chin. Somewhere near Charlie's feet, Toby snored softly. Nan yawned and closed her eyes and soon felt herself drifting off to sleep.

That night they all dreamed of the Sweep.

⤐ COURAGE ⥲

*T*he girl woke to the sound of her own cries. It was the middle of the
night. She and the Sweep had hidden themselves in a barn. The
smell of warm dung and hay filled the darkness.

"Did you have the dream again?" the Sweep asked. His voice was
thick with sleep.

The girl nodded. "I dreamed the charity men got me." Her heart was
still pounding.

Some weeks before, she and the Sweep had passed through a village
where they met some charity men. The men had tried to take the girl away
from the Sweep. They wanted to put her into something called an orphan-
age. The men had grabbed the girl and locked her in a carriage. She had
kicked out a loose board from the roof and climbed out to escape.

The Sweep put his arm around her, and she drew herself close to him.
"You're safe here," he told her. "They're a hundred miles away."

"But what if they follow us?" The girl picked at a hole in his sleeve.
"What if they put me in a wagon?"

"Then you will escape—you will fly free like a little sparrow." He stifled a yawn. "That is what sparrows do." He sounded tired. The girl wondered if he had been in the middle of his own dream. She wondered if he wished she had let him sleep instead of making him talk.

"I'm afraid to close my eyes. I don't want to see them again." She wiped her nose. "I wish I were like you. I wish I could be courageous and never afraid."

The Sweep sat up. Strands of hay stuck to his hair. "Who says I'm never afraid? Of course I'm afraid. You can't have courage without fear, any more than you can have a ray of light without shadows." He sounded much more awake now. "Some things are frightening, and only a fool wouldn't be afraid of them." He scratched the back of his head. The girl wondered if he was thinking about the charity men, too. "Courage is feeling fear and facing it head-on."

The girl swallowed. She wanted to be brave, she really did. "But what if I can't face it?"

The Sweep reached into his pocket. "I have something for you." He pressed a small wooden object into her hand. It was a chessman in the shape of a horse. The girl knew this sort was called a knight. "You hold on to that while you sleep."

"Is it a magic chessman?" The girl ran her thumb over the cracked base. It did not seem very magical. "Will the brave knight fight the charity men in my dreams?"

"It's not magic. It's a reminder." The Sweep mussed her hair. "The brave knight is YOU. And YOU can fight them for yourself."

·⊰ MAY DAY ⊱·

The sky above London was crisp and blue—a perfect day for celebration. Already thousands of Londoners were in the streets, with flowers and coal pies and lucky pennies to throw to the climbers when they marched by.

Nan had forgotten just how many climbers there were in London—thousands upon thousands of small children, all dressed in black coats. Normally they would all be wearing clean clothes and flower garlands, but it had been decided that they should dress as they always did. She was shocked at just how young most of them were. She looked out over the sea of hungry faces and wondered how many of them would still be alive a year from now.

She could hear music in the distance. Market girls were throwing flower petals along the path. Jugglers and clowns danced alongside them. The big finish to the parade would be the march of the sweeps. And what a finish it would be.

Most of the master sweeps were already deep in their cups, enjoying free drinks in public houses all across the city. Masters never bothered to march in the actual parade. As with all other matters, they left the work to the climbers.

The May Day parade followed the path of the Great Fire, but in reverse. The parade started at the Golden Boy of Pye Corner in Smithfield and went across the city, ending at the Matchstick on Pudding Lane. Miss Bloom passed out the signs that she and Nan had made the night before. "Make sure to keep them hidden under your coats until we reach the memorial."

It had been decided that Charlie would remain at the back of the group, where he could keep an eye out for trouble. To prevent anyone from seeing him, they gave him a disguise.

The Green Man, also called "Jack-in-the-Green," was an ancient May Day tradition. The Green Man always marched with sweeps—it was a union as old as fire and smoke. Usually it was an honor given to one of the senior climbers to dress up as the Green Man and walk on stilts and shout silly rhymes at the crowd. But on this May Day, the Green Man would be Charlie.

"Do I look very green?" Charlie asked. A small climber named Shins had stayed up all night making his costume.

"I wouldn't be surprised if Dent tries to build a nest in your ear."

"I do not have an ear," Charlie said.

Nan fought back a yawn and steadied herself on Charlie's leafy shoulder.

"Did you sleep last night?" he asked.

"Barely," Nan said. "My head was too full of too many things." She had dreamed of the Sweep again—it was about a memory she had forgotten from when she was very small. It was about being frightened. It was about courage. "In less than an hour, the march will be over, and then we can sleep as long as we want."

"We could have a napping party." Charlie loved napping parties. "Just you and me."

"Just you and me." Nan knotted a vine around his shoulder.

"And Dent."

"And Dent." Nan wedged some loose branches under his armpit.

"And Toby."

"Never," Nan said, but she smiled to show she was teasing.

"Just one last piece." Shins held up a leafy mask with two holes for eyes. He had attached forked branches to either side of the brow.

"Let me." Nan stood on her toes and slid the mask over Charlie's head. She stepped back and smiled. "Would you look at that!"

"Would I look at what?" Charlie asked her. He tried to see his forehead.

"You finally got antlers," said Nan.

"Did I?" Charlie touched the antlers gently. "Maybe I am a questing beast after all."

Nan laughed, but then she felt the laugh catch in her throat. She remembered how small Charlie had been when he had made his body.

It seemed like a lifetime ago.

She looked over her shoulder. A few of the bigger boys from Finn O'Gready's crew were watching the perimeter for any trouble.

Charlie shifted his feet. "Do you think we will see Crudd today?"

Nan shrugged. "We might. But I'll stay hidden in the middle of the march. And I'll have you to protect me. Everything will be fine. I promise."

"There are a lot of people here. What if I can't see you?" He pushed at his mask, and Nan wondered how well he could see through those little holes.

"See that golden torch?" She pointed toward the east, at the flame of the Matchstick. "That's where we're going. So long as you move in that direction, you'll be fine."

Miss Bloom appeared behind her. "It's time," she said softly.

·❖· ·❖· ·❖·

Charlie liked being the Green Man.

The climbers had woven a cape for him that went all the way around his body. The Green Man's mask had enormous, leafy whiskers that went nearly to the ground—longer than Father

Christmas's. Whenever Charlie moved, he could hear all the leaves and branches and vines *swish, swish* against one another.

It was a nice, green sound.

He was standing beside a little gold statue on a place called Pie Corner. He had been looking for pie all morning. All around him were boys and girls he did not know. They were dressed in black coats, with black hats and black brooms, just like Nan.

Charlie had never seen a parade before. When Nan told him what it was, he worried that it might be frightening, like Bonfire Night. She promised him that this would be different.

He rocked back and forth. His cloak tickled him where it touched his sides. He tried to imagine what all the other people in the crowd would say when he walked past them. *Look at that Green Man*, they would say. *He's a man just like us. Only very green.*

Charlie peered across the square. He could not see very well through his mask. He wanted to see Nan. She was somewhere on the other side of the street.

"Do you know Nan?" he said to a maybe-girl beside him. But the girl did not answer. Most of the climbers were not looking at him. He could tell they were afraid of him, even though Nan had told them that he was nice.

Charlie faced the warm sun. In the hazy distance he saw the pointy top of a golden tower. Nan had called that the Matchstick. He did not understand why it was called that. Beyond the tower, he could hear the bells. He always heard the bells, no matter where he was. He wished he could hear them better. He knew they had something important to tell him. *Soon it will be time*, he thought. *Soon.*

"Thank goodness I found you!" said a voice.

Charlie turned around. There was a boy right next to him. He was dressed like all the others, but he was a little taller. He had a scarf over his chin and a cap pulled low over his eyes.

"Hello," Charlie said. "I am the Green Man."

"You have to come with me," the boy said. He took Charlie's hand and tried to lead him away, but Charlie did not move.

"The Green Man is supposed to stay in the back of the parade," Charlie explained. "That is my job." He was very proud to have a job.

"I know that," the boy said. "But this is a *new* job. Nan told me to give it to you right away."

"You know Nan?" Charlie said. This made him feel better. "What is my new job?"

"She found a gang of climbers—little boys and little girls—who need your help. They're stuck inside a boat at the docks."

"Oh, yes." Charlie knew that a boat was a house that floated on water. "Can the boys and girls swim? Nan says she will teach me to swim someday."

"They're stuck. Their master learned about the march and locked 'em inside. Nan needs you to bust them out before the march starts. They're trapped in there with no food or water. And big hungry rats." The boy grabbed Charlie's arm. "You have to save them!"

Charlie looked back at the crowd. He wished he could see Nan. "Are you sure she wants me to go?"

"I told you—it was *her* idea." The boy stepped back. "Think how disappointed she'll be if I tell her you wouldn't do your new job."

Charlie had not considered this.

Nan followed Miss Bloom to a side alley, where Toby, Shilling-Tom, and Whittles were waiting. Lying on the ground was a pine box.

Not a box, Nan thought to herself. *A coffin.* "It's so small," she said.

Toby knelt next to it. He patted the lid. "I had an old pal out in Stockwell who gave me a fair price—one shilling exactly." He winked up at Shilling-Tom, whose face beamed with pride.

It was plain but well crafted. It certainly cost more than a shilling. Nan wondered how much Toby had traded out of his emporium to make up the remainder of the cost. Nan knelt and touched the lid. "Newt? He's inside there?"

"William is still at London Hospital," Miss Bloom said. "Once the march is through, we'll transport it there and then take him to Highgate Cemetery. Lady Wilde has insisted we give him a proper burial."

Nan stood. "Tell Lady Wilde thank you. From all of us."

"I have to get to the friendly society," Miss Bloom said. "Remember, don't let anyone see the signs until you reach the monument. We can't afford anyone interrupting your progress."

They all knew what she was talking about. The moment the master sweeps realized what the climbers were doing, there would be trouble.

Nan looked to the east. "He's out there," she whispered. "Waiting for me."

"That's what the Green Man's for." Toby nodded toward the back of the crowd. Charlie was talking to someone—Nan couldn't quite tell who. "Plus, Crudd won't even be able to see you. One face in a crowd of thousands. Stay in the middle, keep your head down, and you'll be fine."

"I don't suppose you got a bag I can put over my head?" Nan tried to smooth down her hair, which had grown long and unruly in recent months.

"I brought you this." Toby opened his emporium and removed the Sweep's hat. Nan hadn't touched it since it had burned in the fire. "I tried my best to rebuild the brim and patch the crown. Not exactly good as new, but at least it'll keep your head warm."

Nan supposed she should have been angry at Toby for stealing the Sweep's hat, but she wasn't. "You did a fine job." She tried the hat on and found that it fit perfectly atop her head. "It's heavier than I remember."

"I had to rebuild the crown with steel rods," Toby said. "You could jump right on top of that thing. Not that you'd want to."

St. Paul's and a dozen more churches struck eight o'clock. From this elevation, Nan could hear half the bells in the city. Somewhere, far in the distance, she thought she could even hear the bells of St. Florian.

Whittles jumped atop a barrel and raised his broom. "Brooms up!"

"BROOMS UP!" came back a thousand voices. Brooms went up all across the square, a forest of little black trees.

It was time. Nan pushed her fists into her pocket. She could feel a buzzing in her stomach, the feeling she had whenever she had to jump across a gap between rooftops. "You know, none of this would have happened if it weren't for that talk you gave me about Isaac Ware," she said to Toby.

Toby cocked his eyebrow. "Suppose that's as close to a thank-you as I'm likely to get."

"Nan!"

There was a murmur close by as Shins pushed through the crowd at a full sprint.

"What is it?" Nan said.

"It's . . . Charlie . . . ," Shins said between gasps. "He's gone."

⊰ ADRIFT ⊱

Charlie followed the boy down a narrow alley. They were moving away from the giant golden matchstick that Nan had shown him. He tried to glance back to make sure he could still see it, but it was difficult with his mask on.

"This way!" the boy called. He was nearly around the corner.

Charlie had trouble running, and it was difficult to keep the direction in his mind. He turned another corner and then another. These streets were twisty and strange. He wasn't sure he could find his way back. "The parade is going to start soon," he called out, adjusting his mask, trying to see. "Is it very much farther?"

"Almost there," the voice echoed. "Keep going!"

Charlie turned another corner and found himself at the edge of the river. Boats floated back and forth across the dark surface. He didn't know how they stayed on top of the water. "Toby lives by here," Charlie said. "Do you know Toby?"

The boy ran to the end of a narrow wooden dock that stuck out over the water. "They're in there." He pointed at a small boat that was tied to a pole with a thick rope. "Quickly!"

Charlie walked on the platform, which groaned under his weight. He reached the boat and hesitated. "I don't see any children on that boat."

"They're trapped in that little room." The boy pointed to a green door. "Just go!" He gave Charlie a small push and Charlie stepped down onto the boat. The boat leaned to one side, and dark water sloshed around the edges.

Charlie steadied himself and told himself to be brave. He walked to the green door and pulled it open. The room inside was empty. "There are no children here," he said. "Maybe this is the wrong boat?"

"Nan was right," the boy said from the dock. He was doing something with the rope. "You really are like a little child."

The boy tossed the end of the rope into the water. It landed with a *splash*. "Wait!" Charlie called, running toward him. But it was too late—the boat had drifted away from the platform. "I have to be at the march!"

The boy tipped his cap. "I'll give Cinderella your regards."

·⚜· NAN'S SONG ·⚜·

Nan felt as though she might suffocate. She was in the middle of the parade—packed so tight she could scarcely move. She craned her neck, trying in vain to see Charlie. But there were just too many people, too many brooms blocking her view.

Toby was next to her; his emporium clanked against her shoulder as they walked. The street had been strewn with fresh flower petals, but by the time Nan and Toby reached them, they were a mashed sludge that made the stone slippery—even more so with boots. She cursed herself for not going barefoot like everyone else.

Toby had been the one who pulled Nan away from Pye Corner. She had wanted to keep looking for Charlie, but he reminded her that the only way to keep hidden from Crudd was to stay in the crowd. She strained to see to the front of the parade, which was turning on to King William Street. Shilling-Tom and Whittles were up there somewhere, carrying Newt's coffin. On either side of the march were men and women and children who had gathered on the sidewalks to cheer the climbers as they approached Eastcheap. But as the procession passed, the onlookers' faces all turned to confusion. These people had come out expecting celebration and gaiety. And instead they found a sea of filthy, silent children dressed in black rags. Nan could only imagine how they would react to the signs.

A few people threw coins or coal pies at their feet. Usually the climbers would scramble to pick up whatever they could and offer blessings of luck. But not today. Nan turned the corner and saw the Matchstick looming over the scene. It was a stone column, two hundred feet tall. At the top was a viewing platform packed with men and women, clapping and waving banners. Above them shone a giant golden finial in the shape of a flame.

The square around the monument was packed with thousands of London's wealthiest citizens, all wearing bright clothes and parasols and colorful hats, all cheering for the sweeps. Nan scanned the crowd with her eyes. She caught sight of a few master sweeps, who were watching the march with looks of puzzlement. Crudd was out there somewhere—she could feel it.

She wished she had Charlie.

Toby nudged her shoulder and nodded toward the corner of Monument Street. A section of the sidewalk had been cordoned off with rope, and wooden stands had been erected for the very wealthiest attendees. Miss Bloom was sitting there, along with a dozen other women. There was a very old gentleman with them, withered and frail. Nan thought it might be Lord Shaftesbury.

The cheers from the crowd had already begun to die down, replaced by an uncomfortable silence. Those in front had seen the coffin, but they still didn't seem to understand what it signified. What were these children doing? Why weren't they celebrating?

Whittles's raspy voice broke the silence. "BROOMS DOWN!"

A hundred of the climbers dropped their brooms, which clattered against the stones. They reached into their coats and removed their signs. They children held them high, facing the crowd that encircled them, forcing them to read the words. Each sign was different. Each sign was true.

Georgie Hicks
6 years old
Chimney Fire

Eliza "Twigs" Brown
10 years old
Fall from Roof

Philip "Preacher" Wendell
4 years old
Consumption

These were the climbers who had lost their lives on the job. The crowd stared at the names—and at the little wooden box at the front of the procession.

And then: realization.

A few understood straightaway. Nan saw a young man place his hands over his mouth in horror. But most reacted differently. They were angry. And not for the right reason.

She felt a swelling dread in her chest as people began to boo and jeer. "May Day, my eye!" a woman hollered. "I didn't spend half my week baking pies for this!" More shouts rippled through the crowd. A few people threw coal pies and other food. Nan ducked as people hurled pennies from the top of the Matchstick—they came down on the climbers' heads like hailstones.

"It's not working," Toby said. "They still don't care."

Nan stared out across the square. Thousands of angry voices filled the air. "So we *make them* care," she said.

Toby looked at her. "What are you talking about?"

"We have to find a way to make them understand what it's *really* like." Nan drew a breath. She took off her hat and set it on the ground. She stepped on it with one foot, then the other. Toby was right—it *was* sturdy.

He caught her arm. "Crudd will see you."

"So will they." Nan's head rose above the sea of climbers. It was just like singing for work in the market. She could even use the same melody. But she needed new words. What could she possibly say to make them understand?

At once the words came to her.

She took a trembling breath, closed her eyes, and sang—

> *A little black thing among the snow;*
> *Crying weep! weep! in notes of woe!*
> *Where are thy father and mother? Say!—*
> *They are both gone up to the church to pray.*

As Nan sang, she felt the whole world melt away. One by one, the shouting crowd fell silent—they were listening to her song. She did not have the char to hold, and so she held Toby's hand.

> *And because I am happy, and dance and sing,*
> *They think they have done me no injury,*
> *And are gone to praise God and his Priest and King,*
> *Who make up a heaven of our misery.*

She finished the final lines and opened her eyes. The entire square had gone completely silent. The other climbers were staring at her. Nan looked among their faces—young and old, rich and poor. Many of them had tears in their eyes. All of them, staring at her.

"It worked," Toby whispered. "They heard."

"Oi!" a man's voice snarled from the alley. Every head in the square turned to see the sweep named Martin Grimes marching straight toward the climbers. His face was red and full of fury. "What do you ungrateful rats think yer doin'?" He sounded drunk.

Climbers screamed as the man shoved his way through the crowd. He grabbed Lucky John by the arm and threw the boy to the street. "You dare speak ill about our Sable Fraternity?"

"P-p-please, sir!" John cried, covering his face.

"I climbed just like the rest of you, twelve years I did it, and it didn't kill me none!" The man snatched John's brush from the ground. "You wanna moan about the work? I'll give you somethin' to moan about!"

The crowd gasped as the man brought the brush down on the boy with a *thwap*.

There was another rough shout as a different master sweep pushed his way into the crowd, Bill Burke. He snatched a boy's sign and ripped it to pieces. More sweeps converged on the crowd and assaulted their climbers. This was something usually done behind closed doors, but not today.

Screams rose from the square as people tried to defend the children. The sweeps—drunk and enraged—attacked anyone who touched them. Whistles rang out, and policemen ran in to break up the brawling. A thousand shouting voices echoed across the square.

Nan was nearly toppled as the climbers scattered and tried to escape their masters. "Charlie!" she shouted above the roar. "*Charlie, we need you!*" She spun around and searched for him in the crowd.

Nan took an elbow to the back of the head and fell to her knees. The crowd was pushing against her, trampling her.

A firm hand grabbed her arm. She looked up, expecting to see Toby, but instead she saw a different face. It was an unshaven man with a scalded brow and broken nose and missing teeth and sunken eyes.

"Crudd," she whimpered.

The man showed a poisonous smile. "Well, well . . . if it isn't my favorite climber."

❧ SMOKE AND WATER ❧

Charlie!"

Nan's voice rang from the shore.

Charlie peered through a cloud of black smoke. "Nan?" He had been running from one end of the boat to the other, trying to find a way back to land. The boat had floated into the middle of the water and was bumping into other boats. Men were yelling at him to "clear the way."

"Nan!" He rushed to the edge of the boat, which sloshed to one side. "I'm stuck!" Nervous smoke was billowing from Charlie's shoulders. The hem of his Green Man costume had caught fire, and now the boat was on fire, too. He knew that the boy had tricked him onto the boat. Tricked him into not doing his right job.

And now he could hear Nan calling him. She needed help, and he could not help her.

Charlie stared out toward the buildings along the shore. He saw the golden Matchstick rising up above the rooftops. That was the place Nan had told them they were going to.

Charlie looked down at the river. It was so dark. It looked very deep. He wondered what would happen to him if he went into the water.

There was a crashing sound as his boat struck the side of a bigger boat. The men on the bigger boat all shouted things at him, but Charlie couldn't understand them. Crackling flames had spread all around him, and he couldn't hear above the roar. He thought his boat might be sinking.

"Do you know Nan?" he called. "I need to help Nan!"

He fell back as his boat struck something hard and tipped to one side. There was a snapping sound as one end of his boat broke away and slipped into the black water. He had crashed into a big stone column that was part of a bridge called "London." Charlie knew about this bridge because he and Nan sang a song about it sometimes.

Charlie did not hesitate. He jumped from his burning boat and landed on the base of the bridge. The stones were solid and familiar. Charlie was not as fast of a climber as Nan, but he could climb. He pulled himself up the side of the bridge until he was standing on top. His Green Man clothes dangled, smoldering from his shoulders. He could tell people on the bridge were staring at him.

He thought he heard someone whisper the word "monster."

Charlie didn't care. "Nan!" he shouted, running toward the Matchstick. "I'm coming!"

⤛ LAST CLIMB ⤜

N an had barely gotten a scream out before Crudd pulled her up by the arm and covered her mouth. He held her close to his face. "Lovely day for a celebration." He bared his teeth—or what remained of them. "I almost couldn't find you—until you blessed us all with that song."

"You let her go!" a voice cried behind them. Nan craned her neck to see Toby coming toward them—

Whap! Crudd struck Toby in the face with his fist. The boy fell backward and collapsed to the ground, unconscious.

"Toby!" Nan tried to twist herself free. "*Charlie!*"

Crudd held her fast. "Seems you haven't any heroes to protect you." He made a sound of mock concern. "I do wonder where your pet monster could have got to. He gets confused so easily."

Nan heard these words and realized what they meant. They were the things she had told Roger in Lambeth. Crudd must have found some way to lure Charlie away. She remembered seeing Charlie back at Pye Corner, talking to a boy she didn't recognize—Roger. "If you hurt him, I will kill you."

Crudd jerked her face close to his. "I believe *I* will do the killing today."

Nan winced at his foul breath. His skin was still pink from his burns; his nose, bulbous and bent.

Nan threw her head forward—striking him straight in the nose.

"*Aghhhh!*" Crudd let go of her and gave an animal snarl.

Nan sprang to her feet and ran as fast as she was able. She pushed her way through the other climbers—all contending with their own masters—trying to get to safety.

"Get back here, you filthy brat!" Crudd was right behind her, throwing children out of his path.

Nan needed to get away from him. She needed a rooftop. But she was caught in the middle of the mob. The only structure close by was—

The Matchstick.

She jumped over a fallen climber, racing toward the base of the monument. On one side of the stone plinth was a narrow archway, cordoned off by a small iron gate. Well-dressed onlookers were crowded around the base, pushed there by the swelling chaos around them.

"Out of my way!" Nan screamed, shoving past people seated beneath a canopy. She vaulted over the gate and scrambled into the monument. The stairs were cut in a spiral. Nan raced up them two at a time. The soles of her boots were slick with mashed flower petals. She felt a throbbing in her leg and realized she must have gashed herself hopping over the gate.

She kept running up the spiral steps. Her heart pounded in her chest, and her vision was spotty.

"There's no escape, Nan Sparrow!" Crudd's voice bellowed up from below. "It's up, down, or in the arms of angels!" His footsteps echoed up the stairwell, slow and methodical.

Nan didn't need to escape—she only needed to get to a place where Crudd couldn't reach her. She gripped the iron railing and ran as fast as she could. Nan had climbed steps before, but never this many—hundreds and hundreds of steps that never seemed to end.

At last she rounded the landing to see a patch of gold—the flame of the Matchstick. She lunged ahead and burst onto the open platform. After climbing so long inside the windowless tower, she was made dizzy by the vastness of the sky. The wind howled around her, confusing her sense of balance. A few men and women who had been watching from the viewing platform cried out in alarm.

Nan spun around, gasping for breath. She had hoped to find a door she could bar, but there was none.

"Nan?" Crudd's voice rang out from below. "How are you liking the view?"

She ran a circle around the platform. There had to be someplace to hide, someplace Crudd couldn't reach her. Years ago, the city had built a cage around the area to keep people from jumping over the edge. Nan looked at the top of the cage and saw a gap in the bars. It was narrow, but not as narrow as a flue.

She heard another cry from the observers as Crudd burst from the stairwell, breathing heavily. "There you are," he said. "I was afraid you'd flown off."

Nan grabbed hold of the railing and hoisted herself onto the ledge. She climbed up the inside of the cage, hand over hand, faster than she had ever climbed anything in her life. She thought of the charity men and the locked wagon and how she had worked her way to freedom. She reached the gap at the top of the cage and pulled herself through.

Now she was atop the cage with neither rope nor rig. The wind whipped around her. The golden torch above her was blinding against the sun. Nan squinted at the street below. The entire square seemed to have gone silent. Thousands of faces were all staring up at the Matchstick, staring up at her.

"Come down, little bird." It was Crudd. He was standing directly beneath her. "I promise I won't hurt you . . . more than I have to."

"I'm fine up here!" Nan glanced down toward the street again. She could see figures in blue running toward the base of the monument. "Policemen are coming right now."

"Then I'd better get on with it." Crudd pulled off his coat.

Nan watched in horror as the man climbed up the bars— quickly, expertly. "You forget—I was a climbing boy myself once." He grabbed hold of the gap and pried it wider, pushing his head through. "I'll admit, I thought my last climb was behind me. I remember my master well. Mean Seamus Lint—now, *he* was a brute. It was such a pity when he slipped from that rooftop and left his business to me."

Nan tried to inch higher up the sloped stone, but her foot slipped from its purchase. She grabbed hold of a golden tine around the base of the flame. Her legs swung out over the square. Nan could hear screams from the streets below. "You won't do it!" she shouted, her voice faint against the wind. "Not with all these people watching."

"Do you really believe that?" Crudd pulled himself through the gap and crouched beneath her. "These are the same fine people who watch dozens of boys and girls die inside their very own homes without shedding so much as a tear!" He was shouting now, his voice echoing out across the city.

Nan struggled to keep hold of the flame, but her grip was slip- ping. She stared down at the street, two hundred feet below. She was searching for someone, anyone who could help her. Where were the police? Where was Toby? Where was *Charlie*?

Crudd seemed to know her mind. "You will find no help from below, Nan Sparrow." He moved closer, his own steps uncertain on the smooth stone. "These people will watch you die, and they will do what they have always done when a climber is lost—*nothing*."

He reached out and snatched her ankle.

"No!" she screamed and kicked out her leg—

She felt her grip break loose from the monument—

And then Nan Sparrow fell.

THE GREEN MAN OF
PUDDING LANE

If you asked any two Londoners what happened on May Day, 1875, you would likely get conflicting reports. Some said that climbers tried to incite a labor riot. Some said that it was their masters who started the violence. Some said that policemen tried to stop the fighting—others said they were behind the whole thing. Whomever you asked, they would assuredly claim that they had been among the crowd on that morning, and that they alone knew the truth.

There were some facts all agreed on. The climbers had formed a sort of protest, a march remembering one of their ranks who had died only days before. They brought signs with them, each decorated with the name of a child who had died on the job. How uneducated climbers had managed to make signs was any person's guess.

The signs seemed excessive. Everyone knew that the work was dangerous. But so, too, were fires. Nowhere better to remind them of this fact than at the foot of the Monument to the Great Fire of London. There was discord between the master sweeps and their young wards, and somehow the march devolved into violence and chaos.

Things might have continued in the fashion of a typical riot were it not for the girl. Many believed that it was the same girl who had sung on behalf of the climbers—impossible to verify, for they all looked identical. This girl's master, a disfigured fiend, chased her up to the very top of the monument.

Somehow, the two of them had broken free of the cage, and before anyone could intervene, they were scaling the golden flames. There was an altercation, and when the man tried to seize the girl, something happened, and the pair of them fell screaming from the top of the monument.

They struck the ground with tremendous force. The man died instantly. The girl seemed to have been spared—if only momentarily—by falling through a canopy that had been erected for the celebration.

All of London held its breath as this slip of a girl lay bleeding on the street, moaning in pitiful agony, her body shattered beyond repair.

It was then that the Green Man appeared.

Some claim that he had been noticeably absent from the march, while others swear they saw him hiding in the mews. Reports differ on his appearance. Some say his body was grotesquely wide. Others say he was hauntingly tall. Some even say his body was smoldering and black—a monster hidden beneath greenery.

The Green Man raced up King William Street—pushing through the crowd, throwing grown men out of his way with inhuman strength. When he reached the fallen girl, he knelt down and took her in his broad arms—picked her up as though she weighed no more than a twig.

The Green Man carried the girl across the square without a word of explanation. Policemen tried to apprehend him or at least block his progress. But the climber children all rushed in behind the man and formed a sort of blockade to protect him.

The Green Man carried the girl down Pudding Lane and out of sight.

He and the girl were never seen again.

·⊰ THE SWEEP'S GIFT ⊱·

Nan heard the brushing of leaves—

       Swish–swish . . .

          Swish–swish . . .

              Swish–swish

                     —branches moving back and forth,

like a forest in a storm.

It took her a moment to realize there was no forest.

The storm was Charlie.

He was holding her.

And he was running.

Nan forced her eyes open and saw her own legs, crumpled and cradled in Charlie's smoldering arms. But she could not feel any warmth. She could not feel anything but the pain.

Nan had always thought burning would be the worst way a climber could die. But this . . . *this* was worse. It was slower. More helpless. She couldn't move her body. She could scarcely even breathe. It took all her effort to hold on to her consciousness. She knew that if she fell asleep, she might not wake. She thought of Newt. Was this how his final moments had been?

Nan felt Charlie's arms tighten around her. He was running somewhere. She was dimly aware of having been amid crowds of people, but now they were gone.

"Charlie . . ." she said. Tried to say. The word came out as a croak.

Charlie kept moving. His greens had burned away from his head and shoulders. His eyes were set in determination. Nan saw houses sliding past her almost in a blur. He was taking her somewhere.

She tried to reach a hand up to his face but found she could not move. She was too weak. Her body too broken. She recognized the houses, the narrow alleyways of Tower Hamlets. She tried adjusting her head, and the pain came back like a knife. "Where . . ." The word raked her dry throat like sandpaper. "Where are we going?"

Charlie did not look down. "Home."

Somewhere in the distance . . .

. . . beyond the fog . . .

. . . she heard bells.

✦ ✦ ✦

Nan woke to the sound of groaning metal. She heard Charlie grunt as he adjusted her weight in his arms. She opened her eyes. They were not at the House of One Hundred Chimneys. They were somewhere else. She glimpsed a wall of ancient stone. A rusted iron gate swung wide. And before her—

The Church of St. Florian.

It was stout and square, more like a fortress than a church. She turned her head and stared at the grass beneath her, still wet with dew. In five long years, she had never once passed through these gates. She wanted to ask Charlie why he was taking her here.

But she knew why.

The churchyard was serene and vacant. Charlie carried her past huge tombstones and crypts and statues—monuments to rich men and women long turned to dust. He continued past the smaller headstones and markers. Behind the church was a sort of marsh, hidden by shadows, hidden from view. Nan knew what this was. "Potter's field," she whispered.

Potter's field was where they buried the poor, those who could not afford even a coffin. They were dumped here so that they could be forgotten.

Everything felt faint. The light, the smells, the sounds. It was as though Nan's entire body were wrapped in a gray fog, deadening her senses. "What . . . are you doing?" Her words came out as a whisper.

Charlie glanced down at her for the first time. "I'm listening." He stared out across the field. "I can hear him. The Sweep."

Nan took a stabbing breath. "He's *here*?"

Of course he was. She thought of all those years she had waited for the Sweep to return. He was already with her, not three blocks from where she slept.

"I think this way." Charlie turned his head and stepped toward a bare patch of earth near the back wall. "There are . . . so many of them."

Charlie stopped. He gingerly bent to his knees, taking care not to drop Nan. "Here," he said. "He is here."

Nan wanted to stand, but she could not move her legs.

"Does it hurt?" Charlie asked, holding her close in one arm, like an infant. He brushed her hair from her brow with his stone thumb.

"Only a little," Nan lied. "Can you still hear him?"

Charlie nodded. It was a very small nod.

"What . . ." Nan winced, swallowing. "What is he saying?"

Charlie closed his eyes, as though trying to hear. "*There . . . are . . . all sorts . . . "* he said slowly. "*There are all sorts of wonderful things a person might see very early in the morning.*" His words were halting at first, and then came more quickly.

"*You might see your parents snoring in their beds. You might see an ambitious bird catching a worm.*" Charlie spoke in his own voice, but somehow the words did not sound like his words. It sounded like someone else speaking through him. It sounded like the Sweep. "*You might see an unclaimed penny on the sidewalk or the first rays of dawn or steam rising from the rooftops. And if you are very, very lucky, you might even catch a glimpse of the girl and her Sweep."*

Nan blinked and felt her vision blur. Charlie was speaking her dreams. The dreams she'd had night after night. She listened to his talk of their nights wandering between towns, her riding atop his shoulders. The both of them singing for work. But there were other things in the story that she did not remember. She could hear the Sweep's voice, choked by disease. She could see his caved cheeks as he refused the last bite of food. She could see his face as he watched the girl fall asleep beside him for the last time.

"No," Nan said. "Please don't go . . ."

Next Charlie told her about story soup. About the treasures he kept with him always. Nan remembered begging for that last story, remembered feeling that the Sweep was teasing her. But as she listened now, she could hear the fear in his voice, the knowledge of what telling this story would mean.

Charlie told her about each of the ingredients—

> *A feather for kindness*
> *A doll's eye for wonder*
> *A thimble for mending*
> *A chessman for courage*
> *A cloth for swaddling*

Nan listened. With each new story, she could see every precious second of her life through the Sweep's eyes—she could see how helpless he was to protect her from the world.

The stories moved backward through Nan's life. She could almost see herself growing younger and younger. She listened to her escape from the charity men. She had felt so grown-up in that moment. But now she could see just how tiny, how fragile she had been. She couldn't have been more than three years old. And she could see the Sweep—how losing the girl had left him wild with terror, how truly he thought he had lost her.

"I didn't know," Nan said when Charlie had finished telling the story of courage. "I never knew."

She would have wiped her face had she been able to move. Instead, Charlie brushed the tears from her eyes with his warm hand.

"The last story is very far away." His face became worried. "I don't think it's time yet—"

"Tell me," Nan said. "Try."

Charlie closed his eyes. "I see a man," he said slowly. "And he is alone." His face was strained, as though he were trying to hear an echo's echo. "I think he is tall like the Sweep. But he does not look the same. He is very thin. And very sick. His hands are shaking. The man has nothing. He is . . ." Charlie's face went dark. "He is empty."

Nan held her breath. She did not remember this story. She did not like it. "The man is standing on the edge of a bridge," Charlie went on. "He is staring at the water. The water is cold, but the man is even colder. The man is crying. He is wondering if it would hurt to be in that water. He is wondering if it would hurt to . . ." Charlie shook his head, as though he did not have words for what the man was wondering. "But then . . . the man realizes he is *not* alone. He hears a sound and realizes there is *someone else* there with him.

"The someone is in a bundle on the ground. The man steps down from the ledge and walks to the bundle. The someone is there, at the foot of the bridge, crying. The man unwraps the bundle—a thin blue swaddling cloth—and finds . . ." And here Charlie's face broke through with wonder, his eyes lit from within. "A baby girl." He shakes his head, blinking. "And she is *so small*."

Nan felt her vision blur. She listened as Charlie told the story. Of how the man took the child and stepped back from the water. How he carried her in his arms and fed her milk from a bottle. How every day the man knew he had to stay alive because that little girl needed him.

This was the last story. The one he had been unable to tell.

"You saved him," Charlie said, when he was done.

"It's like Toby said." Nan blinked tears from her eyes. "We save ourselves by saving others."

"I think that is why he made me," Charlie said. "He wanted me to tell you. He wanted you to *know*."

Nan was trembling all over now. She could taste blood in her throat. Every breath was a battle. It wouldn't be long before she would be with the Sweep. She remembered story soup. Remembered the Sweep telling her there was one more ingredient—one she never saw.

"Is that everything?" Her own voice was faint in her ears.

Charlie looked down at her. "There is *one thing* left." Nan felt his rough hand on her brow. The hand was so warm. "It's time to wake."

Nan stared into his eyes and realized what he was telling her. "No," she said, shaking her head. "You can't . . ."

Charlie drew her close to his chest. "Thank you," he whispered. "For everything."

There was a smell of embers. The air turned crackling and warm. "No, Charlie!" Nan fought to get free. "Please!"

But Charlie held her fast, staring down at her with his pained eyes—dark as a shadow's shadow. Nan could feel a flicker of warmth spreading through her broken body, bringing her back. She could hear his breath, shallow and rasping. She could feel his arms turning rigid around her.

"Not you," she begged, clinging to his cold body, even as she felt her own body getting stronger. "I can't lose you, too."

Nan thought of everything that had happened in these fleeting months. She thought of Charlie's face. His kind, sad smile. The touch of his crumbly hand against hers. His warm arms wrapped around her. The home they made together. The reading lessons. The first snow. Their Christmas adventure. The broken egg.

"Don't go . . . ," she whispered over and again. "Don't go." She held him tight, tight enough to shatter him.

At last she let go and drew herself from his arms.

Charlie did not move.

His body had turned to stone.

⊰ THE GIRL AND HER SWEEP ⊱

Nan woke to the sound of bells. She was lying in the Orchard. That was what the boys were calling the Nothing Room these days on account of the oak tree growing through the roof. The roots had spread in the last year to create a sort of cradle that was just perfect for her to sleep in.

It had been a cold winter. Nan could hear icicles dripping outside her window, and she could just make out her own breath as she released a great, lazy yawn. She massaged her right leg, which was always sore in the mornings. A few floors below, she could hear Miss Bloom's voice—it sounded as though she was giving an alphabet lesson. Her students were so used to rising before dawn that she had been forced to start her classes early.

In the months since Charlie's death, Nan's world had changed dramatically. The Climbing Boys Reform Act had miraculously passed in Parliament, outlawing the practice of employing children under thirteen years of age. Miss Bloom and her friendly society had purchased the captain's mansion—taxes and all—and made a school for climbers. Whittles, Shilling-Tom, Ham-n-Eggs, the Twins, and dozens more had all been brought into the home, where they were fed and clothed and taught to read. Roger had not gone with the other boys. Instead he took on apprenticeship with a master sweep named Bill Thwackary (though having no climbing boys to work beneath him, Roger remained as miserable as ever).

Nan, too, had changed. The pit in her stomach seemed to have sealed itself up. And though she still thought of the Sweep often, it did not undo her in the same way. Even the memory of Charlie, whose death at first blazed inside her, seemed now to have diminished to a kindling warmth. It helped, she thought, that Charlie and the Sweep were together.

She heard a *tap, tap, tap* at the window. She climbed down from the roots and wiped the fog from the glass. Outside sat a robin redbreast.

Cheep!

"Dent?" Nan pulled open the window. "Where have you been?" After May Day, Nan had searched the entire house for Dent, but the bird had disappeared. He spread out his wings and fluttered in a small circle. "It looks like your wing finally sorted itself out."

The bird cheeped again and hopped back to the gutter. He wanted her to follow him. "Fine," she said. "But I'm taking the stairs." Her right leg had never quite recovered from her fall. She wasn't sure she could scale the roof even if she tried.

She pulled on her boots and coat and descended the stairs. She passed Miss Bloom with her students in the study. Nan could barely recognize the boys, all seated neatly at little desks. Their faces were all scrubbed clean, and their hair, which had grown out, had been combed.

"Brooms up!" she called as she raced past the open door.

At once, every boy in the room dropped their slates and leaped to their feet. None of them had brooms, of course. A few of them held up bits of chalk instead.

"Be back in time for supper!" Miss Bloom called after her.

Nan met Dent outside. The bird seemed annoyed that Nan could not fly. "You and me both," she muttered as she limped down Harley Street.

She followed the bird through London and into Tower Hamlets until they were standing at the gates of St. Florian's. "Are we going to see Charlie, then?" she asked.

This was a place Nan had visited many times. On this morning the path felt heavy and wet under her new boots—even a year later, she was still getting used to having boots on her feet. Snow had melted to reveal patches of brown grass coming up to taste the open air. Drops of water fell from the bare branches, flashing in the warm sun. There was an earthy smell in the air.

Dent hopped and flapped and led Nan down the path she knew all too well. She turned the last corner beyond the main cemetery to find Charlie as he ever was, kneeling above the Sweep's grave, arms cradled, his body frozen just as it was when he had carried Nan to this place.

When he had saved her life.

His downcast gaze, which had once looked so pained, now appeared calm, almost peaceful.

The church groundskeeper had at first been alarmed to discover such a large headstone on such a bare plot. He assumed it had been mislaid by some careless masons. But no matter what he tried, the statue could not be moved. And so it remained over the Sweep's grave. A sentinel. A companion.

Today Nan noticed something different. Snow had melted from Charlie's body to reveal his arms. And nestled in the crook of his elbow was a small cluster of twigs.

"Is this what you wanted me to see?" she said. "You've built a nest."

Cheep!

A flutter sounded in her ears, and she saw a second robin circle her head and lower herself into the nest. Dent joined her. "Well, well," Nan said. "This is exciting."

The female robin gave a protective *cheep!* Nan stepped closer and saw three small eggs beneath her body. They were light blue, speckled with flecks of brown.

Dent lowered his head and blinked at Nan before getting back to the work of tending his nest. Nan could almost see the eggs shudder and twitch with anticipation. Very soon there would be a little peeping family, all safely held in Charlie's strong arms.

Nan watched the birds and thought of Miss Bloom's riddle—the eternal question of birds and eggs. Her gaze moved to Charlie's frozen face, which seemed to be watching them. "Even now, you're a protector," she said to him. "They're lucky to have you."

Nan turned and looked out across the city, which gleamed against the bright morning sun—snow melting away to reveal a world newly born. Spring was coming.

This change seemed all of a piece to Nan. After everything that had happened, Nan Sparrow was her own person—free to roam as she pleased. At first, she had tried sweeping chimneys with Toby's mechanical brush, but she quickly discovered that chimneys no longer compelled her. (She did, however, make an exception to play Father Christmas for the boys at Miss Bloom's school.)

The chaplain of St. Florian's Church, who had heard Nan singing on May Day, had offered to pay her a small amount to sing in his choir. And Miss Bloom had offered to hire her to help teach the boys. The friendly society even offered to send her out to give testimonials to other parishes about the hazards of child labor.

But none of those things really appealed to her.

Instead, she did odd jobs with Toby, fixing the junk that he found on his rambles. It turned out she was quite skillful at fixing things.

Truthfully, she had been spending a lot of time with Toby. It turned out that he really did know every inch of the city. They spent long hours watching steamships come up the icy Thames. Listening to the haunting chimes of the great churches. Watching the carriages parade around Piccadilly Circus. Once they even threw acorns at the guards at Buckingham Palace.

Nan knelt and set to work cleaning the icicles off Charlie's arms. She didn't like the idea of him being so cold. "Especially now that you have a family to watch over." She worked slowly, humming softly to herself.

Dent gave a startled *cheep* and flapped into the sky.

A voice called from the ridge. "Hullo, Smudge!"

Nan felt a small flutter in her stomach as she turned to behold Toby racing up the path. His cheeks were flushed red and his eyes were bright as jewels. He was breathing hard—either from the weight of his emporium or from the slope of the path.

"Where have you been?" Nan asked as he came near.

"Down by the river," he said, still catching his breath. He heaved his emporium off his shoulder and set it on the ground. "Still can't believe I didn't think of it before." He crawled into his bag and started digging for something at the very bottom. "It's a lucky thing there's still some snow on the ground, else I would have walked right past it!"

"What is it?" Nan said, peering closer. "What've you got?" She wondered if it was another present for her. She had begun to rather enjoy getting presents from Toby.

"Here it is!" He emerged from the bag a moment later holding his prize. He pressed something very small and very warm into her hand. *"Just the thing."*

Nan opened her hand and felt the air leave her lungs. For once in her life, she had to admit that Toby Squall had truly found *just the thing.* It was dark and warm and smelled faintly of ash. "It's . . . Charlie," she whispered.

"A piece of him, at least."

Nan's hands were shaking. She clasped the ember tight, feeling the warmth through her entire body. "But where did you find it?"

"Really, we've Prospero to thank." He pet the rat, whose head poked out from the edge of his coat pocket.

Nan looked up. "It was his Christmas gift! I remember! He gave Prospero a little piece of himself to keep warm."

Toby nodded. "I was walking along the old bank when I came across this one patch—right where Prospero and I used to make our camp. And there, right in the middle of the snow, I saw this great fat dandelion pushing up to the sky, petals and all. I started digging and there it was—just where he'd left it."

Toby had done it. He'd found the last flickering bit of Charlie. It was small, barely a sliver, but it was something.

"What should I do with it?" said Nan.

Toby scratched the back of his neck the way he did when he was afraid of being teased. "There's no replacing Charlie, but . . . I sort of wondered if we could maybe try to make another one?" He tapped his boot against the side of his emporium. "We could mix in a few ingredients and see what happens." He shrugged. "We could raise him together."

Nan looked at the little flickering speck in her hands. She tried to imagine it coming alive—with eyes and a voice and a mind of its own.

She looked up at the figure of Charlie kneeling before her. Her dear, sweet, simple Charlie. She blinked as tears welled in her eyes. These tears felt different somehow. Sad, yes, but also overflowing with every drop of love she had ever known.

She knelt down and wiped the snow from the ground. She dug her bare hands into the slushy earth. She took the ember and pressed it into the hole and then covered it again.

"I think this belongs to you," she whispered, and pressed the soil down.

Nan could feel the change almost instantly. The snow beneath her boots melted to reveal black soil. And there, pushing up from the earth, were little shoots of green grass.

Nan stood with Toby and watched as the patch of cemetery around them came alive—vines and grass and blossoms unfolding and stretching up toward the sun.

"Would you look at that!" Toby said. "Flowers in February. Wonder what the old grave keeper will make of it."

Nan shrugged. "He'll think it's a miracle. And he'll be right."

She turned and adjusted her coat against the cold, which didn't feel as cold as it had before. She passed Toby and started back down the path. To whatever life awaited her. And as she walked, she hummed softly—

With brush and pail and soot and song!
A sweep brings luck all season long!

STORY SOUP

How does one create a story? In the case of *Sweep*, the answer is *slowly*. It took over fifteen years to find the ingredients for Nan and Charlie's story. Let me tell you about them:

A CLAY GOLEM FIGURINE

This figurine came from a gift shop in Prague. When I was nineteen, my father was invited to teach a course at a seminary in the Czech Republic. He took me along with him. At the time, I had only a dim notion of golems, gleaned from a handful of fantasy stories. I had no idea about their connection to the city or their Jewish heritage. Four hundred years ago, the story goes, Rabbi Loew created a golem to protect the Jews of Prague. The creature has since become a mascot for the city—appearing on posters and T-shirts and statues. I became fascinated with golems, reading everything I could find. For years after, I would play a game in which I attempted to draw golems made from unusual substances: barbed wire, newspapers, sugar, eyeglasses, pudding, and yes, soot.

A BATTERED COPY OF *THE WATER BABIES*

Ten years ago, my wife, Mary, handed me a copy of Charles Kingsley's *The Water Babies*, a text she was writing about for her doctoral thesis. "Wait until you read about climbing boys," she told me. "It's horrifying." This particular edition was beautifully illustrated. It was part of a university library collection and was slated for destruction at the end of the semester. I tell you with utmost pride that my wife rescued (stole) the book from the stacks, and it holds a special place on our bookshelves to this day.

The Water Babies is one of the earliest books from the "Golden Age" of children's literature. It tells the story of an abused climbing boy who finds himself caught in a chimney fire (lit by his master). In his frenzy to escape, he is transported to an aquatic wonderland full of talking fish, fairies, and wordplay that never quite lives up to the promise of the book's early chapters. Prior to that, my only experience with chimney sweeps came from *Mary Poppins*. Could sweeping chimneys really have been that horrible? A little research revealed to me that it was actually much worse.

I knew at once that I wanted to write my own story about climbers—one that stayed *inside* chimneys straight through to the end. It did not take long for me to realize that the soot golems I had been doodling for years belonged in this story. And thus, Nan and Charlie were born. After countless false starts, I wrote the first chapter almost exactly as it appears in the final book. With "The Girl and Her Sweep," I knew at once that I had finally found my story—that it was not just about a girl and her monster, but also about a parent losing a child. As exciting as this discovery was, it was also daunting. At the time, I had no children of my own. My own childhood had been safe and idyllic. How could I possibly write about such things with the wisdom and honesty they required? I resolved to put the story away until I was able to tell it right.

A SWADDLING CLOTH

In the ensuing years, Mary and I had three daughters. People often ask if becoming a parent has informed my writing. "I bet they give you lots of material!" they joke. This is true, but not in the way people mean: My children have taught me what it means to love unconditionally. Our youngest child, Hazel Sparrow, has proven the most crucial piece of the puzzle. She was born with Down Syndrome and a severe congenital heart defect that required open-heart surgery and countless medical interventions. At any other point in history, Hazel would likely not have lived to see her first birthday. She is now a healthy two-year-old. I wouldn't wish the experience

on any parent. But as with much suffering, wisdom followed. I had
to make the choice to love someone who I knew could very likely
break my heart beyond repair. It was living through this experience
that made me finally able to tell Nan's story.

A TUCSON PUBLIC LIBRARY CARD

Writing is an act of séance—it's a chance to summon up the ghosts
of authors past and have a chat. In the case of *Sweep*, I was trying
to have a conversation with a number of writers I first discovered
when I was Nan's age—books I brought home from the Tucson Public Library in the summer between third and fourth grade. These
are the stories I read over and over again while writing *Sweep*. In
many ways, they proved to be my most essential research. I learned
about the girl and her Sweep from Roald Dahl's *Danny, the Cham-
pion of the World*. The House of One Hundred Chimneys was
discovered inside the magical attic of Frances Hodgson Burnett's
A Little Princess. I learned about Nan and Charlie's friendship from
Arnold Lobel's *Frog and Toad All Year*. And finally, I learned about
saying goodbye from E. B. White's *Charlotte's Web*.

So many people have helped bring Nan's story to life. Thank you
to Jim Armstrong, Tamar Brazis, Courtney Code, Joe Regal, and
Evangelos Vasilakis for tirelessly helping me shape the text. Thank
you to Chad Beckerman, Dadu Shin, and Shawn Dahl for making

the book beautiful. Thank you to Jenny Choy and Hallie Patterson for sending it out into the world.

And thank you to the scores of readers who provided insight, encouragement, and crucial feedback: Sally Alexander, Katherine Ayres, Clare Beams, Lauren Burdette, Caroline Carlson, Rebecca Cole, Erica Finkel, Michael Galchinsky, Adam Gidwitz, Lee McClain, Colleen McKenna, Kenneth Oppel, Avigail Oren, Jackie Robb, Laurel Snyder, Thomas Sweterlitsch, Benny Zelkowicz, and, as always, Mary Burke.

You have all saved me.

⊰ HISTORICAL NOTE ⊱

*W*hat is the difference between a story and a lie?" This was the central question of my book *The Night Gardener*. When writing a historical book, the question becomes even more urgent.

Sweep is a tangled knot of fantasy and fact. Many of the locations and characters are real; a few are made up. Agnes Marshall, Isaac Ware, Lord Shaftesbury, William Blake, and the Green Man are all real. Children really did live as mudlarks. Sweeps really did use children as climbers. I am by no means an expert on Victorian London. After more than ten years of research, all I've really learned is how little I know. Doubtless, I've made a few historical errors. Easter and Passover did not overlap in 1875. In other places, where facts were impossible to verify, I was forced to guess. I still have no idea what a firework cost in 1874.

Still, I did pick up a few things in my studies. Below are some basic facts about Nan's world—a jumping-off point for teachers, librarians, or the historically curious:

ON GOLEMS

The golem has always been a capacious vessel—able to bear whatever meaning the storyteller brings to it. Modern readers might recognize golems from video games and fantasy literature, or perhaps from novels like Michael Chabon's Pulitzer Prize–winning *The Amazing Adventures of Kavalier & Clay*. For most of history, however, the golem has been an obscure creature. In the nineteenth century, the first written stories of golems began to appear (including one by Jacob Grimm in 1808). Early golem tales depicted them as mindless servants who end up wreaking havoc—not unlike the magic brooms in Goethe's "The Sorcerer's Apprentice."

As the golem gained popularity in the middle of the century, he became more heroic—less servant than protector. The most famous of these protectors is the Golem of Prague. As with so much Jewish history, the golem's tale is closely tied to anti-Semitism. In 1580, Jews in Prague were suffering under a vicious campaign of "blood libel"—Christians were accusing Jews of performing evil rituals and then attacking them in response. According to legend, the persecution became so great that Rabbi Loew created a golem to patrol the Jewish ghetto and protect his community from harm. The story has many versions, all of which end in the golem being destroyed when his work is done. Just as Miss Bloom tells Nan: *For the golem, there is no happy ending.*

Today, the golem has become Prague's unofficial mascot. His bulky figure watches over every corner of the city. Readers interested in learning more need look no further than Isaac Bashevis Singer's excellent *The Golem* or the Caldecott Medal–winning *Golem* by David Wisniewski, whose incredible cut-paper illustrations haunt my dreams still.

ON SWEEPS

Whenever I tell people about this story, the first question they have is about chimney sweeps: Was it *really* that bad? Truthfully, it was worse. Children were routinely rented, bought, or even kidnapped by master sweeps. (Some historians have argued that "The Pied Piper of Hamelin" is actually a story of a sweep kidnapping climbers.) By some estimates, the average life span of a climber was just five years. As Nan herself discovers, this was not for want of technology: Designs for a mechanical brush had been publicly available for nearly a century. It was, in fact, homeowners who resisted the mechanical brush most fiercely—claiming that the brushes did not do as thorough a job as young climbers.

May Day is a real holiday that continues to this day in the form of International Workers' Day. Every year, chimney sweeps dance with the Green Man throughout villages across the UK. The protest march depicted at the end of Nan's story did not occur, though the events coincide with the general arc of history. Reformers and friendly societies spent more than a century trying to ban climbing until finally a boy named George Brewster suffered a horrific death on the job. The ensuing scandal changed the tide of public opinion and led to the passing of the Chimney Sweepers Act 1875—at long last marking the end of climbing across England. This act proved a bellwether for child labor reform in other industries, paving the way for changes throughout the industrialized world. Every person today who grew up with free education and worker protections owes a debt to these children. Nan's struggle perhaps feels like a relic from the barbaric past, yet today over 160 million children world-wide are forced into child labor. The battle is far from won.

Those looking to learn more about the fascinating world of chimney sweeps would do well to read historian Benita Cullingford's incredible and exhaustive book, *British Chimney Sweeps*. For those wanting a firsthand account of climbing, I urge you to pick up George Elson's funny and horrifying autobiography, *The Last of the Climbing Boys*. For younger readers, I would recommend James Cross Giblin's *Chimney Sweeps: Yesterday and Today*.

VICTORIAN LONDON

Victorian London has been the backdrop for some of history's most thrilling stories—from *Sherlock Holmes* to *Oliver Twist* to *Dr. Jekyll and Mr. Hyde*. The century was a time of enormous paradox: The Industrial Revolution turned London into a city of unimaginable wealth, while simultaneously casting countless people into desperate poverty. Climbers like Nan would have been some of the few people to witness both extremes of London life.

As the century progressed, the most abused workers began to make their voices heard. Labor demonstrations became a fixture across England (including some bloody revolts on Bonfire Night). Writers like Charles Dickens began to call for change to the way the poor were perceived and treated. Friendly societies, journalists, and reform groups joined the fight. Perhaps the most significant of these voices was Henry Mayhew. Mayhew's *London Labour and the London Poor* was the first large-scale study of London's poorest populations. As a reporter, he traveled to the slums and actually talked to the people whom most others worked so hard to ignore—capturing their voices and sharing them with the larger world. Mayhew's book is astonishing and unflinching. He has entire chapters on climbers and mudlarks and a dozen more of the filthiest jobs you can imagine (I defy you to read about "toshers" and not squirm).

Mayhew's book pairs perfectly with the "poverty maps" of reformer Charles Booth, who in 1899 created a color-coded map of London showing the relative wealth and need of every single block of the city—I spent countless hours poring over this map, tracking every step of Nan's journey. Younger readers interested in this topic would do well to look at John Thomson's *Victorian London Street Life in Historic Photographs*. Inspired by Mayhew's work, Thomson brought a camera (then a cutting-edge technology) into the slums to show these people as they really were. His pictures and accompanying essays are breathtaking—and those looking closely might even spot Shilling-Tom leaning in the background!

The role and position of Jews in Victorian England was complex. The new ideas of the Enlightenment began to find their way into legislation: For the first time in history, Jews were afforded the basic rights of their Christian neighbors—and with that came the opportunity to participate in broader society. The ensuing decades saw Jewish aristocracy assuming high seats of power, including a Prime Minister and the Lord Mayor of London. Simultaneously, London began to see a massive influx of Jewish immigrants—mostly poor families fleeing persecution in Eastern Europe. (Including countless children like Toby Schaal.) This new population led to a fascinating collision of class, faith, and ethnicity in the English Jewish identity. It also, depressingly, stoked anti-Semitism in the larger population. Readers curious about the lives of these immigrant families would do well to read Israel Zangwill's wonderful *Children of the Ghetto*.

For a modern perspective on Victorian life, I would encourage readers to pick up any of historian Judith Flanders's excellent nonfiction books, including *Inside the Victorian Home* and *The Victorian City*. Flanders has a gift for making even the tiniest detail exciting. She was also a historical consultant on the Victorian-set video game *Assassin's Creed Syndicate*, whose digital rooftops I explored for hours in the name of "research."

When I began the journey of researching Nan's London, I thought I was learning about a different world. But I very quickly realized that I was looking into a mirror that reflected my own. Poverty, child labor, and anti–Semitism continue to this day, no matter how much we would prefer to ignore them. It is only in looking back that we have any hope of moving forward.

⚜ ABOUT THE AUTHOR ⚜

Jonathan Auxier is the *New York Times* bestselling author of *The Night Gardener, Peter Nimble and His Fantastic Eyes*, and *Sophie Quire and the Last Storyguard*, which *Kirkus Reviews* noted "should be in the hands of every human young enough at heart to be enchanted by the written word." He lives in Pittsburgh with his family. Visit him at TheScop.com.